monsoonbooks

OPERATION STEALTH

Lt. Col. JP Cross is a retired British officer who served with Gurkha units for nearly forty years. He has been an Indian frontier soldier, jungle fighter, policeman, military attaché, Gurkha recruitment officer and a linguist researcher, and he is the author of twenty books. He has fought in Burma, Indo-China, Malaya and Borneo and served in India, Pakistan, Hong Kong, Laos and Nepal where he now lives. Well into his nineties, he still walks four hours daily.

Operation Stealth is the fourth in a series of historical military novels set in Southeast Asia comprising, in chronological order, *Operation Black Rose*, *Operation Janus*, *Operation Blind Spot*, *Operation Stealth* and *Operation Four Rings*. The first three books may be read in any order; the final two are sequential. The series features Gurkha military units, and the author draws on real events he witnessed and real people he fought alongside in various theatres of war in Southeast Asia and India.

'Nobody in the world is better qualified to tell this story of the Gurkhas' deadly jungle battles against Communist insurgency in Malaya in the 1950s. Cross spins his tale with the eye of incomparable experience.'

John le Carré, on *Operation Janus*

'... a gripping adventure story ... learn the ins and outs of jungle warfare from a true expert'

The Oldie, on *Operation Janus*

T0168832

Also by JP Cross

OPERATION STEALTH

JP Cross

monsoon

monsoonbooks

First published in 2020
by Monsoon Books Ltd
www.monsoonbooks.co.uk

No.1 The Lodge, Burrough Court,
Burrough on the Hill, Leicestershire LE14 2QS, UK

ISBN (paperback): 9781912049783
ISBN (ebook): 9781912049790

Copyright©JP Cross, 2020.
The moral right of the author has been asserted.

All rights reserved. No part of this publication may be reproduced,
stored in a retrieval system, or transmitted, in any form or by any means
without the prior written permission of the publisher, nor be otherwise
circulated in any form of binding or cover other than that in which
it is published and without a similar condition being imposed on the
subsequent purchaser.

Cover design by Cover Kitchen.

A Cataloguing-in-Publication data record is available from the British
Library.

MIX
Paper from
responsible sources
FSC® C018072

Printed and bound in Great Britain by Clays Ltd, Elcograf S.p.A.
22 21 20   1 2 3 4

List of Characters

[Note: except for those with a * in front of their name, all the others were born in the author's imagination]

Bakunin, Soviet Ambassador in Laos

Bill Hodges, Secret Intelligence Service official, London

Bounphong Sunthorn, a senior Lao communist. Ring B

Charlie Law, English name of Thai surrogate son of David Law, Q.V.

Chi, Colonel, South Vietnamese Defence Attaché, Laos

Clifford Bates, Colonel, Ministry of Defence, London

David Law, Sir, Lieutenant General, KCB, CBE, DSO, MC, Director of Military Intelligence, Ministry of Defence, London

Ed Murray, Central Intelligence Agency, listed as Cultural Attaché in the Bangkok embassy

Etam Singvongsa, Brigadier General, Director of Intelligence, Royal Lao Army

Georgi Nechaev, Colonel, Soviet Defence Attaché, Laos

Gerry Elwood, Head of the Southeast Asian Desk, Foreign and Commonwealth Office, London

Gordon Parks, Secret Intelligence Service representative in
   British embassy, Vientiane, Laos

Hamish Charles Cameron, British Ambassador, Laos

Harry J. Vainey, functionary from United States Agency
   International Development, Vientiane, Laos

*Hồ Chí Minh, first Vietnamese leader

Inkham Hatsady, a.k.a. Princess Golden Fairy, Third Secretary,
   Royal Lao Embassy, London

Jacque Grambert, KBG agent

James Redfeather, Sir, KCMG, Whitehall Mandarin

Jason Percival Vere Rance, Lieutenant Colonel, Commandant,
   British Army Jungle Warfare School, Malaysia, later
   Colonel, British Defence Attaché, Laos

James Tomlinson, Treasury official, London

Jay V. Gurganus, Colonel, US Army Attaché, Laos

Jeremy Coulson, Whitehall functionary, London

John (J L B) Chambers, Indo-China desk officer in the Secret
   Intelligence Service, London

Joseph, Mr, supporting clerk for British Defence Attaché,
   Vientiane, Laos

Kaysone Phomvihan, pro-Vietnamese Lao communist

*Kaysorn Bouapha, Lao language teacher, Vientiane, Laos

Khian An, British Defence Attaché's house boy, Vientiane, Laos

Lanouk na Champassac, Prince, Defence Minister, Laos

Le Dâng Khoã, Major, Army of the Republic of Vietnam
   Guiding Officer, British Army Jungle Warfare School. A
   senior Vietnamese communist. Ring A

Leuam Sunthorn, British Defence Attaché's driver, Vientiane, Laos

Mana Varamit, Major, a.k.a. Major Chok Di when in Thai Secret Army

*Mangkara, Lieutenant Colonel Prince, son of Prime Minister of Laos

Maurice Richard Burke, a.k.a. Dally, Central Intelligence Agency representative in London

Neil Gherry, Captain, Adjutant, British Army Jungle Warfare School, Malaysia

Nga Sô Lưư, a Vietnamese political commissar

Oswald Stewart Taunton, British ambassador, Laos

Ouane, Princess, King of Laos' eldest daughter

Percy S. Zollinger, Assistant US Army Attaché to Royal Lao Army's Military Region 2

Phannyana Maha Thera, abbot of Sam Neua, later Chief Bonze of Laos in Luang Prabang

Phou Si, a mythical giant and the name of a small hill in Luang Prabang, Laos

Prachan Pimparyon, Sergeant Major, Thai Frontier Police

Richardson, Colombo Plan adviser in the Ministry of Information, Vientiane, Laos

Roger Daniel, Colonel, out-going British Defence Attaché, Laos

Ronny Hill, Major, British Assistant Military Attaché, Laos and embassy Beaver pilot

Sainyavong Hatsady, Prince, the King of Laos' only full brother, President of the King's Council

*Savang Vatthana, King of Laos from 1959

*Sisavangvong, King of Laos until 1959

Sisavat Abhay, Major General, Deputy Commander-in-Chief, Royal Lao Army

*Soth Petrasy, head of Lao Patriotic Front delegation in Vientiane, Laos

*Souvanna Phouma, Prince, the Neutralist Prime Minister of Laos

*Souvannouvong, Prince, the 'Red Prince' of Laos

Tâ Tran Quán, a.k.a. Tanh Bên Lòng, a senior Lao communist. Ring C

Tan Ying-chao, interpreter to Chinese Defence Attaché, Laos

Teng Ah-hok, Chinese Defence Attaché, Laos

Terry Olsen, Colonel, Australian Defence Attaché, Laos, and wife, Jane

Thong Damdouane, a senior Lao communist. Ring D

*Vang Pao, Major General, Commander, Royal Lao Army, Military Region 2

Vladimir Gretchanine, Third Secretary, USSR embassy in Paris, later Defence Attaché in Laos

Xutiati Xuto, a.k.a. Charlie Law, q.v.

Yvonne Grambert, French language teacher, London

Abbreviations

AMA	Assistant Military Attaché
ARVN	Army of the Republic of Vietnam, South Vietnamese Army
BBC	British Broadcasting Corporation
BE	Buddhist Era
C-in-C	Commander-in-Chief
CIA	Central Intelligence Agency, USA
CPLA	Chinese People's Liberation Army
CTC	Central Training Command, Saigon, ARVN
DA	Defence Attaché
DI	Defence Intelligence, Ministry of Defence, London
DMI	Director of Military Intelligence, Ministry of Defence, London
FCO	Foreign and Commonwealth Office, London
GHQ	General Headquarters
GI	'General issue', a US army private soldier
GR	Gurkha Rifles, British Army
GRU	Soviet Main Intelligence Directorate, a.k.a. Military Intelligence Agency
HE	His Excellency, used for ambassadors, etc

ICSC	International Control and Supervision Commission
LBJ	Lyndon (Baines) Johnson, 1908-73, 36th USA President, 1963-9
LP	Luang Prabang, the Lao royal capital
LPF	Lao Patriotic Front, political wing of anti-royalist faction in Laos
LPLA	Lao People's Liberation Army, more commonly known as PL
LS	Landing Site
MOD	Ministry of Defence
MR	Military Region, Royal Lao Army
NVA	North Vietnamese Army. Its official name was The People's Army of the Democratic Republic of Vietnam but it was always alluded to as NVA
PA	personal assistant
PGNU	Provisional Government of National Union: joint Royal Lao Government and Lao Patriotic Front administration after Pathet Lao military victory
PL	Pathet Lao, military wing of Lao Patriotic Front
PLA	(Chinese) Peoples' Liberation Army
RLA	Royal Lao Army
RLAF	Royal Lao Air Force
RLG	Royal Lao Government
SDECE	French external intelligence service

SIS	Special Intelligence Service, United Kingdom, a.k.a. MI 6
USAF	United States Air Force
USAID	United States Agency for International Development

Lao Terms

baçi	ceremony of prayer and good wishes
ban	village, house
bor	'or not' when at the end of a question
bor pen nyang	it doesn't matter
boun	festival, celebration
Meo	Lao ethnic tribe, now known as Mhong
phee	thirty-two spirits that inhabit a Lao's body
Tan	Mr
thud	attaché
Tu Nong	Your Highness, to a princess
wai	salutation, hands joined in front of face
wat	Buddhist temple

Vietnamese Terms

Dại Tá	Colonel
Chào Ông	Hello, to a man

Prologue

Early April, 1945. Somewhere in north Indo-China: 'Never forget *The Catechism of a Revolutionist*. It was written many years ago but is still true today,' explained the earnest-looking, gaunt-faced man in a chilling, nasal twang to his class of keen, young political acolytes, wire-rimmed spectacles magnifying his malevolent eyes. 'The true revolutionist sees himself as a doomed man, without any personal interests or feelings, without even a name of his own. He has but one idea, the revolution, and for this he breaks with all the laws and codes of morals of the educated world. If he lives in it, pretending to be part of it, it is only to destroy it the more surely; everything must be equally hateful to him. He must be ready to die, having trained himself to resist torture, and he must be ready to kill any sentiment within himself if it stops him in his purpose. If a comrade gets into trouble, his fate is only to be decided by his usefulness and by the expenditure of revolutionary force necessary to save him. As regards the established society, the revolutionist must classify its members not in respect of anything but the harm they might cause the revolution. The most dangerous must be immediately destroyed. As for the others, they must be exploited – those venal, those greedy, those whom the people hate must be allowed to continue being venal, being greedy, being hated so that the people can understand that the present system is rotten and so must be changed. You will be the instruments of that change.

'Our Communist revolution in Indo-China started many years ago. Now those arrogant and feckless French are so weakened that they will never be able to prevent us from achieving our aim. Our victory may still be years away but you young men in front of me,' and in an uncharacteristic gesture, the fore-finger of the instructor's right hand slowly pointed at each one in turn, his malicious eyes piercing theirs so deeply that they sent shivers up each spine, 'are the cutting edge of the impetus of our movement. You will be responsible, to start with, for northern Laos. Never forget what I have taught you. Never forget that your bedrock for success will be relentless planning, remorseless opportunism and pitiless persistence, with no limits to just how harsh your methods are. As soon as the war is over I order you to go out and practise.

'The Politburo plan, called Operation Stealth, will take thirty years for final victory. Over those years your unflinching dedication to our cause will need unstoppable momentum: that means perseverance, perseverance, perseverance ...'

Late October, 1945: News of the Japanese surrender on 14 August 1945, with Hồ Chí Minh becoming President of the independent Republic of Vietnam – the name used before the French imposed their unwanted presence – travelled slowly in the more remote regions of Indo-China. This was certainly so near the northeast of Houa Phan province on the border of Laos and Tonkin where fast-flowing rivers, jungle-covered mountains, massive perpendicular blocks of limestone outcrops and primitive communications ensured that scattered and isolated village communities, disinterestedly self-sufficient and parochially narrow-minded, were almost always out of touch with their nearest neighbours – and were entirely happy with their lot.

One such village, not more than a couple of hours' brisk walk from the district capital, Sam Neua, was Ban Liet. Situated in a valley, it had enough rice fields and pasture for the villagers' needs. It spread along two tracks, rutted by bullock carts, in the shape of a cross and consisted of some fifty small, rickety, primitive wooden houses, built on stilts. The roofs were thatched and steep, the floors were made of bamboo slats and the rooms, partitioned by plaited wattle, were devoid of furniture. Entry from outside was only possible by climbing up notched poles. In one corner of one room in each house was a cooking place built of mud and stones. With no chimney it was squalidly smoky. People slept on mats woven from grass and there was no privacy whatsoever. The space under the houses was used for domestic animals, chickens, farming implements, carts, kindling and junk.

The peasants, small, brown-skinned, black-haired folk with high cheek bones and epicanthic eyelids – the men almost beardless – normally lived quietly but one morning in late October the place was abuzz with excitement and tension. Unusually, a group of about thirty men, women and children had moved west from Ta Lang, a village just over the border in Tonkin, asking for refuge. They were Tai Dam people, Black Tais, so called from the colour of their clothes. They looked the same as and were ethnically close to the local Lao villagers so were made welcome with food and shelter. And what rumours spread as they talked amongst each other that evening and late into the night: unbelievable devastation had been wrought on some country far away and, although no one knew for sure where, some said it could be connected with the strange disappearance of those heavy-handed Japanese soldiers. Other menaces were threatening, according to the visitors: there were roving bands of marauding Tongkinese whose allegiance was to some nationalist hot-head named Hồ Chí Minh in far-off Hanoi, who was preaching that Tonkin, along with Annam and Cochin-China should again be called by their old name, Vietnam; the Chinese were coming from Yunnan; those unbearable French were coming back ... meanwhile was it really true that King Sisavangvong ruled in Luang Prabang as King of all Laos? Was the war really over? If so, why this new terror? When would it be safe to live normally? Not for many years had there been so much speculation. Nobody could guess the answers.

Early next morning the elders of both communities put their heads together. The harvest was in and ploughing for the next crop had yet to start, so with little work to be done, most of the villagers came to listen. It was decided that three men from Ban Liet and three from Ta Lang would go to Sam Neua, find out what had been happening and maybe also get news of the nature of the threat of the roving bands so that they could make plans as how best to defend their village. They had eaten early so they could get there and back well before dusk. Each man's youngest son asked if his father would take him and, although this was an unusual request, it was granted. The boys, between five and seven years old, were sturdy lads used to grazing cattle, so the two-hour walk to Sam Neua would be no hardship and they could always hop on dad's shoulders on the way back if they became tired. Indeed, one man took both his sons – the elder for the fun of it and the younger to study in the wat, as Buddhist temples were known, at Sam Neua for a year.

At the last moment one of the men from Ban Liet suddenly decided he could not go as his buffalo had started to calf. Instead a shifty-eyed itinerant trader, who had drifted into the village with a woman and a young boy some months before and had stayed there doing odd jobs said he would go along with his son. He had told the villagers that he had come from the northeast of Thailand and had been coerced by the Japanese to work in procuring local talent for their officers. He was, in fact, a soldier of the Royal Thai Army, who had changed his surname from Xuto to Varamit, the easier not to be picked up were he to desert. His woman was temporary but the boy, named Mana, had been with him since leaving Bangkok where a younger son, with his mother, had been waiting for his return for several years.

The weather was crisp and cloudlessly clear. As was the custom when any mission of importance was undertaken, many people came to the village bounds to see the little party of six men and seven boys off. The jungle closed in. At a low pass they turned round and gazed back fondly. There were no other villages in view, in fact the whole of that small valley was empty of people save for those three hundred souls living in Ban Liet. It was a peaceful, pleasant scene that the group turned away from and continued on their journey down the jungle path.

Two hours later the track left the jungle, passed into an area of bare fields before joining a red laterite road, Route Coloniale 6. They crossed the wooden bridge over the River Sam and made their way into the small town, which boasted some stone buildings, a primary school, a wat and the provincial offices, now unstaffed. The wat was the natural place for the group to go to. As was normal the men had brought some sticky rice with them as an offering to the bonzes, the monks. They went inside and paid their respects to the saffron-robed abbot, a man in his early forties, whose name, Phannyana Maha Thera, none of the boys could remember although they had practised it one their way.

The senior man from Ban Liet introduced himself and the rest of his group, telling the abbot that the others were from over the border in Ta Lang. 'We will have a serious talk later on towards sundown,' said the abbot before turning to the boys. 'Introduce yourselves. Tell me who you are. Don't be shy. First let me have those from Ban Liet.'

'I am Leuam Sunthorn,' said the lad who had come to study.

'I am his younger brother, Bounphong Sunthorn,' said the next boy and, unexpectedly pulling the other Ban Liet boy forward, 'this is my best friend, Thong Damdouane.'

The senior man upbraided the three lads for not answering the abbot as 'Phannyana Maha Thera' but the abbot waved his objections away and smiled warmly at the boys. 'And the three Tai Dam lads from Ta Lang? No need to say my name, only yours.'

More shyly, as they still felt strangers in a new country, they gave their names simultaneously which caused them the giggles and so broke down their reserve.

Young Mana Varamit churlishly refused to speak. He stared

at the abbot, quizzically and resentfully, his brown eyes deep set and slightly flecked. His father made no effort to correct his son's rudeness.

Leuam Sunthorn was ceremonially handed over to the abbot, his foster father for a year. The visitors also paid their respects to the lesser bonzes. The boys were given a refreshing drink of coconut juice before the fathers joined a group of locals already sitting down under some trees in the wat's precincts and to whom the men from Ta Lang were introduced. The boys had scampered away out of sight, happily exploring this new place but one of them came back, saying he was tired. He squatted quietly and bright-eyed in front of his father, listening to the grown-ups talking to each other.

Yes, indeed, they had heard of some lawless and ferocious Tongkinese gangs; yes, indeed, the war was over and the Japanese had been sent to Hanoi prior to going back to their own country which seemingly had been devastated in a manner never before known to man; and yes, King Sisavangvong was now Head of State and King of all Laos. No, they could not believe the French would ever come back again after the defeat they had suffered by the Japanese ... and so the talk rambled on, everybody engrossed in it.

After maybe an hour, weak, lukewarm tea was brought and handed to the gossiping group but before they had finished drinking it, four armed men, dressed in a strange, sloppy, green uniform, appeared. The obvious senior, a man with inscrutably dark, glassy eyes, behind which were vacant pits where his soul had been and the sort of face that showed it worked for the forces of evil not for the forces of good, pointed at the three Tai Dam men from Ta Lang. 'You thought to get away from us, did you?' he asked abruptly. 'Fools! We have our own way of dealing with reactionaries and collaborators like you. What you cannot have realised is that you will never escape us and that we workers from Tonkin are determined never to allow the Colonialists, the Feudalists or the Imperialists to bleed the true Socialist toilers to death any more. No foreigner will ever be allowed to come back on Indo-Chinese soil again. In thirty years' time there will be one seat of government for the whole of Indo-China and that will be in Hanoi.'

Everybody stared with blank amazement at these men whose faces were, if anything, a shade fairer than those of the villagers sitting around, although to a casual observer the difference would have been scarcely noticed. They had not properly understood what the hostile stranger had said – so many new words. The atmosphere grew tense.

The man whose son had stayed with him stood up, holding his little boy in front of him. He looked hard at the intruders and said, 'We are in a holy sanctuary so want none of your nonsensical talk here. Keep quiet, go away and let decent folk live in peace. You're not wanted here. Why, we can't really understand what it is you were telling us. Go away.'

With terrifying deliberation the man who had spoken took aim at the little boy's head, itself in line with his father's crotch. He let his intentions be fully realised by the whole group, who could not believe he would carry out his implied threat if only because they were on hallowed ground. The report of the weapon being fired stunned everyone who heard it. A raucous, skin-tightening scream from the wounded man pierced the others' still shattered ears as, unable to do anything but gawp stupidly, they saw him sink to the ground, holding a streaming, pulpy mess of bones, blood and brain of his dead son in his hands, his crotch dripping genitalia. Another shot rang out and the man's bowels burst, with long slivers of entrails oozing out onto the ground. Still benumbed by the shock, the man's last jarring sobs and the ghastly red mush in front of them, nobody tried to stop the Tongkinese gang from leaving. The whole incident had taken less than five minutes from start to finish.

The abbot came out from the wat and took charge. Some locals had clustered around, ghoulishly examining the sickening remains. Almost paralysed by fear, they reacted slowly to the abbot's order to them to prepare a grave for father and son, speedy burial being essential. Digging implements were fetched and a grave was prepared near the village boundary. As the grisly remains were being put into it an unexpected shadow fell over them. One man looked up and pointed at it, gibbering incoherently, unable to speak. The rest followed his gaze, heads shaking in utter disbelief; in the otherwise clear blue sky a thick pall of smoke, ominously flecked with black, was curling up over the hills and drifting their way. It could only mean a pyre of burning flesh, and it came from the direction of Ban Liet. Panic gripped them and it was only the abbot's calm and stern orders that got the gruesome task of interment finished. Final prayers for the dead could, and would, come later. Now there was something more urgent to be done.

Leaving the boys with the bonzes, the five men hurried back to Ban Liet. Fearing an ambush, they kept off the track so making their progress slow. When they reached the pass where, only a few hours earlier, they had looked back so happily at the tranquil scene, they now saw what had been a living village was but a smoking bonfire. What had been a peaceful little settlement comprising families, houses, a few worldly goods and animals was nothing but burnt and smouldering devastation. Curiosity, and hope, got the better of them and they continued down the track.

The job had been done with horrible efficiency. Not one survivor remained and the nauseating stench of still burning bone and flesh, fetid and foul, poisoned the air. One of the men turned away and vomited noisily. Here and there blood-stained rags showed that not all the dead had given in without a struggle and one or two scorched remains plainly revealed that some women had been split open from loin to breast before being thrown into the holocaust. Tongues of flame in the repulsive garbage flickered and flared where cattle carcasses, charred and stinking, took longer to burn than did human corpses. As the men searched the ruins something ghastly in a clump of unburnt bushes near a large rock away to a flank caught their eye. They found the six corpses of the wives of the six men who had gone to Sam Neua. Faces snarling in horror and eyes glazed, they lay naked, each with a half-peeled banana mockingly stuck up their torn vagina, the scars of their molested limbs covered with large black flies feeding on the darkened ooze of blood. The men, scarcely able to believe what they saw, carried their women in silent agony to where the flames were the most active and had formed the deepest bed of embers. There they laid them. As best they could, they dragged some of the still burning timbers from the biggest houses to the stacked corpses, knowing that bodies do not burn without intense heat. As the flames took control they quickly left, unable to bear the sight and smell any longer.

The whole occurrence was a savagely cruel act of reason-deadening barbarity and each survivor's mind was indelibly branded by the crazed effrontery of the murders there and in the wat. There was now nothing more that could be done in the remains of Ban Liet so the men, sadly, slowly and silently, returned to Sam Neua, reaching it well after dark. It was only then did they realise that the one-time Thai soldier was missing.

They took their footwear off outside the wat and went inside, saluted the abbot and were bidden to be seated. They sat cross-legged on a rush mat, speechless and in a state of shock. The look on each face was so stricken that no questions were asked. The boys, mercifully ignorant of the tragedy, were being looked after elsewhere by the schoolmaster's wife. After a while the men started to tell their story and, when it had been told, they were given an opiate sedative. They fell asleep where they were, utterly exhausted, and a kind soul covered them with a blanket.

During the night other reports of the marauders trickled in as the abbot and his bonzes, along with the elders of Sam Neua, met to discuss both the short term and longer implications of these incidents. They recalled what they had learnt as children about various groups of Chinese Ho rebels who had laid waste to the region seventy-five years before. First came the Red Flag Hos who were followed twelve years later by two more robber bands, the Black Flags and the Yellow Flags. Those gathered remembered, when children, the Yellow Flag Hos and had been terrified of them. They were followed by Thai invaders who, in turn, were followed by French. For years there had never been real peace in northern Laos – and now, as soon as the war involving the Japanese was at an end, new and deadly dangers threatened. The options that were open would need much discussion, followed by the abbot looking at the omens with the survivors next morning – meanwhile they needed sleep.

On the morrow after pre-dawn prayers, lengthy deliberations took place. The gang, whose leader spoke in a Hanoi accent, might come back at any time so the five men and their sons must flee but there were matters of the greatest moment to be planned first. The abbot took the fugitives into the inner sanctum, a place seldom visited by those who did not wear the saffron robe. In front of the door, on the opposite wall, was the altar which consisted of a large gilt Buddha, in front of which were many small ones. Flanking the altar was the library, fifty-four cubby holes either side, each with sacred, cloth-covered, flimsy sheets of scriptures peering out in red, yellow and blue symmetry. A pew ran down the centre of the room with conch, cymbals and gong near at hand. The walls and ceiling garishly depicted the rise and fall of man. The fallen were shown as having their limbs torn off and being eaten by ravenous demons, as being trampled on and squashed, as being burnt, as being pulled apart by ugly monsters. The risen were sitting in the lotus position of meditation, eyes inscrutably contemplating eternity. 'If you want to earn merit like these,' said the abbot, pointing to the risen, 'keep faith with me, with each other and with yourselves. Sit down.' This they did, cross-legged on the floor, backs against the wall.

The abbot went to one side of the altar and produced a cylindrical container full of slivers of wood, each with its own individual distinguishing mark. He handed the container to one of the men who, taking it in his right hand, tilted it and gently shook it until one sliver emerged and fell to the floor. This he gave to the abbot. In turn the four others shook out their own sliver, as did four of the five boys, the resentful one sulkily declining. The abbot shook out three slivers. He arranged the twelve slivers in the order of their egress and looked at them steadfastly. After that he turned to the scriptures which, if it is known where to look, give an answer to all queries. He took the twelfth sheet from the hole in which those starting with a T were kept. This was for the twelfth day of Tulakhom, the Lao October, and the date the King was put into a position of sovereign power in Laos. From another pile a second sheet was taken out. This stood for the previous day's date; and another ten sheets, each with its own significance, were produced, so that, finally, there were twelve. An air of hushed expectancy filled the stone-walled cloister.

The evidence was carefully studied for nearly three-quarters of an hour, the spectators watching passive faced, not even the boys fidgeting. The abbot stood up and enigmatically pronounced his verdict: 'It will not be you, oh fathers, who will find the path to reconciliation to what has happened, but your sons. I see right not left, blue not red, white not brown as being essential to and in sympathy with the quest for salvation. But above all I see delusion, pain, suffering and great hardship. The twelve sheets I have studied correspond with the lesser twelve-year zodiac: but it will not be that soon that matters come to a head. Thirty agonising years will elapse before the time is ripe for anything that I have read in the divinations to be pronounced true. Patience and stealth will be the watchwords. Much is still obscure and, hate to say it though I do, one amongst you will betray the others. But salvation will be reached: however, the sixty-year cycle will have to run its course before true and lasting salvation is obtained because, in the first thirty years, evil will be in the ascendancy. But the path is there to be trodden, despite the unknown hardships of this life-long journey,' and, turning to look at the five little boys, saw that now there were only four. Mana Varamit, the Thai boy who had been sitting next to the door, had disappeared. The abbot realised that the others had not noticed that boy's absence, so he did not draw their attention to it. He continued talking to them.

'There is much to be done, much to do: much to be learnt and much to be taught. It is I who can start you on this difficult, dangerous and demanding path but it is you, fathers, who will lead these boys along it for your personal satisfaction – maybe "revenge" is not a word I ought to use in this holy place. It is only they who will reach the end of the thirty-year-long path: their sons will have another thirty years to make matters once more bearable to the backbone of the country, the manual workers in the fields and villages. Sixty years: a long wait but it will take that long before conditions revert to what we know and are used to, I fear, because the forces of decency have so much blackness against them, here and elsewhere. Before the evil can be destroyed by outside help, it has to be softened up from the inside. With this act of dedication we have already set foot in the right direction but in order to get properly started on the journey, listen with great heed to what I have to say. You four boys go and look for your friend. Now, fathers, listen carefully to my proposed plan of action ...'

By late afternoon the men had been fully briefed. The two lads from Ta Lang were each given a new name, one Tâ Tran Quán and the other Le Dâng Khoã, both more Vietnamese-sounding than the Tai Dam ones given at birth. These were entered into a ledger with a codeword, 'Black-eyed Butcher', so that proof of the name change could the more easily be found were it ever wanted. Both as a seal to success and so that the four remaining boys would have some sign that would always know each other by, a small black mark, like a '9' with a curly tail – unique to Laos – was tattooed on the inside of the little finger of their right hand. It also placed an unbreakable bond between them. The sign was, in fact, the 'silent consonant' around which vowel clusters are written in Lao and to which initial vowels are tagged. It can stand for the cry of love, of despair, of victory, or hatred or of any heart-felt exclamation, depending on what the next symbol in the word is. The boys were told how to recognise 'the Black-eyed Butcher' if they ever met him again: inscrutably dark, glassy eyes and an evil face.

It was not the abbot but the fathers who decided that, when the time came, the '9' would be covered by a signet ring that had, on the inner edge, something that looked like a badly written '27' in the Roman script. In Lao it read *kha*, meaning 'kill'. However, there was one caveat, none of the 'four rings' was to kill anyone himself.

Late October, 1945. Near Ben Cat, Cochin-China: Captain Jason Percival Vere Rance, to give him his full name, was Intelligence Officer of 1/1 Gurkha Rifles, which had been sent from Burma at the end of the war to disarm units of the Imperial Japanese Army in Cochin-China. Once in Saigon two Japanese infantry battalions, the Takahashi Butai and the Yamagishi Butai, both innocent of any war crimes, were attached to 20 Indian Infantry Division to help ward off the sullen, sulky but efficient Viet Minh forces which were preventing the Indian Army troops from disarming other Japanese units and back-loading their stores.

It was decided to mount an operation some hundred kilometres north of Saigon to clear troops of the Viet Minh from an area they used as a base. Only B Company, 1/1 Gurkha Rifles, commanded by a subedar, was available so the Yamagishi Butai was detailed to operate with it. The surrender orders were that the commander of any unit of the Imperial army, however senior, when operating with the Indian army, had to come under command of the Indian Army senior officer, however junior he be. So it was that Captain Rance found himself commanding a battalion of Japanese troops even though he was many years the junior in service to the Japanese battalion commander.

Orders for the actual operation and a strict timetable of movement were given once the general area was reached.

The convoy left its base towards its target area at dawn on the morrow and the force moved off on foot from the start line dead on time. With Jason Rance and his three Gurkha gunmen were Captain Yamagishi, the battalion commander, and his staff and, on the right, the company of Gurkhas. One of Yamagishi's companies was on its right and the other two away on the left. The force advanced steadily through elephant grass, scrub and patches of rubber trees for about two hours with no incident.

Firing broke out from an overgrown rubber plantation to the front, about two hundred metres away, on the top of some higher ground. The country was patchy scrub that sloped down to a small river. Jason Rance looked around and tried to pinpoint the fire. Captain Yamagishi suggested firing his mortars before any advance.

'Comrade Commissar. Who do you think the forces to our front are? Are they Imperialist British with Indian Army lackey soldiers?'

'I only saw Feudalist Japanese. Why do you talk of Imperialists?'

'Because I saw a European through the binoculars. Surely those cursed French are not once more back in our midst?'

The Comrade Commissar, mumbling 'perseverance', took the binoculars and looked through them at the European. *I have a plan to eliminate him and some Japanese for certain to show the young, unbloodied lads how easy it is.*

Crump, crump, crump. Mortar bombs began exploding round the Viet Minh position. A piercing treble scream was heard and a more muted male sobbing.

'Listen. We will abandon this position,' said the Political

Commissar. 'You: get one brave soldier to hide under the leaves of that ditch, wait till the Japanese troops carry the casualties away – the white men always take enemy casualties with them – and, as they depart, to come out of hiding and make sure he kills the European by firing at him from behind.'

Yamagishi and Jason, aided by the interpreter, conferred shortly after the mortars were ordered to cease firing. Jason suggested a platoon attack on the enemy position but was respectfully asked if he would mind if Yamagishi could have his permission to send a section. Jason gave it – having not much option – and was intrigued to see ten men, commanded by a Second Lieutenant armed only with a sword, disappear down the slope a few minutes later. After a short while they appeared some way up on the far side, below the rubber plantation. On reaching the high ground, the Second Lieutenant turned and waved. *How so very different from only two months ago!*

The main body advanced in extended line. At the top of the hill were two casualties, both badly wounded by large mortar fragment penetrating near the top of the thigh and making a nasty hole in the neck. One was a young man, armed with a rifle; the other, an unconscious lad of about twelve, with a catapult in his hand. Had, Jason wondered, the Japanese mortar fire only wounded those two? If not, why were the other wounded taken away and not those two? *Leave it: theoretical.*

Yamagishi Butai had a medical officer with it. He examined the wounded and gave his decision. 'Death will come soon', he told Yamagishi. 'I'll give them a jab of morphine, bind their wounds and leave them. Knowing these Viets as I do, I expect their comrades will watch us and, if they see we do not take them with us, come and rescue them.'

Yamagishi agreed. 'I'll have to get permission of the English officer. He won't like leaving them.'

Nor did he but under the circumstances there was little else to be done. Through the interpreter Yamagishi pointed out that there was only about another half an hour before the road they were aiming for was reached and the villagers would be told to go back and rescue the wounded – or attend to the corpses. 'We must move on quickly as we are behind time.'

About twenty yards away a section of Japanese soldiers were going through some sort of dumb pantomime. They were excitedly pointing down to something Jason could not see.

'Stop them fooling about,' Jason said to the interpreter, angry with himself about the decision to abandon the wounded.

The interpreter went to speak to the soldiers and, on his return, said, 'Respected sir, they are afraid.'

'Why?'

'They have seen an arm,' was the enigmatic reply.

So Jason went to see for himself. The bank, maybe three feet high, had a ditch on the other side. Rubber trees were planted on the bank and the ditch was to hold water to help their growth. But now it was full of dry leaves and a skinny brown arm was waving about, palm upwards.

'Pull it,' Jason ordered abruptly.

'They are afraid to,' answered the interpreter.

Jason, normally placid, felt his temper about to snap and this was noticed by the interpreter. Sensing that valour was the better part of discretion, the soldiers were quickly ordered to pull the hand. One man, braver than the rest, bent down ready to grasp it. A second man caught him round the waist and a third the second likewise. In one movement the leading soldier grasped the hand and all three pulled. Jason watched, fascinated, as a small man, dressed in a strange, sloppy, green uniform, whose eyebrows were uneven and his face malevolent – a face not easy to forget – was jerked upwards, carrying a brand new machine-gun of curious shape that had a tray-like magazine. Almost in one movement he wriggled free of his captors, looked up at the near-cloudless sky, crouched low and bent both ends of the magazine down, so jamming the weapon. He jumped up and down, shrieking. The Japanese were on him in a flash even before one of Jason's Gurkha escort brought his kukri out of his scabbard as though to decapitate him. He ceased his shouting and looked sullen. The left sleeve of his shirt had been torn, revealing the star of Tonkin tattooed on his left shoulder.

'Why the pantomime?' asked Jason, before realising that the interpreter would not understand. 'Can you explain this?'

'Respected sir, the soldiers were in micturition' – some quick overtime with his dictionary there – 'on the leaves when the arm appeared.'

Then only did Jason understand why the man had looked at the sky on being so unexpectedly pulled out. When he felt the sudden surges of liquid wetting him he had put his hand up to see how heavily it was raining! The two casualties were decoys and his task was to shoot some of the attackers, Jason himself probably, being the tallest by far, as they moved off burdened with the wounded. On seeing that there was scarcely a cloud in the sky, he was furious at having disclosed his position.

'Fancy being saved by Japanese secret weapons,' murmured one of the Gurkha bodyguards. 'Yes,' said another, 'so different from the recent war in Burma.'

Jason Rance, feeling hot, took off his hat and stared at the unusual spectacle. As the prisoner's hands were being tied behind his back he took a long look at the Englishman: tall, a taut, lean body, and the indefinable air of a natural commander. He had strikingly blue eyes, fair hair, almost hawk-like features. The three men with him, certainly not Japanese, looked at him with respect as he spoke with them. *Who are they? They talk in a tongue unknown to me.*

He was led away with the advancing forces, his now useless weapon carried by a Japanese soldier.

I hope the Politburo never hears of my failure. Somehow I'll escape and, anyway, the time is, in fact, nowhere ripe. Another thirty years. Our watchword is Perseverance. I'll never forget that arrogant imperialist's face. Order those feudalist Japanese to piss on me, did he?

Captain Jason Percival Vere Rance never thought he'd see the man again, but he did, many years later …

January 1946. Somewhere north of Bangkok, Thailand: Major David Law, scion of an old Huguenot family, commissioned in the last batch of regular officers in 1939 into the Somerset Light Infantry, had spent most of the war in India and Burma, attached to a Punjabi regiment. He had gone on a month's leave in England to marry his childhood sweetheart but had had to hurry back to Thailand to be Brigade Major of 33 Brigade, 7 Indian Infantry Division. One of his tasks was to reconnoitre the area near the bridge over the River Kwai which the desperately unlucky prisoners-of-war in Japanese hands had built at such an appalling cost in casualties. His task was to recommend which area a permanent site could be purchased from, or given by, the Royal Thai government as a fitting memorial and war grave cemetery.

On his way back a Thai woman stepped out from the side of the road, her small boy trailing behind her, and, not looking where she was going, Major Law's jeep knocked her down. The vehicle slewed to a halt. David Law jumped out. The woman died as he was binding a broken leg. The law concerning such a death was explicit: the last person to touch a person before he or she died was responsible for looking after that person's family. There was no escaping it.

The police soon arrived and the necessary formalities were undertaken. In this case the family was a small one; an elder boy of about seven, he would have been when last seen, said a neighbour, taken north by his father, a soldier in the Royal Thai Army, who had disappeared somewhere to the northeast it was thought even before the war had come to an end. No news had ever come back of either. No, the name the father had registered for military service was not known: it would certainly be different as it was so much easier to desert and not be caught when using another name. His wife, now his widow, had been *Khun* – Mrs, the police explained – Xuto, so the neighbours confirmed, and her small son said that his name was Xutiati.

In the fullness of time, Major Law managed to get Xutiati Xuto over to England and educate him along with the rest of his children. During his schooling he was mildly teased about his name but he took it graciously and the kidding soon wore off. Family and friends knew him as Charlie. David was well off, having inherited a fortune, so the burden of one extra in the family was more that of conscious than of capital. Nevertheless burden it was. Luckily the lad became part of the family and took full advantage of his English education. Nor did he ever forget that he was a Thai.

CHINA

NORTH

VIETNAM

TOMKIN

Yunnan

BURMA

Dien Bien Phu
Talang
Annam
Hanoi

Ban Hom
Keuang
Ban Liet
som ltteua
Nong Kang

Xieng Lom

Pak Beng
Houa Phan

Luong
Prabang
Bouam Long
Xieng Khouang
Long Cheng
Ban
Ban

Saraboury
Plain of
Jars
Barthelemy
Pass

Gulf

of

Tonkin

Vang
Vieng

Phou Khao
Khwoi
Nam Ngeum
Vinh
Nape
Pass

Vientiane
Nam Theon

Mu Gia
Pass
Ban
Karai
Pass

DMZ

SOUTH

THAILAND
VIETNAM

Saravane

Pakse
Kong mi

Champassak
Attopeu

CAMBODIA

LAOS

———— Military Region boundary
———— Province boundary
o   Province capital
— — —   Road
- - - - Trail
Ⓐ   Route number
        Approx ceasefire line 1973

0   25   50   75   100
Statute Miles

Traced by Resham Bahadur Pun

1

New Year's Day 2515, BE (Year of the Rat) / 5 April 1972. Northern Laos: This was the day people had been looking forward to, when everybody would enjoy themselves in a prolonged *boun*, as the Lao people called their holy days and celebrations. The fervent hope was that the King would announce a date for his long-delayed coronation and surely a crowned King would act as a shield against those troublesome Communists and the Lao People's Liberation Army, known to the Western world as the Pathet Lao or PL. Excitement and expectation were intense, almost palpably, in the royal capital, Luang Prabang, situated on the left bank of the River Mekong.

Before dawn His Majesty the King, as Head of the Buddhist Church in Laos, had gone to worship at the royal wat, surrounded by elderly, shaven-pated bonzes, who, in turn, were flanked by similarly clad and shorn youths. Here the scriptures were read and prayers intoned for a speedy end to the twenty-seven-year-long war which had split the country so tragically in two, for a return to their home for the refugees and to their family of the many men under arms with, finally, in confirmation that Laos was an independent, sovereign state, the coronation of His Majesty, King Savang Vatthana.

The King, a tall and dignified man in his late sixties, was worried, though he tried hard never to show it. His father's sovereign power, the last gift of the defeated Japanese at the end of the Second World War, had been revoked by the returning French soon after. On every New Year's Day since his father had died, thirteen years before, the scriptures had been read and the divinations foretold to him by the senior abbot, Phannyana Maha Thera, now stiff-backed and a little hard of hearing, but renowned for his knowledge of omens. He had been of great value to the royal family ever since he had moved to Luang Prabang from Sam Neua twenty-seven years before, when he had become the Chief Bonze of Laos. Every year he had had the same sad message which he always interpreted to his royal master in the same quiet, measured tones: 'The King who is crowned when the wild buffaloes are trampling the grasses of Laos will be the last crowned ruler of Laos.' Thus it was that the King was still uncrowned and had, as yet, no plans for his coronation, for the war still raged in his kingdom.

Before walking back to his palace, His Majesty offered sticky rice and fruit to the senior bonzes while outside, in the town, spectators gathered for the processions of virgins, hoping to catch more than just a passing glimpse of them.

By now it was hot and the early morning mist had cleared so the small T-28 fighter-bombers of the Royal Lao Air Force had started to fly their routine missions to warn the Royal Lao Army of any Communist advances from their positions in the hills a few kilometres to the northeast of the town where the Pathet Lao forces were dug in. In previous years there had been shelling and mortar attacks during public holidays, with the Communists patrolling even as far as the King's orange groves to the Southeast of the town, and nobody wanted their *boun* spoilt yet again.

The processions started off as numerous individual trickles of virgins, bonzes, jokers and musicians from the many wats scattered around the town. First would come eight pretty girls walking in front of a ninth, and prettiest, who sat on a large model of a rat, carried by four stalwart youths with glistening, rippling torsos. Behind the girl on the rat came the virgins, six abreast and maybe four or five rows deep. The heat, the noise, the excitement, the water that was thrown around seemed to have no effect on them as they walked demurely along with heads held high, tantalisingly nubile. Their long jet-black hair was put into a bun on the right-hand side of their head, signifying virginity, and a thin gold chain and a comb kept the shiny tresses in place. They wore a silk blouse of peacock blue, emerald green and damson red, each trim little figure scarcely discernible. A silver belt around their waist held up their skirt, more subdued in colour than the louder tones of the blouses, but each had a strip of brightly coloured, intricately designed needlework round the base. Bare-legged, they wore sandals with low heels. Each oval face had high cheek bones, each nose deliciously and delicately snub. Their brown eyes gazed with unfocussed indifference – almost disdain – as they passed through the ever-thickening crowds of spectators with their raucous applause and ribald comments.

Behind the virgins came the bonzes, shaven heads darkly stubbled, walking bare-footed, with saffron robes girdled and folded over left shoulders. In their midst, carried aloft under a large orange umbrella, came the head monk of each group. Behind him came the musicians playing flutes, drums and giant xylophones carried on a stretcher with the player between the end two carriers.

In the rear came the jokers, some stripped to the waist, covered in yellow dust, others with soot-covered faces, dressed any old how. They sang and danced, twirled and pirouetted, veered and shuffled their way, carrying buckets and throwing the water over the crowd who joyously responded by trying to tear the jokers' clothes. At predestined places, the jokers' buckets were refilled. As the last of the jokers passed, some of the crowd joined them while others waited for another procession to pass, replenishing the water supply for their buckets.

In the middle of the town is a sacred hill, on the top of which is a golden wat named Phou Si, after a mythical giant. A wide avenue runs round the hill and, on one side, a steep path from the wat joins it in front of the King's palace. The royal wat that the King had visited earlier on was the destination of all the little processions from various wats which were so routed that the trickle became a stream, then a torrent and finally a flood of moving, pulsating, tramping, dancing, singing, banging, happy, torn, wet people with their own quiet patches of virgins and bonzes making the rest of the commotion more concentrated.

One and all they squeezed into the courtyard of the royal wat, the earlier ones being forced against the walls where there were intricately carved fabulous beasts, gold-leafed pillars and large bells, a wonderful riot of bright colours. Finally there was no more room for anybody else to come and gradually silence fell, with even the jokers restrained.

The hushed crowd heard the heartfelt and vibrant chants of prayer from inside the wat, '... peace in the land ... a return to the farms ... menfolk back home ... our King crowned on his throne ...' The praying became subdued then ceased and the pent-up emotion of the crowd welled out with a long audible sigh and excitedly they spoke among themselves, '... peace in the land ... and the King crowned on the throne ...'

But to nobody's real surprise yet to everybody's real disappointment, no announcement of His Majesty's coronation was made.

By early afternoon all was quiet again and the crowds of the morning had dispersed. It was stinkingly hot and humid, with a few low clouds. The rains proper were still some weeks away and the ground was parched and dusty.

Suddenly at about half past four there was a sharp clap of thunder and a short but violent dust storm. As it died away a single rifle shot was heard, then another and a third. Within a few minutes shooting was heard all over the town, rifles and machine-guns. Traffic and pedestrians vanished and Royal Lao Army troops appeared at street corners in the town and on the outskirts. Tension mounted while, in their hotel rooms, little groups of diplomats counselled among themselves, feeling a tinge of induced heroism, composing telegrams for their ministries at home. The firing died away and life slowly returned to normal.

By sundown no enemy attack had materialised so, at 7 o'clock, dressed in ceremonial uniform, members of the Royal Lao Government, local dignitaries, senior members of the Royal

Lao Army and the foreign diplomatic community started to arrive at the palace for the culminating ceremonies, when they would be presented to Their Majesties before a banquet was served and a long drawn-out presentation of Lao classical dancing, based on the ancient Ramayanas.

On foot or by car guests converged on the gates of the palace. Those in cars got out and joined those on foot, leaving the police to sort out the traffic chaos. They passed two young sentries of the King's bodyguard, dressed in red coats and white trousers, and armed with long, old-fashioned rifles nearly as tall as themselves, and went in through the gates into the ornate palace grounds. Members of the Protocol Department then guided people to their rightful places. The majority of the guests went to one side where there were chairs and tables set out in the open ready for the evening's entertainment. Only those privileged few to be presented to the King and Queen went to the palace itself.

Once at the palace the diplomats were confined to the verandah flanking the large reception room. There they moved slowly around, with the polished ease and insincere shallowness of their profession. Accompanied by their womenfolk, they smiled, bobbed, bowed, shook hands and passed empty pleasantries or veiled and cryptic comments – Ambassador to Ambassador, First Secretary to First Secretary and Defence Attaché to Defence Attaché. A close observer would have seen the pointed ignoring of Soviet and Chinese, the hauteur of the French, the cockiness of the Australians, the brashness of the Americans and the diffidence of the British, with only their Ambassador and the Defence Attaché the odd men out. The Ambassador was shunned by those the

British would normally deem their allies and was sycophantically made much of by those not immediately considered in that category. The Defence Attaché was a thick-skinned little man with a misplaced sense of humour whom the rest of his colleagues found difficult to stomach, despite the military freemasonry of the soldiers that allowed for less constrained and more sincere conversation than enjoyed by other diplomats. He approached his Soviet colleague, a Russian, and cornered him.

'As military representative for the British Co-Chairman of the 1962 Geneva Accords for Laos and the 1954 Geneva Accords for Indo-China,' he began pompously and long-windedly, 'can you tell me what the firing this afternoon was all about?'

The Russian eyed him speculatively through thick glasses, wondering what this petty little man was aiming at. As a member of the Soviet Intelligence Service, the KGB, he should have known the answer and indeed his Ambassador, a more senior KGB official, had earlier upbraided him for not knowing; but then, in Laos, so often the inexplicable had a deceptively simple explanation.

'I do not know,' he answered in guttural English, 'but I too am the military representative for the other, the Soviet, Co-Chairman,' a slight pause, 'and I think it was some imperial provocation.'

'No,' countered the British colonel with heavy humour, 'I expect it was a scare put about by your agents acting for the Pathet Lao or the North Vietnamese Army …' He broke off as he saw the Deputy Commander-in-Chief of the Royal Lao Army, a podgy, foxy man of small stature, a born intriguer and cold-bloodedly ambitious to become the next prime minister after Prince Souvanna Phouma.

'Excuse me, *Mon Général*, but can you please tell me what the firing was this afternoon?' he continued in fluent French. The Russian, who pretended not to understand French, looked on impassively.

The General smiled momentarily, with his lips, but his eyes remained brownly impassive. 'It was firing at the moon to dispel the wind demons,' he explained as casually as though he were pointing out something of no significance to a wayward child. 'To make sure that it did not rain tonight,' he added, 'rather a lot of ammunition was expended but that is of little matter.' Here he glanced at the impassive Russian. 'The Americans will doubtless give us more. Translate, please, Colonel,' he ordered.

The Russian listened and asked, through the Englishman, 'What did you do, General?'

'Nothing at all. I didn't hear any of it as I was asleep. My wife told me about it later. She knows better than to wake me up just because firing is heard,' he said, moving off to meet somebody else.

'Ah well,' said the British Colonel, 'this is my last New Year *boun*. I'll be away before the next one and some other poor sucker will have taken my place to try and make head or tail of it.' He said it in a tone of voice that was meant to imply that, whoever that might be, the task would be beyond him.

The French Defence Attaché, who had joined them during the conversation, sniffed disparagingly. 'I was a Lieutenant in 1946 when we French came back to Indo-China after the war. Then the brave General was an idle Sergeant. Still should be just that,' he added disdainfully.

To meet Their Majesties and the royal family, a member of the palace staff called the guests into the large audience chamber and formed them up in protocol seniority, Lao guests on one side of the room and foreigners on the other. The French Ambassador, having been longer in the country than any other Head of Mission, was the doyen of the Diplomatic Corps and so the first foreigner to be presented to the royal entourage as well as having to give the loyal address. On his left stood his wife and behind them the First Secretary with his wife by his side and, at the rear, the Defence Attaché, also with his. Next to the French, likewise arranged, were the South Vietnamese. There was no North Vietnamese representation. There were fourteen groups of diplomats, some of whom had come from Bangkok, as well as representatives of the United Nations Organisation and the International Control and Supervision Commission.

The Communist world was represented by the Soviets, the Poles and the Chinese, to say nothing of any fellow traveller, recognised or not.

The King made his address in impeccable French. He clasped his hands in front of his body, looked around and started to speak. '*Altesses, Excellences, Mesdames, Messieurs; la Reine et Moi ...*' he continued, 'thank you all for your presence here tonight and the loyal address of welcome and warm wishes for a happy New Year that you have extended to the Queen and Ourself.' He outlined the general situation and blandly ended up, 'Indeed We hope for a just and lasting peace for Our united kingdom, a return to homelands and of Our loyal subjects – now refugees and soldiers – and, as soon as practicable after peace has returned,

Our coronation which We regard as indispensable to lasting unity and Our political identity and freedom.' He turned and smiled at the Queen before leading the way out, smiling no more.

The fact that there was no mention of any date for the coronation was noted by the Communists who passed the information on to their fraternal colleagues, just in case their own palace spies had not told them.

Then came a procession of lights descending to the palace from the Phou Si wat at the top of the sacred hill. After a banquet the long evening finished with an exquisite presentation of Lao classical dancing, based on the ancient Ramayanas.

In the remote, jungle-covered hills some eighty kilometres from the Laos-Tonkin border, at Bien Dien Phu, where the French colonial death knell in Indo-China had sounded on Easter Monday, 1954, was a small army camp. Dispersed, equipped with underground shelters, well camouflaged and surrounded by barbed wire and booby traps, it had escaped nothing worse than superficial damage during the interdictory attacks by B-52 bombers and F-111 fighters of the United States Air Force. It was in Military Region 959 and it contained the highly secret Office 95, guarded by the People's Army of the Democratic Republic of Vietnam, more commonly alluded to as the North Vietnamese Army or NVA, controlled from the country's capital Hanoi, and PL, whose capital was in the limestone hills, honeycombed with caves, at Sam Neua, not far away over the border in Laos. It was staffed by dedicated Political Commissars and civilian functionaries.

Office 95 was so called because the chief Vietnamese

representative worked in room number 9 while his Lao counterpart was in room number 5. It was responsible for planning, coordinating and directing clandestine activities, such as subversion, sabotage, the running of intelligence and counter-intelligence networks, disinformation and brazen strong-arm tactics designed to further the revolution by exerting political pressure wherever necessary. It had tentacles all over Laos, especially in the eastern part of the country that was dominated by North Vietnamese men and supplies moving to South Vietnam and Cambodia down the infamous Hồ Chí Minh trail. North Vietnamese influence was strong, too, in the small strip of Laos still in government hands. Only in the northwest of Laos was it nugatory because the Chinese, Communist or otherwise, historically antipathetic to the Vietnamese, dominated that region. Vietnamese uniforms showed Soviet influence: they wore badges of rank and regimental insignia aping the Soviet armed forces, whereas the Pathet Lao, Chinese-style, wore neither. As for the teaching side of Office 95, it was based on Marxist-Leninist principles as dilated and modelled on the KGB Training School No 311 in Novosibirsk, Siberia's largest town. Various courses and seminars were also run in the camp, as was now the case.

Despite their outwardly cosy political relationship, the North Vietnamese looked down on the Lao and had done for centuries. Being harder, more resilient, more dogmatic and more stubborn themselves, they despised their softer, less fervent and more happy-go-lucky neighbours, criticising them for their lack of ideological stamina and condescendingly regarding them as the children of Asia, the hyphen between 'Indo' and 'China', who never took anything, except merry making and flirting, seriously. For their part, the Lao were brought up on the saying that 'the day a Lao is born is the day he starts to hate the Vietnamese'. The Lao resented the Vietnamese superiority but were not strong enough to counter it. The new bonds of Communism were still only strong enough for an outward show of solidarity so, although the Lao were contemptuously disdainful of Vietnamese priggish rectitude, their fervency of purpose and the sparrow-like twittering of their speech, they feared and respected their 'elder brothers' who, resilient as lacquered bamboo, had had any natural spontaneity knocked out of them by the dour Puritanism and unimaginative rigidity of their Communist faith.

The 'imperialists of the western world' were the main target of North Vietnamese vituperation but even so they kept the most poisonous of their venom for use against any American combat personnel who came into their hands. The North Vietnamese Political Commissar in Office 95, Nga Sô Lựu – secretly nicknamed the Black-eyed Butcher because of his inscrutably dark, glassy eyes and his cold-blooded killer instinct – was giving his closing address to a course of ranking Pathet Lao cadres who had been studying Political Solidarity. He was objectionable and narrow-minded, a short-statured, humourless man with close-cropped hair and rimless glasses; he spoke Lao with a Hanoi accent and sometimes made himself difficult to understand by rendering Lao grammatical constructions as though they were Vietnamese. This sounded amusing to the less intense Pathet Lao but they refrained from showing any amusement as, with good reasons, they were dead scared of him.

He walked with a limp, the result of being captured and tortured by the French. He hated all fair-skinned races but swallowed his pride to realise that Soviet Communists were of help for promoting the cause.

The previous day he had had an opportunity to impress his students by demonstrating what to do to any enemy caught and proving that his actions matched his revolutionary teachings. Two American airmen, who had had to bale out of an aircraft damaged by a surface-to-air missile, were brought into the camp on their way to Hanoi for imprisonment. Both men were tired, thirsty, hungry, unwashed, afraid, dazed and in need of urgent medical treatment. One had a broken leg, the other a shattered knee. They had been carried into the lecture room where there was a cage, so restrictive in shape that they could not stand, sit or lie naturally. Into this they had been forced and, making matters worse, had been handcuffed together behind their backs. Both were pain racked and the man with the shattered knee passed out in sheer agony as he was being stuffed into the cage. An English-speaking Vietnamese cadre had vilified them mercilessly for about an hour in front of the students, recounting their heinous crimes against the peoples of Indo-China and threatening them with even worse treatment unless they recanted their crimes by signing a full confession of their guilt. The second airman, beside himself in pain breaking his code of conduct, managed to croak, with a look of utter disdain, 'Go get stuffed, you cock-sucking son of a syphilitic bitch.' The fury of Nga Sô Lựu was such that he yanked his pistol from its holster and shot him through the head, killing him outright. He then shot the other captive, still unconscious, in the gut, letting him bleed slowly to death.

'Those Americans are worse than the arrogant and feckless French: they wound themselves by indulging in what our revered Helmsman calls "sugar-coated bullets", such as condoms and talcum powder in their Mess supplies,' and he spat his disgust.

Now seated on benches the course listened as the Political Commissar was giving them long-term political instructions. 'Today is 5 April 1972. Our armed struggle has been waged for the last twenty-seven years and may continue for another four or five but the political struggle will be with us for always. You, Comrades, will have these three aims always in mind during the political struggle whenever that supersedes present conditions.

'The first is to maintain combat readiness – notably against the USA imperialists and the Lao reactionaries and Thai feudalists – always having regard for the importance in this respect for political study. The second is to be good at increasing production and practising thrift, bearing in mind the community of interest between the Lao people and their armed forces, and the need to encourage self-reliance and self-sufficiency.'[1]

He paused in his dissertation and looked around at his class. The students looked back at him, showing neither enthusiasm nor boredom at the meaningless clichés that were the staple of all such lectures. Nga Sô Lựu continued, 'The third aim is to mobilise the people to build up the basic political organisations, prior to and after the forming of the Lao People's Democratic

---

1 This speech was actually monitored by the BBC so presumably the North Vietnamese cadre was reading it from a prepared Government handout.

Republic. The present reactionary and feudalist clique must be replaced as soon as we are prepared to implement the change. You are revolutionaries and you must never forget what your business is, namely destruction – terrible, complete, universal and pitiless – like I showed you yesterday with relentless planning, remorseless opportunism and a ruthless all-pervading fear.' He paused, panting slightly with the effort of his proselytising zeal. 'I have taught that since 1945.'

The senior Lao student, a man in his thirties named Bounphong Sunthorn, said, 'Comrade Political Commissar, may I ask you two questions?'

'By all means.'

'Comrade, yesterday you more than adequately demonstrated how to deal with US imperialists in the framework of being a true revolutionary. But how about their friends the British in the context of their being the right-wing Co-Chairman of the 1954 Geneva Accords for Indo-China and the 1962 Accords for Laos? You have already explained what we have to do in relation to our Soviet comrades, who have, earlier on in the course, told us how they are manipulating their part of the Co-Chairmanship to the advantage of the socialist camp. The Soviet Defence Attaché also hinted broadly but was not particularly enlightening when he referred to the danger of pro-Chinese tendencies among our cadres.'

Bounphong Sunthorn was, by now, used to working in a milieu he inwardly loathed but outwardly tolerated. In the heart of his heart he lived in hope, still not understanding the code in which the abbot at Sam Neua had spoken those years ago: 'I *see right not left, blue not red, white not brown as being helpful and in sympathy with the quest for salvation'. But the abbot had certainly been correct in saying 'above all I see delusion, pain, suffering and great hardship.'*

Comrade Nga studied a piece of paper in a file on his desk close by. 'Comrade, our Soviet comrades are looking after the economic and political aspects by working against the British when it comes to Co-Chairmanship matters and, I may add, highly successfully too. I am given to understand that the present British Ambassador is a true socialist and also indiscrete enough to be positively enlightening, whilst the British Defence Attaché is a useful link, although he doesn't realise it, to the Americans. Certainly, the British brand of socialism is full of fallacies and inconsistencies. As regards the military side of your question, our military representative can tell you about somebody studying the British methods right now. Colonel?' He asked his military counterpart.

'Comrade, yes. British jungle warfare tactics and teaching are of a much higher order than ever the French or the Americans could evolve. It will be no secret to let you know that a most keen comrade, a Major Mana Varamit, now masquerading in the Royal Thai Army, is even now at the British Jungle Warfare School in Malaysia, acting as Guiding Officer to a course of Thai students.' He sat down with a smug look on his face, not having given away any details that mattered. He had no idea the inward jolt that gave the grave-looking questioner.

'And your second question, please,' invited the Political Commissar.

'Comrade, this may not be completely relevant to this discussion but it is something that has been troubling me since the lecture given by the Soviet Defence Attaché: why did he stress the danger of pro-Chinese tendencies when both fraternal countries are aiding the struggle in Indo-China?'

The Political Commissar tried to hide his inner vexation at the question before answering. 'The Chinese aspect doesn't concern this course but you may rest assured that it is constantly receiving our attention. Let us say that our Soviet comrades are worried lest, after the war has been won, the Chinese try and make Southeast Asia into a carbon copy of their old dreams of a Nanyang Empire, a Southern Seas Suzerainty,' he mockingly concluded.

'Thank you, Comrade. Most helpful and clear answers.' *Stealthy enough?* and he grinned inside himself.'

Bounphong Sunthorn was an enigma to his Vietnamese superiors and his own Lao classmates. He seemed to have an insatiable appetite for work and a most unLao-like habit of studying Vietnamese personalities and their methods. His background was a mystery: some said he was an orphan from a village, Ban Liet, near the border of Laos and Vietnam but others said that that was impossible. Ban Liet and its inhabitants had been mysteriously wiped out soon after the Japanese war had ended. The new Ban Liet was a military staging post, not a village as such. Others said he came from the ancient kingdom of Champassak, ruled over by a hugely fat, rapacious and utterly corrupt prince whose proud cousin was even now the Minister of Defence in right-wing Vientiane. Bounphong spoke, at times, with a northern accent, not a southern one, but no Communist ever showed too much interest in others lest they themselves became a target of too much interest.

But although he was an enigma to the Vietnamese, they had no doubts as to his devotion to the cause, his dedication and his capabilities. He had been marked out to go to Vientiane, that den of right-wing imperialist, reactionary depravity and iniquity, that was the administrative capital of Laos, and where, alongside the Morning Market, the Boulevard Circulaire and the Rue Mahasot, lived the small, virtually beleaguered group of his own people, the Lao Patriotic Front, LPF, representatives, still nominally and legitimately part of the Royal Lao Government. Headed by Soth Petrasy, an ageing schoolmaster, it was due for reinforcement towards the end of the year. Comrade Bounphong Sunthorn was obviously the man to send there. Such a move would redound on the Political Commissar who had recommended him to the Politburo. If only the wretched fellow would stop twiddling that large ring he wore on the little finger of his right hand when he was deep in thought, as he was so obviously now.

A few kilometres into the jungle from the north bank of the River Mekong in northwest Laos, near the riverine town of Pak Beng, was an old road construction camp that the Chinese People's Liberation Army Engineers had used when they rebuilt Route Nationale 46 from a narrow laterite track to an all-weather two-lane highway in the 1960s. As the whole area was deemed of strategic significance and tactical importance to the Chinese, Route 46 was heavily guarded by Chinese infantry and anti-aircraft artillery, the only units of the Chinese Army operationally deployed outside China, less Tibet, at that time. The infantry supported the Pathet Lao and kept pro-Government ground forces away while the anti-aircraft guns had proved effective against USAF U-2 reconnaissance planes flying as high as sixty-thousand feet. No USAF B-52s or F-111s had been used against any target in the area but the Royal Lao Air Force T-28s had, on occasions, been used on local tactical missions, nor had any civil aircraft overflown it since a Dakota of the internal Lao Air Lines, piloted by a Corsican opium smuggler, had been shot down, the wreckage being covered with soil almost immediately afterwards.

The road, bringing the Mekong to within a few hours' motoring distance from Yunnan, was a constant source of alarm to the Thai Government and was conveniently near to Burma to aid the White Flag Communists in their struggle against the authorities in Rangoon, and was also near enough to the Golden Triangle of the illicit opium trafficking for which the region was infamous. Furthermore, the Chinese saw Route 46 as a barrier whereby Soviet influence from India to the west could not meet up with Vietnamese, hence Soviet-tainted, influence to the east. Although the building of the road had been suggested to the Chinese in 1962 and US roving Ambassador Averell Harriman had recommended it to the Royal Lao Government, nobody in Vientiane could find anything in writing about it. Chinese diplomats sedulously denied its existence.

The jungle camp was now used as a training centre for a mixture of Pathet Lao soldiers, dissident Meo and Yao tribesmen from the hilly opium-producing districts of Laos, and Thai Communist guerillas. They were overseen by the Gung An Jiu, the

Chinese Public Security Service of the Ministry of Public Security, and under the instructional guidance of advisers from the Chinese Army People's Liberation Army, the PLA. It was also used as a staging post for Communist movement between Thailand and China. Surrounded by wire and bunkers, its entrance, guarded by two sentries, was in the form of a ceremonial archway on which were two flags, the Lao Patriotic Front flag, red top half, blue bottom half with a white circle in the middle, the emblem of the defunct Lao Issara political party, and the red flag with the yellow star of the People's Republic of China.

Inside one of the huts a group of men dressed in baggy green smocks and slacks, with a round cloth cap, fitted with a small peak and a brown chinstrap, sat listening to a lecture. It was, at first glance, hard to tell who was Chinese and who not, until it was seen that the Chinese wore a red star in their caps and the Lao did not. A Chinese cadre was standing near a blackboard, to the side of which were two large photographs, one of Prince Souvannouvong, the Red Prince of Laos and half-brother to the Lao Prime Minister, Prince Souvanna Phouma, and the other of Chairman Mao Tse-tung. The lecturer, holding a small red book in his right hand, was intoning, with religious fervour, '… weapons are an important factor in war but not the decisive factor: it is people, not things, that are decisive …'

His audience, Lao political cadres, listened respectfully. This part of the Chinese cadre's talk was to illustrate what had been printed and given to each student earlier in the lesson, the meat of which was written in turgid Communist prose, repetitive and deadly boring.

'The present and immediate duty of the armed forces, which must be urgently carried out, is to lead and pave the way for the masses to stage the revolution and seize power, and serve the masses as a strong support force in seizing administrative power from the hands of the reactionaries and feudalists. The armed forces must do everything to facilitate the people's efforts to counter all enemy schemes and divisive activities. It is necessary to use arms in order to surpass and punish the enemy if he remains obdurate.

'The Lao People's Revolutionary Army is a revolutionary army and truly representative of all ethnic groups, it is loyal to the country and the revolution. Therefore, the army must at all times heighten its role, responsibilities and traditions, hold aloft its revolutionary qualities and nature, resolutely carry out its pledges, further consolidate the unity among all the people and enable the people to carry out successfully their seizure of power in a short time after conditions are correct.'[2]

It was signed by an illegible scrawl and bore that day's date, 5 April 1972.

One of the Lao students, who had remained unusually pensive during this tirade, raised his hand and said, 'Comrade, may I ask you two questions?'

The fervent Chinese cadre glanced at his questioner. Nothing showed on his face as he remembered the good reports that had been sent back to China about this student. Here was good material to send to the royal capital, Luang Prabang, when the

---

2 This speech was actually monitored by the BBC so presumably the Chinese cadre was reading it from a prepared Government handout.

time came to install pro-Chinese revolutionaries instead of the present government of King Savang Vatthana and before the pro-Vietnamese clique of Kaysone Phomvihan in Sam Neua could start undoing what the Chinese had been unobtrusively working for over the years. Yes, he would answer any questions asked, sincerely and accurately, and commend him for his assiduity.

'Most certainly, Comrade Thong Damdouane.'

Thong Damdouane was also, by now, used to working in a milieu he inwardly loathed but outwardly tolerated. He, too, in the heart of his heart, lived in hope, still not understanding the code in which the abbot at Sam Neua had spoken those years ago. He, too, had cultivated infinite patience and had as thick a carapace against any unexpected suspicion as any self-respecting lobster. He, too, was an enigma to his Communist masters and his own Lao classmates. He, too, seemed to have an insatiable appetite for work and a most unLao-like habit of studying Vietnamese personalities and their methods. His background was also a mystery but to ask questions about such matters was frowned on by higher authority. Anyway, it was always better to keep quiet about such matters.

'Comrade, my first question is what is our policy if we capture any Lao or Thai lackeys of the imperialist Americans?'

'Damned cat's paws! Send them to us. We'll look after them. We have our own methods of dealing with such vermin. Keep them alive, though: let us judge their value. Remember! Our revolution is irreversible, come what may, but those people can be a nuisance unless properly looked after. May I remind you what Chairman Mao Tse-tung said in 1946? 'All reactionaries are paper tigers,' and so are those Lao reactionaries and Thai feudalists. Your next question, please.'

'Comrade, you were talking about what your Chairman had to say about contradictions. Do you see any contradiction between your Chinese interpretation of Communism and the Soviet Union's interpretation?'

There was a pause as the Chinese instructor looked at an index in the little red book of his hero entitled *The Thoughts of Chairman Mao Tse-tung*. He searched the pages and, finding what he wanted, read out: '"In the final analysis the question is … whether or not we can successfully prevent the emergence of Khrushchev's revisionism in China. We must not be like Khrushchev who served both the interests of the handful of members of the privileged bourgeois stratum in his own country and those of foreign imperialists and reaction." That,' he continued, 'is an extract from a speech made on 14 July 1964 and is entitled "On Khrushchev's Phony Communism and Its Historical Lesson for the World". It is still relevant.'

'I don't quite see the difference between the Chairman's interpretation and that of the USSR. Can you further enlighten me, please?' Thong asked.

'Yes. We in the People's Republic of China care for people. Basically the Soviets don't. They think only the leaders matter. Thank you, Comrade Thong, for your questions.'

'Thank you, Comrade,' said Thong and he smiled, a strangely happy smile, as he played with a large ring on the little finger of his right hand. *Stealthy enough?* and he grinned inside himself.

In a Type A Special Forces camp at Phitsanalok in northern Thailand, a group of American case-officers, seconded for duty to the Central Intelligence Agency, were discussing their training programme for the next course of the Thai Unity Forces soon to be deployed in action as part of the secret army fighting the Communists in Laos. Lieutenant Colonel Broadus Richards, a square-faced, crew-cut ex-Marine Corps veteran from Korea and Vietnam, turned to his Executive Officer, Major Peter Hodge.

'Hey, Pete, will we have that guy, what's his name, back from the Limey Jungle Warfare School in time for our next field training exercise?'

'You're talking of Major Mana Varamit. Yes, sir! I sure hope so. It's April 5 today and he's due here in one month, time for us to include those Brit methods in the final training session. He'll be here for about six months or so. We'll need to evaluate any new teaching before we use it over on the other side of the river. In this Year of Disgrace, 1972, it's about time we tried any and everything against Brother Gook, even Brit teaching methods although they won't join us in Nam.'

'That's right, Pete. And then I think we'll have to use him over on the other side of the river for a spell. If you remember he asked to be considered for a tour towards the end of the year. Scrapping on the far bank of that li'l ol' Mekong can sure sharpen folks' minds, Thais' or Gooks'. That'll be around next November time, I guess.'

It was a typically wet spring day in London. April showers, thought the American who was being driven over Westminster

Bridge towards the south bank, are like so much that is English; predictable up to a point, useful at times but unpleasant if you're caught by them. He sighed, looking out of the blurred window over the murky Thames and then at the untidy spread of buildings on the far bank. It was, he reflected, less claustrophobic than New York and not a stylised as Washington DC, although it was growing just as dangerous. The car left the bridge and plunged into the purlieus of untidy, narrow back streets, its passenger glancing at his watch. *I'll be in time this week*, he mused, *not like last week when I got caught in a traffic jam*, and he fingered a stiff plastic pass in his pocket feeling the metal strip running through it.

Maurice Richard Burke, known to his friends as 'Dally' because his facial expression unfortunately resembled that of a Dalmatian dog, was listed in the US embassy in Grosvenor Square as a Second Secretary Commercial. This was the cover for him in his role of Liaison Officer between his own and the British Secret Intelligence Service, the SIS. His main interest was Indo-China and weekly meetings with the SIS Desk Officer for that region enabled him to keep up to date with details from the British Heads of Station in the area, who sometimes had the edge on the Americans by virtue of their Co-Chairman's status. Although there was considerable in-post exchange of views between the two organisations where both were represented and personalities did not clash, there were some matters of substance that needed clearance before dissemination was permitted. More often than not these routine weekly meetings were anodyne but sometimes, like the one today, they could be important. He had a proposition to put to the Limeys affecting the future, based on a sad premise that in turn was a problem with no easy solution – probably with no solution at all. Period! No papers were carried on these occasions for security reasons and anyway, if you lived long enough with a problem, you had the details at your fingertips so no paperwork was needed.

His car stopped at a large building, not at the main entrance, which could be overlooked by some new high-rise flats, but at a side door. He got out and, without a word spoken, the car drove off. Maurice Burke took the pass out of his pocket and placed it in a slot in the wall. Within five seconds the door opened and he went inside. Almost immediately the door shut behind him.

A hall porter, dressed in blue uniform, sat in a kiosk opposite. 'Hello, Mr Burke. How are you, sir?' he asked.

'Fine thanks, Frobisher. And yourself?'

'OK. Mustn't grumble, but then we always do! Mr Chambers will be waiting for you on his floor.'

During this exchange of pleasantries, Maurice Burke had his pass taken from him while Frobisher, having written down the relevant details in his ledger, gave the American an internal clip-on visitor's pass, which Burke fixed on his right lapel, and detailed another security guard to escort him up to his destination. They got into the lift and, on the fourth floor awaiting his arrival, was the man he had come to see, John Chambers, Indo-China Desk Officer in the SIS.

'Hi, Dally, what's new?' he asked as, accustomed to the American habit, he proffered his hand which was immediately swallowed up in Burke's vast paw.

'Not so dusty, Johnny boy, not so dusty,' he said with a grin. 'I hope you've been able to act on my message about putting out feelers.'

'Yes, I have,' answered John. 'Come along into my office and we'll see what can be done to help. I've got a character coming over from the Ministry of Defence to advise us. He's not due in until 3 o'clock. That'll be enough time for a cup of something hot and to run over anything routine first.' He was referring to the link man between the MOD and the SIS when there was any customer requirement that the army might be called upon to provide or give advice about.

John took Maurice along a corridor to the right and left of which were unnumbered and unnamed doors. 'How the devil you find your way around here just beats me,' grunted Maurice. 'All these damned doors are unmarked ...' and his voice trailed away in humorous disgust.

'Cheer up, Dally,' John countered. 'It helps us maintain a high standard of security but, unless you've got a guide when you're first posted in, it can indeed be tricky.'

John took a key out of his pocket as they reached the last door at the end of the corridor, unlocked it, held it open for Maurice and then followed him inside. It was a small office with a table, an ordinary chair, two easy chairs and a combination lock cupboard. 'Hang your mac up by mine,' said John, indicating a couple of hooks on the inside of the door. 'Sit down and let's get the routine work over and done with before the ministry man gets here. Tea or coffee?'

'Coffee, two lumps, no cream. Haven't yet learnt how to

swallow what you guys call tea.'

While they conferred the secretary brought them their brew and a biscuit, ordered over the telephone. No intercommunication sets were allowed in the offices as they were too easy to bug and switch to alive by remote control.

Shortly afterwards, at 3 o'clock sharp, John's secretary knocked on the door, announced Colonel Clifford Bates and ushered in a tall man in his late forties. With greying hair, ramrod straight back, a florid complexion and a short, crisp moustache, he almost looked like a stage caricature of a military officer. Maurice Burke sighed inwardly but reserved judgement as John Chambers introduced them to each other, with minimal formality. The two visitors sat in a comfortable chair and John Chambers sat at his desk. The Colonel was offered a cup of tea.

'OK, fellows, I'll come clean,' the American began. 'As you know, we over in the States are worried about our future in Indo-China. Public opinion won't stand for many more months of no victory, no defeat. The partial bombing pause of LBJ that started in March of '68 dealt those Viets the Ace of Trumps: big advances in northern Laos and a terrific amount of work done on the Hồ Chí Minh trail that allowed them to complete the preparatory stages of its being a six-lane highway in many places. The North Vietnamese reinforced themselves heavily in Cambodia, especially in the two northeastern provinces of Ratnakiri and Mondolkiri that abut South Vietnam, as well as in the Southeast around Svay Rieng, known as the Parrot's Beak as it juts out towards Saigon – its tip is less than thirty miles away – thereby threatening it and launching many successful Dac Cong, Engineer Commando, raids from there. Many of our GIs are beginning to feel that the pressures of sustaining an unpopular war are intolerable. If it wasn't for those poor guys in the Hanoi Hilton and those still Missing in Action, who possibly are still shacking up somewhere waiting for their chance to get the hell out it, we'd quit even sooner than we're going to,' said the American, wearily shaking his head, vexed with himself for having had to 'come clean'. He finished off his coffee and declined a cigarette. 'I'm trying to give them up,' he explained. He sat silently, composing his thoughts.

What a turn up for the books, mused John. *I've yet to hear any Yank face up to this before quite so openly. It's obviously hurting him saying all this in front of us Brits.*

Maurice Burke cleared his throat and continued. 'As you probably well remember, the Foster Dulles theory of defending the homeland against Communism included having a firm ring of defence running, roughly, north-south through Hawaii and containing the threat of its spreading by fighting it on the mainland of Asia. That is no longer tenable as a theory today: what we've found ourselves doing is propping up regimes that are as repressive as the Communists but whose political power base is not as strong as the Gooks'. Their political will is not conducive to complete victory.

'As far as Indo-China is concerned there is an undercurrent of feeling back home that says only Laos can be saved because the ties of the King there are so strong. South Vietnam and Cambodia, or the Khmer Republic if you will, are certain to go Gook, either pro-Soviet or pro-China, but there is just a slim chance that Laos will remain neutral, if not devotedly pro-West, provided, somehow, we can get King Savang Vatthana crowned and unshakably installed as a permanent feature. If the King goes so does the country. Success will also give Thailand just that more breathing space which it badly needs to put its house in order. Failure in Laos means, therefore, bringing your northern Communism south to the Thai-Malaysia border where it can neatly link up with the Communists already there. Our problem is how to get a safe line to the palace without being suspected, let alone compromised by the sieve-like security in Laos and to be in a position to thwart a Communist takeover, by coup or by direct intervention, were the King to be in a strong position after being crowned.'

John and Colonel Bates glanced impassively at each other, both having noticed Maurice Burke's choice of the word 'our' regarding the problem that was bothering him and both still not sure where this unusually long and frank assessment was leading to. The twenty-seven-year-old war in Indo-China was going badly for the Free World, as those ranged on the American side called themselves, and a reversal of Communism did seem impossible, sad though such an admission was.

'It's no good we Americans manoeuvring this,' continued the CIA man. 'We're discredited, being hated for our blunders and despised for our incredulity. Likewise those political jackals of Europe, the French. Ever since Admiral Decoux rebuffed Hồ Chí Minh just after the war, they've neither been liked nor trusted, this despite King Savang reading Voltaire before going to sleep! Also they're too arrogant. Their motto for keeping the Lao people in order seems to have been "Give them only enough rice to mute but not assuage their hunger and put just enough salt in their water to keep them thirsty". No, it's got to be some country that is not directly involved in the Indo-China quarrel but is acceptable to both sides. That rules out the Aussies and the New Zealanders. The Canadians are also non-starters as it would ruin their precious peacekeeping image. So who's left? It's got to be an Englishman or nobody at all, a soldier, not a diplomat. He must have a flair with Asians, a flair for languages, a malleable personality, a sharp brain, a discerning eye, an understanding of the Communist threat and, at the same time, be of sufficiently eccentric character to be accepted as a harmless curio of no danger, seen as an affable non-threat but be able to work by stealth. He would, also, just to limit the field ever further, have to be of sufficiently presentable calibre both to be accepted by the host country and acceptable to your foreign affairs people, the Foreign and Commonwealth Office as you like to call them, as a Defence Attaché with all that implies.' Burke paused, then said, only half jokingly, 'There must be one eccentric you can spare for Operation Stealth!'

There was an eloquent silence as the two Englishmen considered the implications of this bizarre request. The Colonel looked at Burke and asked, 'When will the storm break and when do you want this unlikely paragon? Supposing there is one such and he happens to be that modern rarity in the British Army, a bachelor, will 'the system' allow it? Bachelor linguists are, in Communist eyes, fodder for brothels or boys, so an obvious target. Also we don't normally send high-flyers to attaché posts, especially so when no British interests are at stake,' and he sighed deeply, shaking his head as he did.

'Our guess is that there'll be some sort of accommodation between the Royal Lao Government and the Lao Patriotic Front some time next year, in 1973, although conventional in-theatre wisdom is guessing much later. Between now, April 5, and whenever, there'll be a lull, probably quite a long one. We'd like your man to be in post by the end of 1972.'

'It'll certainly take until then to get any new man, let alone this fellow,' the Colonel replied. 'I'll have to do some delving. We've got a list of one or two such fellows in the bowels of the office. However, the constraints on British Attachés are that, as licensed collectors of overt military information, no deviation from this state is tolerated; and, being overt, there can be no question of forcing information by monetary or other means. This makes a difficult task almost impossible. Furthermore, although the United Kingdom is the right-wing representative of the two Co-Chairmen of those Geneva Accords, the present financial climate just doesn't allow for anything but the cheapest interest and representation and, despite the colour – blue rather than red – and persuasion – right rather than left – of our present Government, it is such that not only the lunatic left-wing fringe in Parliament but the whole cabinet would buck at, if not veto, any such scheme if it were put to them even were it possible to get departmental approval for it in the first place. That means that your man would either have to be an unconscious agent which makes him into a mind-reader of the highest order or having to operate counter to his government's policy, which makes him virtually a traitor. On the other hand, not to try to rise to the occasion is, in my view, wrong. What a choice! For my part, I'm ready to approach the

Director of Intelligence about it as, in any case, there will soon have to be a change of Defence Attaché in Laos who will need the usual clearance. What are your views John?' and he turned to Chambers in some perplexity.

'The only way an Attaché can play such a situation is by ear. If there are legitimate openings for him to use, then let him use them. If he is to have the slightest chance of success, he has to be within the framework of legality and diplomatic immunity. Let us follow that Lao proverb, "You must fish in the mud if you want to find an eel". Let's get our man to Laos – provided that there is one such of the calibre required and that he is available – and let him fish around. On your net, Dally, could you feed any clues that your boys find from time to time?'

'Yes, sure. Let's leave it like that for the moment and keep in touch as matters develop. And since you're quoting Lao proverbs, let me add another one, "Hasty words lead to a loss of confidence. Hasty feet to a fall". But in our case, this is going to be a race against time and, if our yet-to-be-chosen paragon of military efficiency, virtue and acceptable eccentricity is going to have even the slightest chance of success, the sooner we can start obviously the better for every one of us.'

The Colonel and the CIA man left soon afterwards and John sat on at his desk, deep in thought. *How airy-fairy can you get? Here we are in real life trying to work out something that would sound too improbable for a novel. But it is for real, blast it, too real and too urgent to be ignored.*

After a while he called his secretary and told her to go to

Registry and bring every relevant background file. Three-quarters of an hour later he found part of what he wanted. He read: ... *this situation can best be simplified with an analogy of a boxing ring, which is Laos and belongs to the King. In the blue corner is the Royal Lao Army, (RLA), seconded by the Americans. In the red corner is the Pathet Lao, (PL), seconded by the North Vietnamese. The referees are a panel of three, the International Control and Supervision Commission, (ICSC), comprising a neutral India, a pro-left Pole and a pro-right Canadian. The sponsors are the Co-Chairmen of two lots of Accords who, once again, look left and right, the Soviet Union and the United Kingdom.*

The blues want to keep it that way, the reds don't. In fact, it is not as simple as that because the blues' seconds have some secret Thais and tame Lao guerillas up their sleeve, while the reds have representatives of both Communist empires and their satellites in the background. And, like the grin of the Cheshire Cat in Alice in Wonderland, both red and blue boast their own neutrals – weird, wonderful and insubstantial – yet part of it all.

Dear God, thought John Chambers. *What a mess! No wonder there is talk of British disengagement from Laos.* He flicked through the pages, his mind busily scratching at some half-forgotten memory. Then he found it: ... *and among the many cross currents and shifting opinions, there is a rumour that an as yet unidentified group of four men exists, permanently and unequivocally opposed to their Communist masters ...*

There then came some references to leads found, then lost, by the French and American intelligence services and a summary of their findings: *It is the firm opinion of the SDECE and the CIA that, were only this group to be found and exploited, there would be a firm lead into the Laos part of the Indo-China maze with a one-off chance of a more than rewarding result.*

If only! mused John Chambers after he had given the files back to his secretary for return to Registry. But what could their notional Englishman do with the in-built constraints of his job and the financial restrictions that were applied to a part of the world of no importance to the British to say nothing of the unknown Asian intricacies involved?

He did not ever hear Frobisher's 'good night' to him as he left the building.

2

5 April 1972. Kota Tinggi, Johor Bahru, Johor, Peninsular Malaysia: The Commandant of the British Army's Jungle Warfare School, Lieutenant Colonel Jason Rance, sat at his office desk, staring out of the window at the jungle trees that crowded in, a hundred or so yards away, at the edge of the camp, so making it hot and oppressive for much of the time. A piece of paper lay in front of him, with Far East Land Forces HQ printed in large red letters in the right hand corner and its winged dagger crest in the left. The letter was graded 'Staff – In Confidence' and dated three days prior, 2 April 1972. Written and signed by a senior staff officer, it was evasively superficial, ending up, '… and so, because you will have no Gurkha troops to act as "exercise enemy", you will just have to do the best you can. It will not be easy but, since you personally have had considerable experience with both types of student, Thai and Vietnamese, and know their background well, the General has every confidence that, because of the Army's withdrawal from East of Suez, this last course ever to be run at the Jungle Warfare School before its closure next month will maintain its deservedly high reputation until the very end.'

Pompous ass, muttered the Colonel, *must be out of his mind. He's one of those staff officers who is good on paper but hasn't had the experience on the ground to back up his ideas – unluckily for the modern army, an increasing breed. No Gurkhas for the last ten, most important, days means we can't put the theoretical into practice to do justice to what will have been taught.* He continued staring out of the window, thinking out his problem.

The School had become well known in armies of the 'Free World', especially in Asia. Its main aim had been to teach units and individuals for operations in the jungle and, since being set up in June 1948, the Malayan Communists had been beaten and Confrontation with Indonesia in Borneo had been successfully countered. Besides the British Army, it had taught students from eighteen countries – eleven of them Asian – representing all five continents. Its last ever two courses, one for the Royal Thai Army and the other for the Army of the Republic of Vietnam, ARVN, as the South Vietnamese army was officially named, were in full swing. Language and personality problems, orientation and cultural problems, administrative and instructor problems abounded but had, so far at least, been beaten; but now this final difficulty of those stocky, cheerful and efficiently realistic Gurkha soldiers, who had played the parts of demonstration troops and exercise enemy to the students for so many years, being withdrawn made the continuation of instruction almost impossible and utterly unrealistic. *My only solution*, the Colonel mused, *is to make the two courses work against each other – Thai versus Viet and then Viet versus Thai.* His eyes returned to that wretched letter and he sighed deeply.

Lieutenant Colonel Jason Rance had served in Asia with Gurkhas for many years, in India and Burma during the war and, directly afterwards, a spell in Indo-China, disarming the Japanese Imperial Army and fending off depredations by the Viet Minh. After experiencing the gut-wrenching horrors of partition of the subcontinent, he was posted to one of the Gurkha units chosen for the British Army. For the next twenty years his service was in the Malayan Emergency and Borneo Confrontation, conventionally and clandestinely. Although he was, therefore, fully conversant with jungle conditions, he had no European service so had been warned, 'no further promotion': *a time-expired fish in a quickly drying Asian pool*, as he thought of himself.

He was a bachelor, rising fifty but still remarkably fit for his age. Six feet tall and just over ten stone, he had greying hair, a resolute face and clear blue eyes that had the ability to penetrate into the minds of others. He had been chosen to command the Jungle Warfare School because of his long Asian experience; his affinity with its inhabitants and knowledge of their languages were additional bonuses, although he kept his bilingual Chinese ability and his ability as a ventriloquist as closely guarded secrets. It was not an easy job to do well, nor an easy post to fill. Militarily it led nowhere so was unpopular with the more career-minded, especially as the Far East had been a diminishing military responsibility for some years and, since Confrontation with Indonesia in Borneo had been wound up, no longer in the limelight. Rance might have been sent on redundancy had not this post so obviously suited him. An up-market British weekly newspaper had described him as 'one of those gifted and dedicated eccentrics the British Army spawns from time to time'. The same British Army was suspicious of eccentrics, especially bachelor linguist, eccentrics, however dedicated or gifted they were: docility was preferable to eccentricity and even originality had to be stereotyped if it were to have any hope of being accepted. No, in a diminishing army that was plagued by defence cut after defence cut, neither retention nor promotion came easily. As it was, everybody else of senior or equal rank remaining in the command had received posting orders for their next job and Rance knew he was the only one left with no knowledge of his future. He had, in fact, expressed his views that he'd been forgotten and probably wouldn't be given another job. Did he even want one in Europe now that there was no more soldiering in Asia after twenty-seven years, even if he were offered one?

He turned his mind to the students and what he was trying to teach them in six all too short weeks: basically it was to have an elementary but firm knowledge of the correct military counter to the type of military threat currently being posed. This meant knowing how to live, move and fight in the jungle against Communist troops, chiefly the militia and regional forces during the active phase of Communist Revolutionary Warfare. Quite a task, remembering that the military counter had to be geared in with the political, economic and cultural considerations as well.

Initially the Colonel had been surprised to learn that the British Army taught from outside the Commonwealth but he had quickly grown used to the idea. Now that he himself could no longer actively take part against the Communists, at least he could help in the struggle by proxy, so to speak. One of the less obvious problems he was now faced with was that of background: Thailand had never been a colony, Vietnam had – centuries ago of the Chinese, more recently of the French. Then had followed the Japanese war, more French influence, then American intervention but neither the French nor the Americans had ever had a clear-cut military victory over communism in a tropical Southeast Asian rainforest terrain setting, despite individual battles being won, whereas the British had, in Malaya and Borneo. But the British had not fought in Indo-China since those days in late 1945 when, represented only by those officers who were in the Indian Army that went into what was then known as Cochin-China – Rance remembered being sent to the school master of the small Burmese village his battalion found itself in at the end of the war and have a look at his atlas so he find out where this place was. Nobody had heard of the capital, Saigon! They had disarmed the Japanese and started fighting against the Viet Minh, if only in self-protection.

Rance sighed reflectively. He'd been there and found himself, just turned twenty, leading a battalion of surrendered Japanese soldiers of the Yamagishi Butai against the Viet Minh. He'd been in Indo-China at the very start of their long and agonising war and now, twenty-seven years later, here he was, involved once more, albeit on the very fringes. *Who'd have thought that those damned Vietnamese would be still at it after so long, that they'd have clobbered the French at Dien Bien Phu in 1954 or that the Yanks would be still fumbling around, getting more and more stuck like Brer Fox's Tar Baby?*

Another problem he had on such courses was one of simple communication. Of his sixty students, thirty, representing a strong platoon, were Thais and the other thirty were Viets. They were, in the main, similarly built: small, wiry, black-haired men, with complexions ranging from wheaten to dark tan, having almond-shaped eyes and high cheek bones. Where physical similarities ended, linguistic differences began: they could hardly talk to each other as Thai and Vietnamese were incompatible. The Thais' second language was English while the Viets' was French. One or two Viets who had been on American Army course in Okinawa or mainland USA could speak some English. Even so, the actual instruction itself was a problem. Courses brought their own English-speaking interpreters, known as Guiding Officers. Yet instruction was an uphill task as both Thais and Viets came under the American sphere of influence and so were used to American army tactics, organisations, nomenclatures and, most important of all, thought processes, not British equivalents. Among his eight Asian languages, Rance spoke both, having learnt them during his tenure of command over the previous three years. Not liking to use interpreters, he had buckled down to learning enough of each within six months to sustain simple conversations and addresses of welcome and farewell. The tongue, he thought, was a tactical weapon that …

There was a knock on the door, interrupting his reverie. Captain Neil Gherry, the Adjutant, entered with some papers. He glanced at the letter in front of the Colonel, coughed politely and asked whether he still wished to hold a conference about the implications of the letter and, if so, when?

'Yes, Neil. I think we must have one some time today. Damned nuisance, isn't it? I suppose you haven't managed to get HQ to change their mind about the Gurkhas?'

'No, sir. I rang the Staff Captain to see what sort of reaction you'd get if you were to ring and all he could do was to bang on about Force Levels, RAF flights, Gurkha redundancy and no provision for the Gurkhas at the School in the new financial year. It seems we have been jolly lucky to have had them for all this time. He sounded annoyed that I even broached the subject.'

'So you don't advise me to have a go at the Major General?'

'No, sir. There's no mileage to be got there either.'

He paused and looked at his boss. *Strange fellow*, he thought, *never quite knew what he'd do but, by God, he would back you to the hilt until you broke trust, then he was utterly ruthless, no matter what the rank or nationality of the man concerned. And was he good with Asians!* Most of the permanent staff had difficulty in getting through to these men. He himself was from a British regiment and had served in Germany for most of his time. He, like so many others, could get so far but no further. *But the Colonel can, not only with the Gurkhas, but also with the other Asians who came to the School either as students or staff; Malays, Chinese, Filipinos, Koreans, Thais and Viets. He seems to be able to get right through to them with no trouble. It's not only his language ability, there's something else I can't quite fathom. Yes, a strange man, and lonely too. Didn't drink, didn't seem to womanise, either, not that the women didn't cock their dish in his direction from time to time.* 'We'll have to spread the instructors around a bit thinner, sir,' he continued, after a few seconds, 'and get the students to do more for themselves.'

The instructors, British, Australian and New Zealand officers and long-service sergeants, were already tired. The School was the only unit in the theatre working to bursting point until the very end and, as news of the British pull-out had sunk in, those Asian armies whose countries were threatened with Communism had requested more and more course vacancies. It was ironic, the Adjutant thought, that only when the Brits were to be around no longer were they needed and appreciated.

'All the instructors are tired,' said the Colonel. 'I was watching Sergeant Simpson yesterday. Lost a lot of his old zip. He was being scratchy with his old mucker, Sergeant Dowl. That's not like him in the least.'

Captain Gherry hid his surprise. *Fancy the Old Man seeing that. Normally when the Brits see him they pull out the stops. Didn't say much, mind, but they respect him immensely. Gives them their head, lets them get on with their job, only interferes when necessary and then would listen to reasons, not excuses. If there were no reasons, then the hapless man would feel the full weight of the Colonel's displeasure and could expect to be posted away at the first opportunity thereafter. Punishment did not erase weakness from a man's character, or so it seemed as far as the Colonel was concerned. The man he could no longer trust was better elsewhere. Yes, a man they all respected. He never seemed worried and always had a smile and a kind word for everyone; but they never really understood him. What does make him tick?* he asked himself.

'OK, Neil. It is now 1130. Call a conference for 1600 hours today. All instructors to attend. At 1700 have Captain Kulbahadur Limbu of the Demonstration Company come and see me. He might pass on some tips about the Thais and the Viets that will stand me in good stead when I have Majors Steele and Simms in with the two Guiding Officers to talk with me later on at, say, 1730. Anything else that needs a decision on now?'

'No, I don't think so, sir. The rest of the programme for winding the place up is unaffected. I'll continue keeping my eye on that while you are wrestling with this lot,' said Gherry, smiling at the Colonel. 'If anything untoward does crop up, I'll pop in and get the school solution.'

'I'll be away in a few minutes,' the Colonel said. 'I want to wander around, see what's happening and think things out. This is a challenge and it would be bad if we had a crisis on this very last lap.'

The Adjutant saluted and left the Colonel alone. *There's quite a lot to be stage-managed with this change of plan*, he thought to himself. *Glad it's not me but the boss who's got to work this little lot out.* He heard the door of the other office shut as the Colonel left.

Outside the HQ office block work continued as normal. The two courses were being lectured by their course commanders, both senior majors. The Viets were under Andrew Steele, a burly, red-faced, rugger-playing Light Infantryman and the Thais under John Simms, a one-time orienteering instructor, of the Gurkhas. Simms was standing in front of a map of Southeast Asia. He held a pointer in one hand, showing where the Communist trouble spots were. The Thai interpreter stood a little apart from him. This was Major Mana Varamit of the Royal Thai Army and a veteran of Vietnam. Impeccably well mannered, it was hard to judge his real worth but he did seem to have a grip on his men. He was also armed with a pointer and, as Simms spoke two or three sentences, listened carefully to what was being said and then, in turn, translated it to the students. It was a slow method of instruction but it had the merit of allowing time to think out the next batch of sentences unhurriedly.

Both Steele and Simms had tried to learn to speak the language of their students when they first joined the staff. Steele, trying to master Vietnamese, had been put off by the bird-like chattering and curious liquid tones that cascaded up and down a dissonant scale. It had been said that Vietnamese was harder to learn than Chinese, but for Steele that point was academic. Any tonal language utterly defeated him. Simms, on the other hand, had found Thai less of a problem as he was already able to speak Nepali and he had found some similarities but the script completely baffled him. He never learnt enough to say more than a few phrases and used English for his instruction. He never forgot the day he had been lecturing the Thais on an earlier course on constraints to be expected if one became a prisoner of war. 'Your mail will be restricted,' he had said. The Thai interpreter had looked at him and had something that had more of a reaction from the students than Simms would have expected. The Colonel had been listening in and had had a word with him afterwards. 'Use more simple phrases,' he had said. Your "restriction of mail" was rendered "you won't be allowed any women" and that is why the students looked so glum.' Simms had remembered that and had since tried to speak more lucidly and simply.

'Remember,' he was now saying, 'that the Communists will never stop trying to win. If they cannot win by conventional means then they will use unconventional ones. If they cannot win politically without war, then they will try to win politically with war.' He paused while this was being translated. 'Before I teach you the three phases of Communist Revolutionary Warfare I want to emphasise one point: never for one minute forget that you can never trust what a Communist says. His thoughts and logic are different from yours. Never take anything a Communist says for granted for, if you do, you will come off second best.' He did not notice a momentarily gleam in Mana's eyes as he translated what had been said, nor did the class notice the slight emphasis he put on the last part of the last sentence. Why should they, as neither was expecting it?

The Colonel looked in on the Thai lecture. He had see the Thai hierarchy in Bangkok and had been saddened at how they divided themselves into the First Eleven who got jobs in that sprawling, over-crowded, iniquitous city of politico-military intrigue, and the Also-Rans at the sharp end in the provinces. Knowledge of military affairs did not seem to be a prerequisite out in the sticks – only those with no important social connections were ever posted there. That was where the Communists were making steady advances, slowly, sometimes spectacularly, sometimes stealthily, but always, it seemed, with the initiative. One day the race for time would crystallise but at least the Thais were involved in the Indo-China war. In South Vietnam there was the Queen's Division, unofficially known as the Black Panthers until that name went sour in the United States and, because the Yanks were footing most of the bill and so had much influence over the Thais, it was changed to the Black Cobras. On one of his visits to Thailand, Rance had seen training that reinforcements for Vietnam were undergoing and had noticed the weaknesses of Thai middle-piece officers. On his return to Bangkok, he had been called to Supreme HQ and had been closely questioned by the Deputy Supreme Commander about training methods, both for conventional forces and those Special Forces being trained by American 'Green Berets'. He hoped his answers had been of use. And, apart from the USAF bases in Thailand for the B-52s, the F-111s and the U-2s for operations in Laos and Cambodia as well as in Vietnam itself, wasn't there a rumour of some Thai volunteers in Laos? He listened in to the commentary with one ear, understanding what was being said, storing up the odd phrase for future use, making a note to look up a certain word in his four-volume *So Sethaputra* dictionary: *Chon*, did that word for 'thief' really cover the sense of 'bandit' or 'guerilla' as Mana was translating it now?

He moved on to the Vietnamese lecture. This must mean more to them than to the Thais. When he had last visited South Vietnam, as the guest of ARVN, he had instinctively felt that the American teaching of heavy weapons, wheels and wings was 'a hammer to swat a fly' approach. The jungle could not be dominated that way. It was the man, well-trained, with faith in his own ability that counted. He had seen the Fat Cats in the HQs and the peasant soldiers in the field. The comparison was harsh and stark, and boded ill for future ARVN victory.

The Vietnamese interpreter intrigued him. A northerner by birth – 'lacquered bamboo' was the phrase that came to mind – Major Le Dâng Khoã, apparently, was one of thousands who had voted with their feet against the Communists when they elected to go south after the cease-fire of 1954, following the Bien Dien Phu disaster. How many others on the course were northerners? Once you knew the language, their tones gave them away. Some of the older students, Aspirants or 3rd Lieutenants as they were also known, had been active against the troops of 20 Indian Division that he himself had served in Cochin-China, now South Vietnam, at the end of the war in Burma. Supposing one of them was merely a shorter-term man of the South but still a longer-term man of the North? How about Major Le Dâng Khoã, even? The Colonel shrugged. *Leave it*, he told himself, *I've enough on my plate already without adding ghosts to flavour the dish. And anyway, it can't affect me.*

He left the lecture room and walked down to the armoury where he found the Malay storeman waiting for the Gurkhas to put their arms away.

'*Selamat tenggah-hari. Apa khabar?*' he greeted the storeman. Good day, how are you?

'*Khabar baik, terima kasih, Tuan,*' the Malay replied, beaming. Fine, thanks. The Tuan Kolonel always so greeted him, not like some of the other *Orang Putehs*, but how could call the red-faced ones 'white'? So many of them tended to shout: insolent pork-eaters, unclean and full of alcohol, especially the sergeants. The Tuan Kolonel, however, was different. Wah, how he spoke to the Gurkhas and how his eyes lit up when he saw them – and theirs too.

'How is it all going, Ismail? How're the family and the new baby? Let me know when he's to be circumcised and I'll come and join the party.'

Ismail smiled his thanks.

'When are the Gurkhas due to bring their weapons back?'

'*Ta' tahu, Tuan.*' I don't know, sir. 'Soon, I expect. Certainly before half past twelve when they have their midday tea.'

'How much longer have you to go before your Run Out date?' the Colonel asked. The Malay soldier was one of the ever-dwindling band of Locally Enlisted Personnel who were being discharged as a result of the British pull-out.

'Just over a month to go, Tuan. And then I'll go back to my village. Kampong life will suit me. It seems to suit us Malays very well indeed.'

Yes, thought Rance, *it suits you all. Wait until the coconuts fall and the padi ripens. The soil is bountiful ...* His reflections on the Malay way of life were interrupted by a line of Gurkhas coming to put their weapons away. All of them momentarily stood to attention as they filed past him, smiling, wondering what the Colonel sahib would say next. *Ram Ram*, but he so often correctly guessed their thoughts in an astonishing way and he was a hard man to hoodwink.

'Where have you come from?' he asked a Corporal.

'We've been practising one of the ambushes we have to do during the final exercise,' the Corporal answered. He was a strong man, larger than the average Gurkha. He and Rance had made a number of parachute jumps together and there was a strong bond between them.

'How did you manage?'

'No problem. The Viets are tenacious people once they understand what's wanted of them. Not that we couldn't beat them,' he added, without any arrogance, superbly confident of his, and his countrymen's, martial ability. 'They're tougher than the Thais we've had by quite a bit.'

'Yes, I agree with you. What you say is true. Where's the Captain sahib?'

'Here I am, Hajur.' The voice behind him was slightly hoarse and Rance turned and answered the salute as punctiliously as it was given. They had served together in several difficult situations during the past twenty years so had full trust in each other.

'Captain sahib, I've had news about your demonstration troops' future. I'm having a conference this afternoon and I want to see you at 1700 hours. I'm afraid that'll cut into your basketball time but we have many matters to settle.'

'*Hunchha*, Hajur.' Right you are, sir. Captain (Queen's Gurkha Officer) Kulbahadur Limbu, DCM, MM, 12 Gurkha Rifles, was a tall, paler than normal Gurkha, who commanded immense respect. He had won his Military Medal for gallantry during the Malayan Emergency and his Distinguished Conduct Medal, a rare award at any time, with Rance in Borneo.

'You're to return to your parent units in Hong Kong or Brunei sooner than anticipated. Glad to leave here, I'm sure. It's no fun always being enemy and having to lose to someone whose only victories seem to take place on training.'

The Gurkha Officer grunted and smiled. 'Yes, Sahib,' he said. 'The lads are getting a bit fed up with it. Not that they'd dare complain,' and he growled menacingly. 'Normally, as you know, they get on well with the Thais and the Viets, but both Guiding Officers – I can't pronounce their tongue-twisting names – have somehow upset each other. They just don't get on together. Always like two strange dogs sniffing each other on first meeting. The Viet Major is no slouch and yet he wants us to show him the same drills over and over again. He takes more notes on our methods than any Guiding Officer usually does. We can't fathom why he doesn't behave like they normally do. Not that he's offensive – more of a nuisance than anything else. The Thai Major's no slouch either but he behaves as though the Viet Major was a junior wife's son,' he added enigmatically.

At five to four that afternoon, five minutes before the appointed time, a small group of instructors and administrators of the School's permanent staff foregathered outside the Colonel's office. At exactly 4 o'clock the Adjutant again knocked on the door, went straight in and announced that all were present and ready to come in.

'Bring them in,' said Rance, 'and we'll sit around the conference table.'

They filed in, saluted and sat down. Besides the two course commanders and the Adjutant, there were the Second-in-Command, a sad, hen-pecked, passed-over Major called David Carter, the Quartermaster, an elderly Scot, Captain Iain Calverton, and the Regimental Sergeant Major, William Bailey, MBE and the sergeant instructors.

'Gentlemen, please smoke if you want to,' Rance began. He waited while four of them lit up and then continued, 'I have no wish to keep you away from your duties any longer than necessary but we have a problem to be thrashed out. Far East Land Forces HQ, in their wisdom, have today sent me a letter ordering me to release the Gurkhas by 20 April. Today is the 5th. Your courses are due to finish on the 30th. We therefore will be the last ten days plus another week for them to get packed up and ready to go when we'll be bereft of their services. That means there'll be no Gurkhas from the 14th; seventeen days without them and,' he made a quick calculation, 'only eight more days with them from tomorrow.' He paused to let that sink in. 'The reasoning, such as it is, behind this move, is financial, not political, although, if we make a balls-up resulting from no Gurkhas as exercise enemy, it could well become a political issue, redounding onto my greying pate. In brief, no money has been estimated or obligated for us in Malaysia since the start of the new Financial Year. Enough money is available, however, for us to close down – comes from a different vote, I expect – but for no other purpose. The financiers have therefore laid an embargo on our activities, which includes the Gurkhas having to be out of the country by the stated date regardless of our difficulties, international relations and mucking the men, indeed all of us, about.'

Silence, except for a few dreary sighs, prevailed as those present pondered on the enormity of this sudden and unwelcome news.

'In the end,' Rance continued, 'it's the toad under harrow, lots of toads, with no disrespect to you, Gentlemen, who feel where the tooth-points go. Your job will be made infinitely harder. I am not allowed to cancel the remainder of the courses, not that I would contemplate such a move. They've been paid for, anyway, by the Thai and Viet Governments. However, we'll have none of the normal live props to act as enemy. Without the realism of an exercise enemy, much of the good we can do for these people is wasted. So what do we do? Answer: shuffle and deal again – juggle the final exercise so that the Thais are the enemy to the Viets and vice versa. I've always deplored that as an answer but, as the Gurkhas say, "Oil instead of incense in time of need".' He looked round the table. 'What's your individual reaction to this bomb shell? Think about it amongst yourselves for a few minutes, before giving me your printable answer.'

There was a momentary pause as the implications sank in, then there was a buzz of chatter. Steele and Simms were the most involved and conferred uneasily.

'Right,' said Rance after they'd had enough time for consideration. 'Exercise points first, administrative points second. John, let's hear from you.'

'Well, sir. My Thais may be able to cope mechanically, if you get what I mean, but I don't see them taking to losing when attacked by the Viets on the final phase. They're proud people and there's just something I can't fathom about my Guiding Officer, Major Mana Varamit, and his relationship with his Vietnamese counterpart. If you talk to him nicely, sir, he may accept it.

'The main difficulty will be the juggling between the phases of the exercise, the planning and the rehearsing. The answer is we will if we have to, but I'm afraid I can't be responsible for any ensuing cock-up.'

Rance coldly said, 'I'm responsible for everything here. You are but an extension of me and if you find the position untenable or the problems overwhelming, neither I nor the course will be the loser.' There was an uneasy silence, broken only when the Colonel asked Major Steele for his views on the proposal.

Steele said, 'I agree with the main burden of what John Simms has said about the mechanics of it. Each member of the guiding staff will have to cover more ground and be ready to be more flexible than usual. We'll do it because this is a one-off occasion and, for better or for worse, our last course. But the Viets attacked by the Thais! So far, when anything has gone wrong with these final attacks we have been able to control them to some extent because we've had the Gurkhas. In the present situation, if anything goes drastically wrong, we have neither the control nor the sanctions required to stabilise any complexity: there is no Manual of Military Law or Queen's Regulations to back us up and give us guidance. Not that the ultimate is likely to occur and not that we've ever had to do anything more drastic than bandage a few cuts and sprains or write off some minor losses of kit. I'm being Devil's Advocate, I'm afraid, sir. Also, I've yet to fathom my Guiding Officer, Major Le Dâng Khoã, to the extent that I'd like to, despite the number of courses we've worked together. He may need individual handling.'

'So control is your real worry?' asked Rance.

'That's right, it is. You're speaking to them later on, sir, aren't you?' Rance nodded assent. 'I'm sure any difficulty can be pre-empted then, during your briefing.' Rance nodded again.

They then discussed administrative points for some time and shortly before 5 o'clock Rance dismissed them. As they turned to go, he called to Steele and Simms. 'Join me at 1730.'

At 5 o'clock Rance quickly ran through the movement problems and timetable with Gurkha Captain Kulbahadur Limbu.

As the Gurkha officer got up to go Rance said to him, 'Wait one, Sahib. Before you go, give me your opinion on the two Majors, the Thai and the Viet.'

The Gurkha Officer sensed an urgency to the question and his answer came out pat. 'Individually, they'll be manageable. As I've told you, Sahib, there's something between the two of them that doesn't tie up. The Vietnamese looks at the ring he always wears almost as if it is a fetish and the Thai somehow doesn't like it. They're better kept separated from each other. Without us to help you, Sahib, you'll be on your own so please be careful. Also, you yourself intrigue them.' And once more Rance had to be content with an enigmatic answer. He thanked the Gurkha, who saluted and dismissed himself.

It was a strange situation to find himself in, this having to deal with Asian soldiers who were not in their own country nor his, over whom there were no sanctions of a normal military nature. Sure, the fear of a bad course report from a British military school might have some effect on the way some students behaved during their stay. So far nothing of an unduly serious nature had happened in his time and, touch wood, it wouldn't now. He stayed, sitting at his table, working out what he'd say at half past five, possibly the hardest part of the day's work. He had every confidence that he could handle any normal situation but that was no answer to the unsettling comments made to him about both Thai and Vietnamese Guiding Officers. Kulbahadur had given him, well, he was going to say a clear warning and in one way it was clear yet, in another way, it was just the opposite. But for the normal run-of-the-mill Vietnamese just to be able to go to sleep without the sound of explosives or firing was an uncanny but welcome experience, especially for some of the younger men who had always known war. Yet, it was impossible to predict how any would react under abnormal circumstances.

Yet another knock on the door and Captain Gherry reported the arrival of the two Guiding Officers and the two British majors.

'*Chào Ông; Sawadee krab.*' Rance greeted the Viet and the Thai. 'Please sit down.' He offered them a cigarette each from a packet he kept in his drawer, although he himself never smoked. They made themselves comfortable and leant forward expectedly.

'As you know,' began Rance in English, 'yours are the last two courses being run at the Jungle Warfare School before we British finally pull out from mainland Asia. As you also know both courses have been arranged because of the special request made by both governments.'

The two Asians nodded, their eyes expressionless. So far, so good – routine patter despite the lateness of the hour.

'I myself,' continued the Commandant, 'have welcomed this opportunity to help in the fight against Communism by training you to understand our methods and philosophy of Counter Revolutionary Warfare. Here you have learnt how the British Army operates in the jungle against varying threats. Some of our work here equates to the US Army Ranger work, with the difference that the Rangers are rather special. British troops use these techniques as a matter of routine training.' Rance realised that the Vietnamese Guiding Officer, having attended a few courses, was acquainted with these aspects but the Thai, it being his first course, needed it explaining in considerable detail. Rance thought it politic to digress and reinforce his points by describing what he had seen at the ARVN Training School at Nha Trang and the Royal Thai Army equivalent at Lop Buri. 'If you will pardon me for saying this, the disadvantages I saw in both institutions were that the facilities did not allow students to practise against other students, thus not seeing their good and bad points; as well as your tactical situations being more rigidly controlled than are ours. On this course I am rectifying these weaknesses and you will have to rely far more on your own initiative.

'For your final exercise we will not have the Gurkhas to be your enemy. I am having Majors Steele and Simms rearrange their plans so that the final exercise will afford the chance for your two courses to exercise one against the other. Naturally I don't want to place undue strain on anyone but, remembering that sweat saves blood, this is what I believe is best for you both under the circumstances. Please consider any points you may wish to put to me.'

Le Dang Khoa and Mana Varamit eyed one another speculatively. Although they were partners in arms of the 'Free World Forces' along with the Filipinos, the South Koreans, the Australians and the New Zealanders, and although they had been seen standing at the bar in the Mess having a pint together, basic differences were present. Mana, who had had at least one tour in South Vietnam and would be, as he had been warned, seconded for special 'volunteer' duties on his return to Thailand, got on well enough with the South Vietnamese but had never been seen talking to Le Dâng Khoã socially. It was equally impossible for anyone to guess what either Guiding Officer's real thoughts were;

both certainly took his duties most seriously. Many Vietnamese envied the Thais for not having had a colonial past, for having a relatively stable government and an in-built system of checks and balances everyone understood but Le Dâng Khoã didn't show envy, only annoyance, at Thai slackness. What was it that that American he had met in the gift shop of a PX in Saigon had said? Oh yes, 'The Thais, the nicest people money can buy, who work at their play and play at their work.' He tried to push other thoughts out of his mind. As he sat still, thinking, he played with a large ring that he wore on the little finger of his right hand. Suddenly and unexpectedly he said out loud, 'We'll win. I agree.'

At that, equally unexpectedly, Mana seemed to notice the Viet's ring for the first time. A look of understanding flashed in his eyes that were deeply set and slightly flecked.

Rance took the remark to mean winning in the context of the exercise and said, 'You'll both have to obey the British instructors, you know. They're the umpires.'

The bland remark helped Mana to hide any discomposure he had shown. Normally uncommunicative, he had said nothing up to this point. He was sure that Le Dâng Khoã hadn't been talking about the exercise but to have countered his seemingly harmless remark with anything but a harmless answer would have exposed himself unnecessarily and possibly dangerously. He grimaced uneasily. *I'm glad I've got the Border Police among my students,* he thought, *men who'd never even been to Bangkok and who that strange man, Rance, had often praised and even the Gurkhas had been extended to outwit. Made good bodyguards, too.* He shot Rance a glance, quizzical and resentful. 'I agree, sir,' he said.

'Good and I thank you both. That's a relief to me. You four will have a lot of planning to do. Bring me in if you have to but I am involved with closing the place down and getting the Gurkhas away so am not always available, as you have already realised.'

After they had gone, Rance left the office, telling the Adjutant to close the place up. He passed the soccer ground where the Thai and Vietnamese students were playing a friendly match amid cheers from their supporters. He walked among them slowly, passing remarks and enjoying their obvious pleasure at being spoken to, not only in their own language but also by a senior officer – a rare occurrence in either army. He left the soccer ground and made his way to his own quarters. He passed other soldiers as he went, always a smile and a cheery word for them, but he did not feel as happy as he looked. Something nagged at the back of his mind – nothing specific or tangible but a definite foreboding that something intangible was in the offing. *Sufficient unto the day ...* He'd just have to keep alert.

Until the very end when the roles were reversed and the Viets started searching out the Thai base camp with a view to destroying it, nothing untoward happened. Both Steele and Simms were inclined to be optimistic but Rance reserved judgement. Major Mana Varamit had chosen a grizzled old Thai Frontier Police Sergeant Major, Prachan Pimparyon, to be his aide and had controlled his platoon well. Major Le Dâng Khoã had shown real skill in night movement and seemed to be working intelligently.

On the eve of the final attack by the Viets on the Thai camp,

Rance visited both groups who had by then been out in the jungle for seven days. The scenario was that on the morrow the Viets would attack the Thai 'guerilla' camp, drive the Thais out and prepare to repel a counter attack, which would be umpired as unsuccessful. That would be the end of the exercise. Rance spent the night in the Thai camp so he could watch the Viet attack at close quarters. After it was dark he chatted desultorily for a while with Mana who seemed abnormally pre-occupied. That night Rance slept fitfully. He was up before dawn to see the sentries deployed beyond the camp perimeter in readiness to warn of any 'guerilla' movement. The attack came in as planned. The thick jungle had hidden the attackers from view right up to the time they had been spotted by the sentries.

In the noise and disarray of Viets charging and Thais being driven out of the camp, it was impossible to see everything at once. Smoke emitted by grenades and small generators made the whole area obscure and confused, with battle noises making control between the directing staff and the two sides difficult. It was always in such moments that tempers became frayed, both sides having been under some pressure during the build-up phase.

Le Dâng Khoã was passing by Mana Varamit who, wearing black Viet Minh-type pyjamas and playing the part of the 'guerilla' commander, was urging his troops to escape. As the two men came together, there was a quick movement and, in a flash, they were both on the ground, locked in a ferocious struggle, Mana seeming to be intent on grasping Le Dâng Khoã's right hand. The Thai Sergeant Major, Prachan Pimparyon, was standing by undecidedly and, initially, only Rance saw the incident. He instinctively dashed forward towards them, regardless of whom he bumped into, feeling a chill run through his veins, knowing he could have a lethal situation on his hands. He saw Simms out of the corner of his eye and yelled to him above the battle noise to stop the exercise and to tell Steele that both groups had to be separated. Smoke obscured the three men involved in the fight but it cleared in time for Rance to see Mana Varamit break free, stand up and kick Le Dâng Khoã hard in the face as he lay on the ground. Nearly losing his balance the Thai Major bumped heavily into Prachan, sending him flying, and ran off into the thick undergrowth. Seconds later Sergeant Major Prachan ran after Mana, leaving Le Dâng Khoã lying on the ground. It was over so quickly that still no one else seemed to have noticed anything amiss.

Rance reached the injured man who was bleeding profusely from his lower lip and looked dazed. Helping him to sit up, he took a First Field Dressing from his pocket, ripped it open and gave Le Dâng Khoã the gauze inside to put over the wound. 'Hold this to your face till we get to a medical pack,' he ordered. 'Mana tripped into you and you fell against that tree stump there,' he lied glibly.

Le Dâng Khoã looked down at his hand and patted a breast pocket once or twice. He then unsheathed his machete.

Steele came over and started to talk. 'Keep it till later,' snapped Rance. 'Can't do with it now.'

Simms ran up, puffing hard, red-faced and sweating heavily. 'God, what a shambles.' He then noticed the hurt man. 'What's wrong?' he asked.

Rance said quickly, 'Collect your sergeant instructors, gather up your students and, with minimum explanation, get them to pack up their kit and, regardless of anything else, take them down to the road as quickly as possible. Keep them separate. Transport is due at 1000 hours at Panti village. When you get down to the jungle edge, you, John, get your Thais to cook their meal where we had that contact on Day 3; you, Andrew, use the well water in Panti village. I'll join you when I can ...'

'Christ, watch it!' Simms interrupted shrilly. 'Le Dâng Khoã is running into the jungle with an unsheathed machete in his hand.'

Rance dashed after him, leaving the other two wide-eyed and with the task of having to reorganise the students. In front of him, Rance could hear the Vietnamese crashing through the jungle trying to catch up with Mana and the Sergeant-Major. He soon saw that he was going towards the Viet camp of the previous night. He was by himself and there was about to be a crisis. Could he reach them before irrevocable damage was done? Why the hell had Mana gone to the Viet camp?

Just as Rance was wondering if he'd catch them up in time he heard angry voices in bad English a few yards away. He turned towards them and burst into the clearing. There was Le Dâng Khoã, machete raised, face bleeding, menacing Mana who had his back to a tree. The Sergeant Major crouched warily, ready to jump on the Vietnamese if he could floor him without getting chopped as he did.

Rance slowed to a walk and came up to the trio. Completely confident, he inserted himself between Le Dâng Khoã and Mana. Despite the mad dash, he appeared calm and determined.

'I told you to put this on your face,' he said, proffering some gauze, his voice icily controlled. The effect of the Commandant's appearance was a complete surprise to all three, diverting their attention from each other. 'Give me that machete,' he insisted, putting his hand out and taking it from the Vietnamese. 'I wish no more trouble today and I demand that, when the Thai apologises, you shake his hand.' He spoke in Vietnamese presuming Mana did not understand him.

Turning to the two Thais, Rance said to the Sergeant Major, in Thai, 'Go and stand by that track and let nobody come in. Move!' He then turned to Mana, who had regained some of this earlier lost self-confidence.

'Major, I cannot accept your behaviour. Whatever you did in the Queen's Division in Vietnam is over and done with. I'm not interested in who started this, only that it ends peaceably. *Chab meu*' – offer your hand.

The Thai swallowed, stared a long second at Rance and muttered, 'If you so wish, this once.'

He offered his hand to the Vietnamese, who took it in his momentarily before dropping it. Getting involved in an accident like this was in no way in his brief, but the temptation of getting hard evidence had been great. 'I'm sorry if it was my fault,' the Thai said. 'I lost my head when I saw you attacking. I remembered how I lost a friend like that in Vietnam and I became angry.' Rance translated it to Le Dâng Khoã who meekly said in reply, 'It may have been my fault a bit. It is hard to forget the real war. I'm sorry too.'

Self-control had been regained and to complete formalities,

Rance also shook hands and ordered the Sergeant Major to do the same. He told them to rejoin their group before dismissing them. He kept the machete. The two Thais left immediately but the Vietnamese, having made sure that the two Thais had left, came back into the clearing. He stood looking around him as though searching for something on the ground. He obviously found what he was looking for as he bent forward and, in one quick movement, picked it up from under a pile of cut leaves – *last night's bedding*, Rance thought, noticing the drying edges and squashed appearance of the foliage. *What is this all about?* Le Dâng Khoã, obviously in an emotional state, came back to where Rance was still standing, the machete now in his left hand. 'May I say something, please?'

'Yes, tell me what you want to say.'

'You saved my life today, in fact more than my life. You may not realise it but you did. I want you to remember how grateful I am.' He held out a ring in the palm of his hand. 'I want to give you this. Mana saw I wasn't wearing it. He ran to the overnight camp looking for it. Why, it doesn't matter. I thought I'd lost it – when I found it was not in my pocket. It doesn't matter now,' he ended ambivalently.

He took Rance's right hand and slipped the ring on his little finger. It just squeezed on. Rance was too surprised and too overwhelmed to refuse. Genuinely touched, he thanked the Vietnamese Major and shook hands again. Something made him look at the now bare little finger and he noticed a strange tattoo where the ring had been: a sign like a small 9 with a curly tail. It reminded him of the Lao character of a 'silent consonant' but dismissed it because Le Dâng Khoã was not a Lao. The Vietnamese glanced down at his own finger as Rance was looking at it. 'Có lẽ,' perhaps, he muttered out loud and, to himself, 'stealth'. The Vietnamese then adopted a more formal manner. Withdrawing his hand, he excused himself and departed.

After a couple of paces he turned and came back. 'I saw you looking at the inside of my little finger. Yes, there is a mark on it. It is special. There are only three others. Likewise, if ever you see a similar ring, not that you ever will, you will know that he too is one of us.' And with that totally unexpected and absurdly unrelated remark, he left.

Rance sat down on a log. Reaction took over and he started trembling as he realised what he had managed to avert. Murder possibly, bodily harm certainly, in a third country where no Malaysian national was involved so the Malaysian police would not be particularly interested, everybody would be terribly embarrassed, the Press ghoulish in its quest for gory details and he himself obviously at fault for not having prevented such a situation from developing in the first place. Yes, he was indeed lucky to have cleared it up without more bloodshed, even if he had had to be more devious and dramatic than he really wanted to be.

It started to rain but he sat there, not seeming to notice it. *What a way to finish off*, he thought. *Thank the Lord they'll be gone tomorrow and I'll never see any of them again. It's too involved for me to understand, not that I particularly want to. I'll have to get the others to keep quiet about it, but then, if I never tell them what's happened, only the four of us will know. I'll certainly not mention it to Far East Land Forces HQ. I can't guess what's behind it all.* He looked down at the ring on his finger. He examined it and saw it was made of copper. He noticed that it had a strange emblem on its inner edge that looked like a badly written 27. *So what?* Nothing was really making sense that day.

He got up off the log, wet through and feeling cold. He made his way to the road head, an hour and a half's walk away, where his Land Rover was patiently waiting to take him back to the School.

By 3 o'clock the following afternoon both lots of students, with their Guiding Officer, had departed for Singapore to fly back to their respective countries. There had been no further incidents during those last few hours and the closing addresses Rance gave were routine and outwardly relaxed. Now he felt drained.

He went into his office to clear up the paperwork that had accumulated during the past few days. The Adjutant knocked on the door and entered, with a signal in his hand. *My, but he looks whacked*, was his unspoken comment. 'Here is your posting order, sir.'

'So they haven't forgotten me after all.'

Rance read the signal: 'You have been posted to Vientiane, Laos, as the Defence and Air Attaché, with Naval Representation, to assume duties by the end of November, 1972. Return to London for briefing, indoctrination and language training soonest.'

'Me a DA? At least it is neither Thailand nor Vietnam, so I won't be troubled by anyone like I was today,' he said, a slow smile of satisfaction spreading over his face.

He was not to know that he could not have been more wrong.

3

July 1972. London: Halfway down Whitehall on the north side of the road and not far from the Cenotaph is the Cabinet Office. At half past 10 on Monday, 3 July 1972, a meeting was under way in the fourth floor conference room to consider and make recommendations about Britain's role as Co-Chairman of the 1954 and 1962 Geneva Accords for Indo-China and Laos respectively in the light of the worsening financial situation in and the diminishing credibility of the United Kingdom as a Great Power. It was not a topic to inspire confidence and some of the participants from the Cabinet Office itself, the Treasury, the Foreign and Commonwealth Office, the Ministry of Defence and the Secret Intelligence Service felt that it was an infringement of their valuable time when they had other and more pressing tasks in hand. Sir James Redfeather, KCMG, the remarkably able Mandarin who normally presided over such meetings, had been called away by the Prime Minister just before it was due to start and his place had been taken by one of his underlings, a man in his mid-thirties, named Jeremy Coulson. An up-and-coming civil servant with soft left tendencies and an exaggerated opinion of his status, he annoyed his colleagues by a façade of languid superiority and intellectual arrogance which had etched a permanently sour look on his face. He was showing that he found the proceedings irksome and a bore.

'With due respect to those here who represent different departments of state,' he drawled soon after business had started, 'I must say that the days when we needed to have or could afford to show an interest in Asian natives and their affairs just to keep our place in the world popularity stakes are now over. The war in Indo-China is rising to a climax and even before the Americans have pulled out, either as losers or as the staler of two in a stalemate, we ought to bow out gracefully. Our interests are tenuous, our influence is nugatory and our presence is probably unwanted.' He paused and smirked at the Treasury man across the table who, after a brief silence, took up the same theme from his department's point of view.

Clearing his throat, he said, 'I admit that our annual aid to Indo-China is not great. In Laos the Foreign Exchange Operating Fund, or FEOF as you probably recognise it, pays out a paltry £700,000 a year. A number of Lao students are awarded scholarships in Britain, normally in the fields of electrical engineering and tourism. Since 1954 we have financed the construction of three radio stations and a provincial hospital, to name but four specific projects, at a cost of £12,600,000.'

James Tomlinson, a bespectacled, balding man in his fifties, had an unhealthy grey pallor, considerable middle-aged spread and unusually long fingers that were epicene and crawly. When he spelt out the derisory less than three-quarters of a million pounds annual contribution he made it sound like a king's ransom, which John Chambers, representing the Secret Intelligence Service, felt could well be the case.

'We get nothing back from it,' Tomlinson continued, prodding the bridge of his spectacles with his spidery forefinger,' and I have come to believe it is not only a waste of time and effort maintaining our contribution but that it is not appreciated. Gratitude is an induced reaction and one not normally found in children or Asiatics,' he pontificated pompously. 'Thus I am an advocate of the last speaker's views,' he concluded, glancing up at Coulson and simpering.

The FCO man coughed discreetly and gently gave his opinion. 'Maybe what you say is so, Mr Tomlinson, but nobody could call it expensive. As you must well know, one year's total foreign aid to Laos is equal to forty minutes' trading on the Tokyo stock exchange. While our American colleagues will say that the Lao budget reads like something like the first chapter of Brer Rabbit, the discontinuation of aid is not going to cure our insolvency problems. It is true to say, however, that we still have a moral duty to the Royal Lao Government as the right-wing representative of those Geneva Accords, whether you like the idea or not. Money isn't the only measure of a nation's stature or sincerity.'

An awkward pause followed, broken by Coulson, red in the face, turning to the MOD representative, Lieutenant General Sir David Law, KCB, CBE, DSO, MC, Director of Intelligence, who said, with insouciance, 'General, may we have your Ministry's views, please?'

The General glowered at the younger man, resentful at his disparaging tone. Of razor-sharp intellect and immense vitality, the General had the sense to realise that neither the MOD nor the FCO could ever dictate policy to the government. They could only advise but, even so, soldiers seemed to be looked upon as country cousins in inter-ministry matters by most of their civilian counterparts and sound advice was often ignored.

'Our connection is legal, valid, responsible and useful, albeit not critical,' the General began after a moment's pause. 'What we are witnessing is a Communist versus Free World struggle with the by-now recognisable but little exploited facet of both major Communist rivals, USSR and China, jockeying for influence, power and prestige in Southeast Asia. By our having an established position in Indo-China we have an unrivalled opportunity to study the Indo-China "case book", for want of a better description, and hopefully, by extrapolation, be able to apply its lessons to the northwest European "case book". We'd be utter fools to opt out. Despite the eventual outcome of the struggle probably being a foregone conclusion, namely an all red Indo-China, we ought to do what we can to limit the damage, so we must be represented there for as long as possible. Failure so to be is not only the waste of a golden opportunity but also a dereliction of duty – a court-martial offence in my service,' and the General glared meaningfully at Coulson. 'I'd have thought that even a non-combatant like yourself would have realised that.' The General's definition of a gentleman was someone who was never unintentionally rude.

A longer than usual pause followed that impassioned outburst. 'Mr Chambers, may we have your views, please,' Coulson asked stiffly, thereby avoiding a direct confrontation with the General, whose implication that the Cabinet Office as a whole and he,

Coulson, in particular, were not sufficiently interested about the threat of Communism had not been lost on him; had he not been acting as chairman, he would not have bothered to have sought the views of the SIS, being one of that strange product of post-war, red-brick processing that regarded the maintenance of security and the need to keep a nation's secrets secret as being incompatible with democracy – at least 'democracy' as it suited him.

John Chambers looked around the table at each of the other men before answering, thus getting their attention. 'Gentlemen, our interests are basically similar but we bring with us our departmental baggage and backgrounds that tend to narrow our vision,' he began soothingly. 'Communism, whether in its raw form or in its less obvious manifestations is dangerous and unpleasant; it is terrifyingly insidious and hydra-headed in its deviousness. It, and its allies of unthinkingly blind selfishness and political opportunism, are uncomfortably close to us here in the United Kingdom, whether we like it or not, or even if we refuse to recognise the evidence, stealthy or otherwise, here for us to see. We have, as Co-Chairman in Indo-China, a presence in an area where history is being written, destinies forged and patterns changed. I can almost agree with General Sir David when he says that the result is probably a foregone conclusion.' Here he paused for effect, then continued, 'but even if the rest of Indo-China goes red, it is just possible that Laos can be saved if their King is crowned before the Communists get a stranglehold on public opinion. The King has been on the throne for thirteen years and plans to have his coronation when peace is restored, nor has he made any secret of it. The best we can hope for is that this will happen, having, in turn, the effect of a neutral Laos with balanced, rational policies, so giving a breathing space for Thailand to recover its poise after the Americans pull out, as they one day will have to, and this in turn will keep Communist pressure from Peninsular Malaysia where we do have considerable interests. It needn't be too fanciful to see the clash of interests between China in the northwest of Laos and Vietnam, the Soviet Union by proxy, in the east, resulting in unforeseen opportunities to show up and slow up the expansionist, colonising, proselytising faces of Communism: this is neither the time nor the place to dilate on this aspect of it but it is worth mentioning. My plea, Mr Chairman, is that this meeting recommends no dilution of existing machinery for, say, three or four years, reviewing it annually if necessary.'

It would have been embarrassing for those few dissenters to have cavilled at what Chambers had so lucidly recommended, especially as the stenographer had taken a verbatim record of what had been said and this would be circulated at Mandarin level in due course, then later going to the cabinet in a pruned version. The recommendation was agreed on and the meeting broke up soon afterwards. The General and Chambers walked down the stairs together.

'Well said! You spoke dispassionately after my more violent outburst,' the General smilingly congratulated the SIS man, 'and the points you made were better made by you than by me. As it happens I am briefing our next Defence Attaché to Vientiane at noon today. Your words have clarified my thoughts. You must have a good idea of him after vetting him?'

'Yes, I have. He's one cool operator, especially amongst Asians. Seems to hit it off with them in a way other Europeans don't seem able to. I've read up what he's done: overt, covert, with a gift for the stealthy approach. Tell him to keep his head down, General. We have good reasons to believe that the Soviets are mounting a diplomatic offensive in Southeast Asia and on Attachés going there consequent on the vacuum caused by the British "East of Suez" pull-out. This is now even more important than normal in view of the delicate embassy set-up,' and here he looked at the General who nodded, knowing that the unusually left-leaning ambassador was tactfully being referred to, 'and that he is of that small band of people which attracts Soviet attention – bachelor linguists, rare birds and known targets in the diplomatic world.'

The General had not expected any other answer and, at the front door, they parted.

His first week in London depressed the future Defence Attaché to Laos more than he cared to admit. He was glad when the time came for him to start on his concentrated French language course; it would keep him nicely busy. He had been told to make contact with a portly Egyptian, a speaker of thirteen languages, the director of a language school, Linguist, who told him that a Mme. Grambert would be his teacher. Rance vaguely wondered how he would get on with her – four hours daily in her company would be a strain.

Mme. Grambert, already on Linguistic's books, thus had foreknowledge of who her new pupil was so what and where his next job was. She had telephoned her husband Jacque who worked in France under cover of the air-freight business, based in Nimes Garons, near Gard, in the south of the country, but controlled from an office at 2, Passage conduit, Paris 17. M. Grambert's real job in life was taking part in a courier service operating between Paris and Vientiane. He had fought in General Leclerc's Deuxieme Division near Lake Chad in 1944 and then in Tonkin from 1945 until he had been captured by the Viet Minh. He had spent a number of years as a Vietnamese prisoner before they were convinced of his loyalty to their cause. His wife had told him about Rance and had asked for orders.

M. Grambert had made contact with a Third Secretary in the Soviet Embassy and had arranged a meeting later on that same day.

'Good day, Comrade Gretchanine. I think I might be able to help you in catching a little fish, a Colonel Rance, the next British Defence Attaché in Laos. Here is his background,' and he sketched out the details, not forgetting to dwell on his 'bachelor-linguist' status.

Vladimir Gretchanine, a tall, thick-set, silver-haired and hirsute Muscovite, was attached to the Far Eastern Affairs Section of the KGB that had recently been moved to 10 Znamenskaias Street in Moscow so as to be near KGB headquarters. With the Chinese quarrel showing no signs of mending, this section had assumed an even higher priority than before. Gretchanine listened to M. Grambert in silence then said, succinctly, 'Get Yvonne to compromise him. Normal procedure.'

Jacque Grambert had already contacted his wife, giving her this order before Rance and she met.

His French teaching was concentrated. From 9.30 a.m. till

1.30 p.m. he was closeted with Mme. Grambert in a small cubicle in Linguist. He found his teacher difficult to fathom; she was a good teacher, having patience combined with a deep knowledge of her subject and she intrigued him as a person. He had not met any French people since he was in Saigon in 1945 when, on his off-days, he had brushed up his French with them at the Cercle Sportiff in the Rue Chasse Loubart. But Yvonne Grambert was, somehow, different. Pert, chic, cosy and responsive as she was trying to be, she had no pretensions to beauty. She had a mouth that was wider than normal and, when he was bored by the tedious question-and-answer periods of a particularly inane work script, he amused himself by trying to count her teeth. He was fascinated to see that she reacted by her normally didactic method of teaching becoming simperingly giggly. It was her bad luck that she completely misread the reasons for this attention and her self-congratulations on her success were premature.

Before he had started his French language training, Rance had contacted the Education authorities in MOD and asked them why they had not included any Lao language training. He was told that it had never been considered necessary. With his already considerable knowledge of Asian mentality and his firm belief that a native language produced results, certainly on a personal basis, more beneficial than any second language, he had managed to give officialdom sufficient of a jolt by his persuasive reasoning to get authority for a Lao teacher to be paid for by MOD. She arrived at Linguist at the start of the third week.

The Director of Linguist introduced her as Miss Inkham Hatsady, the Third Secretary of the Royal Lao Embassy at 5 Palace

Gardens near Hyde Park. She was ready to teach Rance basic written and spoken Lao for three hours directly after his French lessons. It meant a heavy work load for him but he instinctively knew it was worthwhile.

The Lao girl was in her late twenties. She had exquisitely moulded features, smooth golden skin, raven-black hair and almond eyes. She held herself almost regally yet had a demure manner. She stood a little over five and a half feet tall and had a wonderfully shaped figure. Her poise and elegance made Mme. Grambert seem coarse and bovinely unattractive by comparison. Miss Hatsady spoke fluent English, French and Thai as well as her native tongue in the not-so-common Luang Prabang dialect of north Laos. Her silvery voice, her rippling laughter, her impish grin made Rance feel a pang of regret he was not twenty years younger. He tried not to show his feelings but his obvious joy at making her acquaintance and his feigned sorrow at bidding farewell Mme. Grambert deceived nobody. *My God*, he thought, *what a winner*, animal sap rising swiftly in his veins.

During their practice conversations, Mme. Grambert had often hinted that, if they got the chance, Rance should go and have supper with her. Rance had shown little enthusiasm for this but neither had he any valid reason for refusal. On the Friday before his military briefing, Inkham did not arrive as due. She had had a message at the embassy purporting to be from Rance saying that he would be unable to study Lao any longer. Mme. Grambert suggested that they relax over a cup of coffee in the café opposite the school till Inkham came. When by half past two no Lao teacher had arrived, the French woman said she would telephone the Lao embassy for news. This she did and came back saying that '*La Laotienne n'arrivera pas aujourd'hui.*' So the Lao girl would not be coming today. *Something wrong somewhere.*

After some desultory talk, Mme. Grambert suggested that now was as good a time as any for M. le Colonel to go home with her but first would he please help her with her weekend shopping? He felt that she was making the running. Her unwonted skittishness and purposeful insistence, coupled with an intensity of manner since Inkham had entered his life had been blatant. That made Rance suspicious. Now politeness, boredom and a desire to get it over and done with overruled his natural inclination not to accept her invitation.

'Yes,' he replied. 'I'll help you with your shopping before I go back to my place to change.'

They left for her special grocery, run by a Frenchman. To his surprise she nodded to the grocer who nodded back. 'Wait here for a few minutes,' she bade her pupil as she disappeared through a door in the rear of the shop, the Frenchman trailing her.

Where on earth has she gone? Rance wondered as he waited. A packet of Gauloise cigarettes lay open on the counter and the smell irritated his nostrils. Ten minutes later the grocer came back and beckoned him over. 'Go up those stairs. She's in the first room on the right.' Rance took a step back as his breath was fetid. A childhood memory came back: Grandfather smoked something that smelt like that … Balkan Sobranie, worse than that French muck. As a child the smell almost made him vomit. Up he went, dutifully. At the top of the stairs, he opened the door of the first room on the right and, without any warning or hesitation, Mme.

Grambert flung herself at him, one arm round his waist, the other starting to unbutton his trousers and her face buried into his, her tongue forcing his lips open. Jason was no prude but there was something forced about this assault. *She is sex-starved*, he thought. *The bitch, I've a damned good mind to stuff her more stupid than she was ever designed to be and then leave her.*

But almost immediately he knew that something was forced. Her breath had a taste of tobacco on it and, as he knew she never smoked herself, it seemed that the grocer had probably had a quickie. He pushed her away hard. She fell over backwards but he left her on the floor to get up on her own. *I didn't like the French in Cochin-China and I don't like them any better now.*

At 11 o'clock on the following Monday, 3 July, Rance arrived at the Ministry of Defence, New Building, off Whitehall. He made his way through the doors to the glass-fronted kiosk, behind which sat two elderly women, also in uniform. 'Can I help you, sir?' one asked in a kind tone of voice.

'Yes, please,' and Rance reiterated his destination. 'I have to see the Director of Military Intelligence at noon.'

'Are you expected?' the more buxom of the two females asked. 'You're very early, y'know, sir,' and she eyed his diffidence speculatively.

She reached for a telephone directory, searched for the General's office number, then dialed it. She smiled at Rance as she waited for an answer.

'Oh, hello. Desk here. Is that you Mr Watson? I've got a – wait a sec luv,' and she covered the phone with her hand and said to Rance, 'Give us yer ID card, there's a dear, it's the DMI's PA.' She spoke into the phone again, 'I've a Lieutenant Colonel Rance here. Do you know anything about him?' She nodded a couple of times at the answer and continued, 'In that case I'll 'ave 'im brought up to you in a jiffy. Bye bye.' She put the handset down. 'You'll have to wait a while, sir, for the General, he's out for a bit but Major Knowles'll look after you.'

She made out a temporary pass, asked Rance to sign it, showed him where it had to be countersigned before leaving the office of the person he had been to see and then asked him if he knew the way. Rance shook his head. 'No, I don't. It's my first visit.'

His guide took him up to the fifth floor and, out the lift, turned left and walked down a long passage that had fire-proof doors regularly spaced along it. They reached 505 and she knocked on the door. A voice called them to enter. She opened the door and announced that 'Lieutenant Colonel Rance come to see the DMI, sir,' and thrusting his pass into his hand, made off back to her desk.

A Sapper Major got up out of his chair and walked over to the visitor. 'Knowles, the General's Military Assistant,' and extended his hand. 'Welcome in. The General will be back from a meeting fairly soon. Sit down, Colonel. Coffee?'

'Yes, please. Sugar and milk, if I have a choice.'

'Mr Watson, two cups of coffee, normal pattern,' Knowles called to the General's Personal Assistant. Rance waited for his coffee before asking Knowles if he knew the scope of the General's briefing and how much the General expected or tolerated his visitors to say.

'He likes to get to know his DAs personally before they start on their mission. He will talk to you in outline yet be succinct. If you have any particular queries, now's the time to ask him. As regards matters of detail, you'll be having a number of sessions with your Desk Officer on the third floor starting ... let me see' and he consulted a piece of paper on his desk. 'This afternoon at 1430 hours,' said Rance who had had a programme already and had memorised the timings.

While they waited for the General to come back, Knowles explained the workings of the Defence Intelligence set-up. Rance listened attentively. Then the General swept in and, shooting a glance at the new Attaché, barked out, 'Give me five minutes,' and walked on into the inner office, No. 506. After the stated time had exactly elapsed, the Major followed suit and went into his master, carrying the folder which contained Rance's details.

'Thanks. I'll give a buzz when I'm ready. This may take slightly longer than I had envisaged. I got talking to John Chambers after our meeting at the Cabinet Office. I want long enough with this new man to see if I can fathom him. I haven't got any more visitors before lunch so I can afford to take my time.'

The MA acknowledged his orders and withdrew. The General, left alone, picked up Rance's file. In it were his service details and a copy of the letter written to him when it had been decided by No. 3 Selection Board that he was to be the new DA. '... apart from the Plowden scale not properly covering your allowances as a bachelor in an attaché post so that you may find that you have to live off capital, you do not qualify on three counts: you have not done a Grade Two Staff job, you are not Staff Qualified and you are not married. However,' the letter continued, 'your selection is implicit in the belief that you can bring some personal experience and knowledge to the job others might not have ...' The General, brought up in the belief that a military career was lop-sided unless an officer had been to the Staff College, resisted the temptation to wonder how an officer with Rance's limitations had reached Lieutenant Colonel's rank. Instead he asked himself the question, why was it that someone with Rance's intellect had not bothered to become properly qualified. The brief contained outlines of two most unusual and successful operations, *Janus* and *Blind Spot*, and adequately told its own story of experience, knowledge and dedication. The list of Asian languages that he had passed already was impressive enough as what he had achieved in Malaya and Borneo. He also knew what he had achieved in Burma. *Why no decorations? Should have been awarded at least a couple ...* He himself had fought in Burma as an officer in the Indian Army so could understand Rance's empathy with Asians: *must be a man of simple tastes and of solid standards.*

Having refreshed his mind on some of the more relevant details, he rang the buzzer and there was a subdued knock on the door. The new DA was shown in and went over to the General's desk and stood to attention. The General also stood up and, having shaken hands, offered him a seat. Before starting his briefing, he noticed a deep look of authority and inner confidence in the younger man's eyes that nevertheless looked troubled. *Will he be successful without his Gurkhas?* the General asked himself, glancing at his watch.

'Right you are. Let's get down to business. We can clear up any other points later,' he began. 'There are four aspects to your new job. You probably know them already but I will rehearse them.' He went into the relevant details, stressing that being an Attaché is more than cocktails and gossip.'

Rance considered what Sir David had said for a few seconds and then said he understood entirely. 'In that case, come over to this wall map,' the General ordered. 'I'll give you a broad-brush run-down as I see your job is Laos.'

He finished off, 'Internally you have rightists, leftist and neutralists. It's confusing and complicated and there's more to it than that, but as has been said , "a little inaccuracy saves wealth of detailed explanation", and you'll learn fast enough once you're in the chair. However, the pivot of the country and the one man who could prevent it from going Communist is the uncrowned King, Savang Vatthana.' A thought struck him. 'You have a Lao teacher, haven't you?'

Rance told him her name, where she worked and that the King of Laos was her uncle.

'I've read all about how you have managed to successful when great odds were against you. I have a gut feeling that you many, just, hit it off with her to be able to get use her to talk to her uncle secretly.'

Jason gave an involuntary start.

The General's eyes lit up and in an uncharacteristic mood of either extreme flippancy or utter conviction and a broad grin, said, 'Such a ploy has already been christened "Operation Stealth". Get him crowned and you'll get the OBE.'

Rance grinned back. 'If you have nothing more for me, sir, I'd like to talk something over with you, if I may, because, right now, I'm not rudderless so much as chart-less. I'm up against the frontiers of ignorance.'

'Carry on,' said Sir David and Rance told him about his French teacher. The General was a good listener. He saw how embarrassing it was but appreciated the frankness with which the story was told. His mind raced with implications. 'You certainly didn't go to bed with her or act indecorously "off your own bat" in front of any camera as far as you know. Nothing else is there?'

'No, General. That's about the sum of it. I think that the grocer's shop,' and here he gave the General the address written down, 'could do with some sort of surveillance.'

'I agree. Who have you mentioned this to other than to me? No one, I hope.'

'Correct, sir. Not a word to a soul, nor about "Operation Stealth".'

'Good. Keep it that way. I'll leave word with Peter Rigby, your Desk Officer, if I want you here once more. But if I don't see you again before you go out to Laos, may I wish you the best of luck and a successful tour.' He stood up, signalling that the interview was over. They shook hands once more and Rance left, it not having occurred to him to mention the strange happenings on the final exercise at that last Jungle Warfare School course as neither of the two men concerned were from Laos.

As he handed in his pass at the glass-fronted kiosk, the banality of the conventional scene contrasted forcibly with the graver affairs upstairs.

Rance spent most of that week on the third floor of the building, closeted with the fraternity who would be the group through whom he would work. He immediately felt at home amongst them. Late that first afternoon they sat together having a cup of coffee. Rance had been reading a number of reports, personality studies and military appreciations, the various types of force he'd meet and had learnt that the country was divided into five Military Regions, No 2 being out of bounds to the British. 'If you can get a report about the place, we'll be more than interested,' said Peter Rigby, the thin, sardonic-looking, one-time Marine.

'There's more than enough detail here,' said Jason, 'most of it tiringly complex. How can you tell if it is only superficially correct or if it is reliably backed by irrefutable evidence? I see you've pins on your map showing North Vietnamese Army units, Chinese People's Army units, American-dominated Thai Unity Forces units to say nothing of Meo guerillas, the Royal Lao Army and the Pathet Lao Communists. Who is interested in such details? With our tenuous and residual interest as Co-Chairman to whatever-it-is in Geneva, what can we do about it anyway? In short, why do we bother with it to this extent?'

Peter Rigby looked at Rance and said, 'Colonel, we know that we can't even keep our own house in order here in the UK. We know that, except in general terms, nobody in the government or even in that impediment to positive thought, the FCO, could give or care a stuff about it. I don't want to disillusion you but, as I see it, despite our narrow-minded and inward-looking politicians – some of whom are so wet you could shoot snipe off them – there are a number of people, apart from the Yanks, who do care a lot, the right-wing Lao themselves for instance. For us not to care would be to let them down. And the more alert we, you, show the Communists that we non-communists are, the more they'll be on their mettle to try and defeat us. The harder they try, the more likely they are to expose themselves and to make mistakes. The more we know about them, the more that knowledge can be put to our use. Long shots, I grant you, but since we're in the job that, to me, seems to be a workable rationale for us. The detail you've questioned is not, to my mind, necessary but if we felt it were all a waste of time, we'd go mad. There are some benefits to be gained from the therapeutic value of self-engendered heat.'

Rance grinned broadly at this. 'I like it. You give me encouragement. A new country, a new language, a new people and a new challenge – but apart from the military trivia to get to terms with, I've no real target; or, if I have, I've yet to identify it. It so indeterminate.'

As he said that, he remembered the General's remark about the King, but Attachés simply never had their sights that high. And yet, how come that he, a searcher, was already a target himself?

Before the week was out a number of moves had been made. On the administrative front Rance arranged for his Lao lessons to continue in Miss Inkham's flat at 18 Holland Road, Acton, W 3. On the tactical front, the General contacted Colonel Bates who, in turn, called up John Chambers. Maurice Burke was alerted but he did not appear at a conference held on the Wednesday morning, 12 July, when the DMI, Peter Rigby, Clifford Bates and John Chambers got together, the outcome of which Rance was merely told in outline and 'unattributably' that the surveillance on the grocer's shop had produced some interesting background facts, to be even more chary of strangers than hitherto and to keep the closest contact with his Desk Officer. Meanwhile, unbeknownst to him, MI5 had been called in to keep a watch on Mme. Grambert, with the French Intelligence Service, the SDECE, collaborating with the SIS as, in fact, she had interesting and suspect links in France.

M. Grambert had been alerted that the action to discredit the new British Defence Attaché had failed. He was angry and suspicious but had decided to take no action with the Soviets until he had more details. His wife's letter had said that he had not reacted as she had expected, he seemed less excitable than the others had and probably he was *un triste homme* – a homosexual. Nothing was lost and maybe something gained.

Blast it, thought M. Grambert angrily, *how much better to have got Rance in his very early days.* No matter, the Soviet would have an answer. These bachelor linguists always have a weakness. My wife is probably correct; boys, in this man's case: Asian boys, golden, smooth-skinned and, if not homosexual, heterosexual. It might even work out better if he were discredited in Laos as the Attaché rather than while still in England. The transvestites or catamites or whatever they called those creatures would sort him out. That gang that lived around the Thad Luang area in Vientiane are especially vicious. Even if they failed to do the trick there would be some other perversion but, whatever it was, there'd better be no second mistake. He reported the case to Vladimir Gretchine who, in turn, forwarded it to Moscow. Luckily for Rance's peace of mind, he knew nothing about it.

The following week Rance started his interrupted Lao lessons again with Miss Inkham Hatsady in Acton. It was hard going at first but his knowledge of Thai helped him and by the end of six weeks' instruction, he was reasonably fluent. His relationship with Inkham flourished and she was, by then, calling him Jason. On their last day he took his ring with him, quite why he did not know, except in his mind's eye it marked the end of a period, the turning point in a crisis.

'Jason, do you know what my name means?'

'No, I don't. Please tell me.'

'"In" means "fairy" and "kham" means "gold". I'm really "Golden Fairy" although it sounds strange in English,' she explained, smiling at him radiantly.

Rance then remembered the ring. He took it from his pocket where he kept it as a talisman and slipped it on the little finger of his right hand. As soon as she saw it, the smile left her face and she looked perplexed.

'Where did you get that? Who gave it to you?' she asked. 'But before you answer, I'll tell you something that I hadn't meant to tell you, Jason. I am the King's niece. I am not plain Miss really but a princess of the royal house of Luang Prabang in my own right. That's why my accent is different from the other people's in the embassy as you remarked when you telephoned me that time. That's the accent I've taught you.' A pause, then, 'My father is the only full brother His Majesty has.' As she said this, with a wonderful combination of regal poise and unaffected charm, Rance's heart melted but his professional instinct prevailed.

Play this one carefully, he told himself, *this could prove a winner*. He was musing on what the General had said about the King as he turned the ring over in his hand. As he did he saw that something had caught her attention. She took it from him and scrutinised the underside of it. A look of horror passed over her face as she stared at it. 'Have you seen this, Jason?' she demanded abruptly, fear in her eyes.

'I have noticed that it has a strange emblem on its inner edge that looks like a badly written 27.'

'Look at what is engraved there. It is Lao.'

Rance said nothing, being too stunned to think of anything relevant to say. 'It was given me by a Vietnamese who was quarreling with a Thai. I had taken it for a badly written '27'. I can now read it as *kha*, to kill, in Lao.'

'Yes, that's right. It does mean "kill": whoever gave you that ring was either a professional killer or a man under the gravest oath of revenge. It's like a curse that nothing can stop ...' She paused, frightened.

'Go on,' prompted Rance yet again. 'Please tell me more. I must know.'

'I can't. I can't,' she sobbed, 'because whether it is you or the man who gave it to you, the wearer is destined to die a savage death because of it.'

It was all he could do not to comfort her physically. 'Please, Inkham, please,' he pleaded, perplexed and wondering why she had broken off suddenly.

She wiped her eyes.

His mind had flashed back to the scene in the jungle where a Vietnamese, not a Lao, had given him the ring. He had always thought it an unusual motif but he had never imagined its significance. Was there anything deeper to it? But why did a Vietnamese wear something that was Lao?

'Now it is my turn to tell you a confidence,' he said, and went on to explain the '9' he had seen tattooed on the ring wearer's little finger.

Inkham explained it. 'It is, in fact, the silent consonant around which we build vowel clusters and our initial vowels.'

'Yes, of course. I now recognise it.'

'What I have not told you is that it can stand for the cry of love, of despair, of victory, or hatred or of any heart-felt exclamation you like. It depends on what the next symbol in the word is. It is an old device in Laos and one which we royal family are brought up to regard with much reverence.'

Jason thanked her, declining to tell her that it was not on a Lao's that he saw the mark but on a Vietnamese' finger, a long, long way from Lao royalty. It was no use bothering her ... but it gave an added and serious dimension to his mysterious discovery. *Who are the other three? Four rings and four '9's. The writing Lao but neither of the two men quarreling Lao nor royal. Do I start worrying? Leave it ...*

They said their farewells with sorrow, Jason thanking 'my own princess' – as he now thought of her – for her hard work, valuable time and friendship.

As for Princess Golden Fairy, she had seldom met a man who appealed to her more ... so she stood on her toes and gave him a surprise, and unroyally warm, kiss.

4

November, 1972. Vientiane, Laos: It was with mixed feelings that Colonel Rance followed the Duty RAF Movements Officer who led him deferentially into the VIP lounge at Brize Norton aerodrome in Oxfordshire on Sunday, 12 November 1972, Remembrance Sunday. He had been given the local rank of Colonel which meant no increase in pay although he had been given £99 as a uniform allowance to help make the necessary changes from his Gurkha black buttons, Highland pattern brogue shoes and black belt to the General Staff brass and brown. For all other purposes he was still as he had been, a Lieutenant Colonel, drawing, so he had been told during his briefing, only seventeen and a half percent of the allowances his married diplomatic colleagues got. But he was not duly upset about the imbalance or the implication that, certainly in FCO eyes, the military were second-class citizens. There was comfort to be drawn from the vagueness of no set solutions and few ground rules. Even so he felt very much the new boy.

The VC 10 took off shortly after dawn and for most of the flight Rance was lost in thought about everything that had happened since the previous April, rehearsing them over and over again. They still did not make sense; the Thai, Major Mana Varamit who had assaulted the Vietnamese Major, Le Dang Khoa, who had them given him the ring that he had feared lost which, in turn, had had such an effect on Princess Golden Fairy – was it an asset or an incubus? – the unpolished and heavy-handed behaviour of Mme Grambert – who had smoked that peculiarly scented tobacco? Concerning the ring, he had decided he had no option but to play it by ear, so to speak, having realised that the effect of wearing it could be irrevocable. His thoughts alternated between pleasure and gloom: he became lost in reverie with enchanting scenes of Princess Golden Fairy in his mind's eye, unconscious of the glances at him of the cabin staff and of the faintly-heard and monotonous whine of the high-powered Rolls Royce Pegasus engines that kept up their background threnody: at other times the hopelessness of his mission engulfed him with dismay. Whoever heard of an Englishman in Laos where American pressures, French idiom and the communist Big Brothers were all jostling one another so blatantly and the situation so complex – whoever heard of an Englishman making any difference at all? Laos – he had always mentally rhymed it with 'chaos' before learning to pronounce it like 'mouse'. What had his Desk Officer said: the only under-populated country in Southeast Asia, not far off the size of Great Britain, with a population of less than three million, a twenty percent literacy rate, fifty-eight different languages, to say nothing of a plethora of dialects and a life expectancy of between thirty to thirty-five years ...

In Hong Kong for twenty-four hours, Rance managed to spend a nostalgic night with his Gurkha battalion in the New Territories in Queen's Hill camp, where he met up again with his old friend Captain (QGO) Kulbahadur Limbu, DCM, MM. The wise old Gurkha Officer felt that all was not well with the Colonel sahib, gleaned from a strained look in his eyes, but forbore to say anything. *I smell danger*, was all he said to himself.

On the morrow Rance reported in to the Royal Lao Air counter in the civil part of Kai Tak airport for the last lap of his journey. He flew in a quarter-full Lockheed Electra, painted in its red and white livery with its badge a three-headed elephant surmounted by a nine-tiered parasol. They dog-legged south of the Demilitarised Zone of Vietnam (the Dee Em Zee as he later learnt to call it), to southern Laos and northeast Thailand, crossing, for the second time, the Mekong, the world's thirteenth longest river, as the plane dropped into Wattay airport at Vientiane, shortly before dusk on 15 November. He had been happily stimulated and secretly flattered by the effect his Luang Prabang accent had on the charming air hostess whose unbridled flirting was only just short of being indecorous. Had Rance been wiser, he would have realised that she was angling to be his mistress. It might have led to fewer complications had he succumbed.

He was met by a number of people, the arrival of a new boy being of considerable interest to the other Attachés. The outgoing incumbent, Roger Daniel, was already on the tarmac; a short, balding, plump man who, as Rance was to find out in the next few days, had an inflated idea both of his importance and efficiency, a sense of humour that was lost on the other Attachés and an abrasive outlook on life generally. Rance noticed some white cords round his wrists and as they walked together to the terminal building, still under construction and dustily resonant, asked if Daniels had hurt himself.

'No, no. These are *baçi* strings. I'm having another *baçi* in my house next Thursday and,' condescendingly, 'you might as well come along too and learn about it. They're quite fun until the novelty wears off.'

Without any more explanation they entered the building where Rance met Major Ronny Hill, the Assistant Military Attaché, whose other task it was to fly the embassy Beaver aircraft, and the third military member, Mr. Joseph, the supporting clerk. The Australian Attaché and his wife, Colonel Terry and Mrs Jane Olsen, were also there, a gesture Rance much appreciated. Mr Joseph, a gangling, amiable, north countryman, relieved him of the immigration form he had filled in on the aircraft, his baggage tags and passport. As the bits and pieces were being checked, Rance looked around him and gazed intently at the Lao functionaries' and baggage boys' faces, mentally comparing them with the Gurkhas he knew so well and noting how alike they looked. He had no idea what made the Lao laugh or what happened when one scratched them: he wobbled his eyebrows independently of each other and one particularly happy youth saw him and immediately became convulsed with laughter. Others turned to see what was happening and joined in the merriment.

Rance looked at the arrival and departure boards, finding he could read the Lao script alongside the French. He noticed a large European standing by them, staring at him intently. Their gazes met and the man turned quickly away to examine the departure notice, glancing at his watch as he did. On the spur of the moment, Rance said to Daniel, 'Roger, are there any more departures today?'

'No, Jason, there aren't. Why the interest?'

'Oh, nothing really. Just idle curiosity.'

Daniel shot him a glance of quizzical impatience. 'Time we went. All ready?'

Rance caught sight of a black car as it drew up at the entrance and, out of the corner of his eye, he saw the European turn on his heel, go down the steps to the car and get into it. The car immediately drove away and Rance noticed the rear number plate was 124 CD 052.[3]

Daniel moved outside and signalled for his own car. Up drove a white Ford Zephyr, flying the Union Jack, defaced with crossed swords and crown, surmounted by a lion, also crowned, the emblem of the UK Ministry of Defence. The driver, a Lao aged about forty whom Daniel barkingly addressed as Leuam, jumped out and opened the left rear door for him. As Rance walked round to the other side of the car he saw that the number was 24 CD 050. He got in, on the right hand side behind the driver, so that Daniel could have his seat with the uninterrupted view that protocol demanded.

'I see the British Embassy has 24 as a Corps Diplomatique plate. Who has 124 CD?' Rance asked.

'Let me see,' said Daniel. 'Yes, that's the Soviet number.'

So why was the Soviet DA waiting in the background with no more flights? Can he have been waiting to see what I look like? Perish the thought.

---

3 The diplomatic plates of the Soviet and British embassy vehicles were as given in the text.

'Yes, Comrade Ambassador,' said the Soviet Defence Attaché, Colonel Georgi Nechaev, who was also a member of the GRU, 'you are right. The new Englishman is certainly eccentric and shows definite signs of homosexual tendencies. At the airport, where I'd gone to meet the new political cadre, Comrade Bounphong Sunthorn, who flew in from Sam Neua in the AN-2 to reinforce the Lao Patriotic Front's effort at the peace talks, I watched Colonel Rance gazing intently at the Lao men on duty and making positive advances to one youth. I think it will be easy to arrange to fix him,' and he smiled, his thick spectacles making his blue eyes glint coldly.

'Good idea,' said Ambassador Bakunin and, as an afterthought, 'Comrade What's-his-name – I find these Lao and Vietnamese names jaw cracking – is he a good man?'

'Yes, Comrade Ambassador, one of the steadiest we could ever trust. 'The Black-eyed Butcher', by that I mean Political Commissar Nga Sô Lưu, regards him as one of his best.'

The following morning Daniel fetched Rance from his temporary accommodation, the Hotel Lane Xang, on the left bank of the Mekong, and drove him to the British embassy. As they motored along the rue Lane Xang, past the Morning Market and the Lao Patriotic Front HQ, Daniel talked about the British Ambassador, His Excellency Mr Oswald Stewart Taunton.

'Lord alive! You'll find that he's a queer fish. He's an ardent pacifist, anti-American, anti-military and has strong left-wing tendencies. The stresses and strains of his first diplomatic post ever in a country at war, Manchuria, coupled with the frustrated worries of a broken marriage and his impending retirement have made him peevishly intolerant of normal procedures, outspokenly critical of American policy and openly sympathetic to those who portray themselves as underdog fighters for social justice – in short, a perfect and unconscious subject for Communist ploys. The Yanks mistrust him and, regrettably, us, that is now you and was me. His indiscretions at various social functions are an embarrassing commonplace. The right-wing Lao faction, whom we are here to represent, are most unhappy about him and he's the darling of the left wing – for these reasons alone I can't tell you how glad I am to be leaving.'

They turned down a narrow, bumpy road, rue Pandit J. Nehru, and stopped outside a single-storied building with the royal coat of arms on the wall by the entrance. 'Here we are. This is where it all happens and where you do your work. Come on in and I'll introduce you around before we settle down to anything serious,' said Daniel and Rance entered another world.

As he walked up the three steps into the foyer, still happily ignorant of what he was to find, he saw men with limpid brown eyes turned on him. He took a plunge and smilingly greeted them in his northern accented Lao. The effect was pleasantly reminiscent of a group of Gurkha recruits, not previously believing that this tall, silver-haired, blue-eyed, straight-backed man could communicate with them in their own language, being astonished to realise that he had cared enough about them to speak to them fluently: smiles and nods greeted his efforts.

'French or English is perfectly adequate,' sniffed Daniel depreciatingly. 'You'd better get used to the fact that any European

speaking Lao to anyone of note is considered to be in bad taste.'
If Rance had any reaction to this pompous snub, he kept it to
himself.

They turned left down a long corridor, flanked by barred
windows on one side and shut office doors on the other. Daniel
stopped at the third office and went inside. There was Mr Joseph
at his typewriter. Daniel asked him for the key of his office and left
without saying anything else.

'Good morning, Mr Joseph. You were a great help last night.
Thank you. I'd have been lost without you,' said Rance. Mr Joseph
flushed with pleasure and thought what a change and about time
too. 'And how come the Defence Attaché opens his own office?
Why wasn't it opened before he came in?'

'Security, sir. No office can ever be opened without the
occupier being present and he has to shut it and lock it, taking
the key with him, whenever he leaves it. The key must never leave
the embassy building. It doesn't take long to get used to. These
rules are new and are the result of laxity in high places elsewhere,'
and Mr Joseph smiled with pleasure at being able to show his
knowledge off.

Daniel came back to fetch Rance. 'What's the hold up? Let's
get these introductions over now and they we'll have time to talk
before we go and see His Excellency the Ambassador, HE.'

He led Rance away and introduced him to the various
sections: consular, aid, chancery, administration and the security
guard. Rance did not say much. The surly way the various people
greeted Daniel was a fair indication as to how they regarded him.
He quickly found that the embassy was indeed different from the

crisply efficient military life that he had till then known. Here he was to meet a longer haired, less incisive, more verbose and first-name orientated set-up. He was to find punctuality a thing of the past and the morning repetition of the previous night's cocktail party trivia as irritatingly banal as it was spuriously inaccurate. In silence they went back to the Defence Attaché's office. It was a small room that stank of Gauloise cigarettes, Daniel being a chain-smoker. Rance involuntarily recoiled.

'Sit down, Jason. We've a few minutes before we go and see HE. I don't know what, if anything, you were told about His Excellency the ambassador when you were in London. Nothing, I expect. A tradition of reticence hangs heavily over all organisations, especially in Whitehall, which makes taboo even the most veiled understatements about other people. Has to be, I suppose, but the tradition is now so enshrined that, coupled with benevolently uncritical annual confidential reports, it perpetuates the odd miscarriage of common sense. That having been said, let me run over the rest of our programme. We've a very hectic week before I leave on the twenty-second. We have a protocol visit to FAR HQ at Phone Kheng, followed by one to HQ MR 5 at Chinaimo.'

Rance held up his hand and brought Daniel to an unwilling halt. 'Let me check whether I can remember those initials from my briefing. FAR is Forces Armées Royales, also called RLA, which is short for Royal Lao Army. MR is straight forward Military Region. That's about it, isn't it?'

'Yes. You've also got that strange organisation, FAN, the Forces Armées Neutralistes. With some French terminology and some American, it does take time to understand it all. While we're at it, PL stands for Pathet Lao, which we use loosely for all the left-wing baddies, while they prefer LPF, the Lao Patriotic Front. As regards the MRs, there are five: MR 1, commanded by one of the King's half-brothers, is based on the royal capital, Luang Prabang.' Here Rance pricked up his ears at the mention of the King whose reference had no effect on Daniel as he continued with his discourse. 'MR 2 is the remotest and the hardest to get to. Its HQ is situated to the southwest of the Plain of Jars and it is commanded by the unpredictable and legendary Meo, Major General Vang Pao. MRs 3 and 4 are down in the Panhandle in southern Laos and MR 5 controls the capital and the Vientiane plain. It also holds the HQ of the military rump of the Prime Minister's forces, the Neutralists I've just mentioned.'

As he spoke he pointed out these places on the wall map. 'OK? Right. Well, today we're going to FAR HQ and to HQ MR 5. We have our monthly attaché luncheon at the Tan Dao Vien restaurant, given this month by the Thai as he has hardly any English and no French. You'll no doubt ask why he has been chosen to be the Attaché. Business interests, I expect, lie at the bottom of that one. He deals in rings. Why are you looking so surprise?' Daniel asked as he saw Rance visibly flinch. As before, he continued without waiting for an answer. 'Anyway, none of the other Attachés have got any Thai – nor, strangely, when you think of the mix, any Lao. After lunch we'll pay a courtesy visit to MR 5 and on the way back we'll drop in on the Yanks. All the others you'll have to fix for yourself after I've gone. The Yanks are the only ones who know what's happening but I find them very difficult to deal with. They blow hot and cold. The Australian is smarmy to them and seems to be nearer to them than are we. I put this down to their Vietnam connections. However, I have had one piece of luck with the Americans – we have been allowed to go and visit the Thai Unity Forces, the secret army run by the CIA, and the Meo Irregulars of General Vang Pao on Saturday morning. Early next week we have a whole day in white uniform when the King comes down to Vientiane and attends a number of ceremonies, including a visit to the Trade Fair, where we have a pavilion. That's at Thad Luang, near my villa. We may also be visiting the Royal Lao Air Force, RLAF to you, because you'll be the Air Attaché as well. There'll be a number of parties to say farewell, including a *baçi* and a hello to you. You'll find it hard going.'

'My, but that's one hell of a programme. I'll be punched, bored and counter-sunk before we're even halfway through! It's lucky you'll be here to remember it all. How long did it take you to fix that lot up?'

'Quite a bit of time.' He glanced at his watch. 'Come on. Time to see HE. Don't say you weren't warned.'

They reached the Ambassador's door and knocked.

'Come in,' came the shrill, nasal reply.

In they went. On the left of the room at a large desk sat a tall, bespectacled man with grey hair and a cadaverous face, with a pronounced hook nose. He was dressed in a tropical suit and sported a wide pink tie.

'Good morning, Your Excellency. May I introduce my successor, Colonel Jason Rance of the Gurkhas?'

'Gurkhas? Nasty people who take tops off. I see you're both in fancy dress.' His voice had turned into a whine. 'Why?'

Daniel replied with more than a tone of asperity. 'We are in uniform because, after this, we are making some protocol calls and so are being representational, sir.' That last word was too heavily stressed for politeness. Rance looked the Ambassador straight in the eyes and saw he was looking at an unhappy man, probably out of his depth.

'I suppose you like killing people, Colonel, and that's why you joined the army,' was the next extraordinary outburst. 'Just like those wretched Americans and their beastly bombers. Get this, too, will you: when you give me your briefings at our weekly meetings, never mention casualties,' he added querulously. 'I don't like hearing about them. And if you find out anything sensitive that I can use to embarrass the Americans with, let me know. I want to punish them for their madness.'

Again Rance kept silent. *Dear God!* he thought, *the bastard's a nutcase if ever there was one. I can now see I'll get nowhere fast with him.* Daniel then outlined their tentative handing- and taking-over programme, omitting any reference to a Saturday morning trip to MR 2 that had never been visited by a British DA since the present Ambassador was appointed.

'Are you meeting that madman, the Minister of Defence? He really is the most unbalanced of right-wing hawks. No?' as Daniel shook his head. 'I shouldn't bother if I were you. The weekly Tuesday morning peace talks would have been settled and done with by now if it hadn't been for that maniac. Have you heard that he's going to Paris to divorce that French wife of his? I was told about it at the Polish reception last night given for the new Patriotic Front man who flew into Vientiane yesterday from Sam Neua.'

'Your Excellency, we won't waste any more of your time. Colonel Rance is living at the hotel Lane Xang until I go and then moves into the same villa near the Thad Luang.'

They left and went back to their own office where Daniel asked Mr Joseph to make them each a cup of coffee. 'God save me, Roger. How on earth does a man like that ever get to the position he's in? He's a nervous wreck besides being a dangerous nutcase. Surely the people in the FCO back home know about him? I simply can't understand it. I find it frightening.'

'Frightening it indeed is, Jason. I'm not sure whether being a Grade 4 here is a reward for past services or just the Old Boy network showing its unacceptable face. In HE's past I can't believe he was as bad as he is now. The Communists must see him as a "fellow traveller". I can't think they don't know about him back in the FCO, as you said earlier. What is certain sure is that my position was and yours now will be well-nigh impossible. We are shunned by the Yanks, who know everything that's going on and are chary of telling us anything sensitive, spurned by the right-wing Lao and mistrusted by most of the other embassies, except the Soviets and the Chinese. He's the darling of the left-wing Pathet Lao who not unnaturally use him as much as they can. I don't know how I've stuck it out for these past two years I have been in the job.'

For the rest of the day their programme included going to Phone Kheng, as the GHQ compound was known, and meeting the Commander-in-Chief, whom the Yanks called Jubilation after some strip-cartoon joker, his Deputy and various other important people as well as attending an attaché luncheon at the Formosa Chinese eating house. A number of expensive cars were already parked outside. Inside they were greeted first by their host, the Thai, and Rance was introduced to the rest of the Attaché Corps; the Australian, the American, the Frenchman, the South Vietnamese, the Filipino and the Soviet, a Russian. The three military members of the International Control and Supervision Commission, ICSC, were there also, an Indian Brigadier, a Polish and a Canadian Colonel. It was an all-male group, it not being the custom to invite wives. The Chinese were not represented, taking no part in such frivolities, and anyway, apart from the Formosa Chinese eating house being off-limits to Communist China, they and the USA did not recognise one another diplomatically.

Everybody was interested in the new Brit, especially the Russian, Colonel Georgi Nechaev, who now had the opportunity to examine him from close quarters. Conversation alternated between English and French and was anodynely bland until the Thai ordered champagne. As the corks popped, Daniel looked at Nechaev accusingly and said that it was like the North Vietnamese Army using Soviet ammunition. As the NVA's presence was still being sedulously denied although it was widely known to be in Laos in force and to be supplied by the Soviets and the Chinese, the remark was considered to be in offensively bad taste. The American smirked and the Russian glowered because, although Rance had not yet learnt of it, relations between the two were strained, Nechaev's driver having recently defected to the US embassy and granted asylum in the States. Nechaev turned to Rance who was toying with a Pepsi Cola and tried to nettle him by saying it was an imperialist drink. The remark failed to rankle.

'I hadn't thought of it like that,' smiled Rance. 'There's not much choice really. I don't like champagne anyway. I'm teetotal, in fact.'

Nechaev tried to bring some cordiality into the conversation. 'I am neutral. I don't take sides. See, I am drinking Portuguese wine. I don't know how to be anything but neutral.'

Daniel's voice rose above the hubbub. 'Georgi, you don't know anything. You are a product of the Revolution and were probably born in 1917, weren't you?'

Nechaev's blue eyes frosted behind his thick spectacles. 'No, Colonel, in 1916. I had to prepare myself for the Revolution, like you will have to one day.' As the laughter swelled up, he continued loudly, 'You don't know anything yet.' His eyes were steely and his lips pursed into a pretence of a smile. 'You have it still to come.' There was further mirth at the Englishman's discomfiture. Nechaev turned to Rance, lowered his voice and said, 'You, on the other hand, know everything about everything. Soon you will have to learn Russian and when you go to Moscow to learn it, I will take you there.'

Before Rance could find anything suitable to say, the Russian got up and joined another group. At that moment the Thai stood up and, reading from some prepared notes, he bade farewell to Daniel at this, his last attaché luncheon. The party broke up at half past two.

Before the end of the day, Daniel and Rance visited the HQ of the local Military Region, No 5, and the American embassy. As they entered it Rance shivered on the temperature dropping several degrees, the whole building being reliant on canned air continuously being pumped into it for ventilation. They waited while a sweetly smiling Lao lady receptionist telephoned for someone to fetch them. The intrusion of local femininity in such a sensitive establishment struck Rance as decidedly odd. She looked intently at Rance as he stood viewing his surroundings. *The Committee will be interested to learn what I think about this new one*, she thought.

'Come this way, please, Gentleman,' said a plain-clothes serviceman, leading them down a corridor to a spacious office.

'Come in, come in. Hi, Roger! Hi, Jason! Nice to see you both. Take a pew, take a pew. Make yourselves at home.' The American moved over to them, shook their hand although they had met less than two hours before, then turning to Rance, said, 'Jay V. Gurganus, from Texas, and the United States Army Attaché. We are the only embassy where there is no Defense Attaché, regarded by many in the Pentagon as an anomaly. The Air Attaché is a different man. His office is in the main building. You're of the Gurkhas, if I heard aright at lunch. Coffee? Abigail, three cups, if you please,' he called out.

'Cream and sugar?' came the nasal twang of a gruff female voice.

'Yes, please,' said Rance.

'Black and no sugar for me,' said Daniel. 'I've got to watch my weight.'

'I think,' continued the American, 'that the kindest thing we can do to each other in the Attaché Corps is not to give each other too much to eat. As regards the drink, well, it's every man for himself.'

There was a pause while the coffee was brought in by Abigail, a flabby, middle-aged career woman, savagely ugly, complete with tinted hair, grotesquely beaky nose and whose flaccid fingers were heavily ringed.

'Thanks, Honey,' said Colonel Gurganus and Daniel butted in with 'Jay. You and Jason have plenty of time to swap your *curricula vitae* later. I want to know what's happening up in MR 2. I hope the Agency is arranging for us to visit Long Cheng on Saturday morning, the nineteenth, and since I'm on my way home on posting, I'd like to be sure that that strong probe to the west of the Plain of Jars by elements of NVA 335 Regiment that your weekly hand-out told us about won't either prevent us from going there or, come to that, from returning.'

'Well, Roger, your guess is as good as mine. We have some Assistant Attachés in the field so we're only one step ahead of you but you Brits are good at the counter revolutionary game so maybe after your visit you can tell us.'

It was skilfully done, Rance had to admit. The American had given nothing away, Daniel's vanity had been pandered to and he, the new boy, was being cleverly kept at arm's length.

That evening, after he had come back from a farewell cocktail party given by the French Attaché for Daniel, Rance, exhausted and not hungry, went straight to bed. His head was in a whirl.

He knew it was premature to make any reasonable comment, let alone come to any conclusions but never had the start of any job he had previously tackled seemed so discouraging, depressing or inauspicious. He remembered at the Jungle Warfare School teaching that the Communists used unconventional methods, never for one moment thinking that he would come across such a mirror travesty. He fell into a troubled sleep and awoke still tired.

On the morning of Saturday, 18 November, Daniel and Rance, wearing plain clothes, drove back down the wide road to the airport. Viewed by day, Rance could see the unmade-up tracks that led to the Mekong on the one side and padi fields on the other. One particular road led off near a workshop for Citroën cars; 'that road goes to the French Military Mission, a low-level training concern allowed by the 1962 Geneva Accords,' was explained to him.

They reached Wattay airport but, short of the civil terminal entrance, they turned into an entrance marked Continental Airways and reached a barrier opposite an office building. Telling Leuam to wait, they got out and went inside where a number of Lao and Americans were busily engaged in preparing various details for the day's tasking. Daniel went to one desk and asked a crew-cut, cigar-smoking pinhead if Mr Harry Vainey had arrived. 'Nope, wait,' was the laconic response, Pinhead observing them suspiciously. The two Englishmen sat on a bench outside under a tree and Daniel told Rance that Continental Airways was the branch that carried VIPs and CIA Case Officers and advisers, while Air America had the contract for troop movements of the

CIA-inspired Thai and Meo Irregular Forces, and their stores. No one else could go to HQ MR 2 in Long Cheng without explicit permission, rarely given, from both Lao and American sources, nor without a CIA escort if a foreigner and this was what they were now waiting for. They had to go by air as there were no roads into the region and there was never time to walk that, even were clearance granted. Rance was later to learn that, instead of being allowed to wait inside, sitting where other passengers sat, they were kept away from the crew-briefing room which was an office where talc-covered maps had pins showing pilots where to expect NVA anti-aircraft artillery or missiles – the Strella 7 was then becoming a danger – as well as areas to be bombed and strafed by USAF B-52s and F-111s, and positions being shelled by conventional, own-force artillery. Such was the lack of trust that the Americans showed to the British, the visit to HQ MR 2 was not confirmed until the last minute. This mistrust stemmed partly from the British Ambassador and partly from Daniel's own talkative nature. The visit was undertaken on the express understanding that no subsequent mention was made of it and no notes taken during it. Before their CIA escort arrived, they were joined by the Australian Attaché who was a favourite of the Americans, the Vietnam connection being the reason. Little love was lost between him and Daniel.

'Hello there, Poms. Sitting outside, eh? What's new?'

He was a small man with large sideburns which he fondly believed made him more attractive to the Lao maidens who, he had been told, regarded such adornment as a sign of virility. His hair was flecked with grey but his brown smiling eyes gave the impression of youthful vitality, although he was fifty-four years of age.

'You can thank me for this visit. The Yanks were blowing hot and cold over it and were wanting to fill their Beechcraft up with some guys from Udorn but I persuaded them to take you along instead.'

Thick-skinned Daniel was on the point of retorting when a car arrived and a man wearing a blue Dacron safari suit and suede shoes got out.

'Hi Terry. Good to see you,' he greeted Olson. He turned to the two Englishmen and, holding out his hand, introduced himself as 'Harry J. Vainey from USAID, the United States Agency for International Development, *siree*, and let's never forget it.'

He went into the office and returned almost immediately with three bits of paper. 'Tickets,' he explained, 'to let you drive past the barrier and get you into the aeroplane. OK. Let's go.'

They drove over to the dispersal point without the Lao guards on the barrier showing any interest in them whatsoever. Back in the office one of the Lao cleaners turned to his mate and said, 'Not often you see two Englishmen here. We'll have to report it to our Committee representative.'

Their plane flew in from the USAF base in Udorn, Thailand, stopped behind a large hanger and unloaded some passengers who hurried away. The pilot gave Harry Vainey the thumbs up sign and they climbed in, engines still running. The plane taxied out, did its checks then, receiving clearance to leave, took off. It circled left over the town and river, gaining height. Headsets were not provided for the passengers nor was there an intercom loudspeaker, so Rance was not distracted as he observed the countryside below. Being November, the dry-weather heat haze, so common in this part of the world, had not yet started its build-up, so visibility was clear and extensive.

The terrain grew more spectacularly precipitous with beetling limestone crags and thick jungle. In the valleys and on the lower slopes Rance saw where the Meo tribesmen had slashed and burnt the jungle so that they could plant their dry padi.

A while later Daniel shouted, 'That's the Plain of Jars forward right,' pointing to where there was a valley just visible to the northeast. 'NVA 335 Regiment is over there.'

His ears told him they were descending as the pitch of the engine changed. The little plane was making a tactical approach by circling tightly downwards. He gasped as he saw a concrete runway with yet another high cliff of limestone at the far end, Skyline Ridge. The plane straightened out, flew over a small hill with only feet to spare and was forced down at the end of the runway, the pilot fighting the up currents. He saw wired and sandbagged 5.5 millimetre medium gun emplacements; a straggly, dusty road; civilians dressed in black clothes with lemon, red or blue sashes round their waist and hanging down behind them like a tail; six radial-engined T-28 training aircraft used as fighter-bombers; H-34 helicopters and C-130 Hercules transport aircraft.

The Beechcraft drew to a stop and the got out. There were a number of Americans about, dressed in civilian clothes of a style so close to being military that it was not hard to tell what they were: technicians, advisers and administrators. Uniformed Lao and Meo soldiers shambled about, either getting themselves and their kit into bundles so that they could be flown to some outpost or engaged on some local fatigue. The air was considerably cooler than down in Vientiane and Rance wished he had an extra sweater on. Harry Vainey said, 'Come on, let's go get some chow,' and led them to a disreputably dirty Jeep that had driven up to meet them. They clambered in and drove two hundred metres before turning right and on past two imposing buildings, on which bullet and shell marks were clearly visible. HQ MR 2, it was explained and, if we're lucky, we'll meet the General before we go back. On they drove, into an administrative complex, and stopped in front of a temporary wooden hut. Rance noticed they all had sandbag emplacements in front; to keep us safe from the in-coming, it was explained by the young American Jeep driver. They went inside and joined a queue of Americans and locals all getting their chow. They, in turn, were asked what they wanted. Rance declined everything except a cup of coffee but Daniel, despite his incipient weight problem, made a hearty meal of waffles, followed by eggs. As the tramped out, Rance saw they were expected to pay cash, in American dollars, for what they had had and was embarrassed because he hadn't thought to bring any US currency with him, even had he any.

Behind him the Australian gagged, 'Don't worry. I'll pay for you. At least my country isn't bankrupt.'

Harry Vainey joined in the general laughter and Rance burnt with humiliation as he realised how easily such remarks were being said, how much they were meant and how true they were.

They left the mess hut and were taken into a similarly

constructed building that was the control centre from where orders were given for the defence of the complex and the operational activity against the communists. It struck Rance as decidedly odd that this should be run by a handful of Americans when just down the road was HQ MR 2 with a major general. They were introduced to a man who was obviously the boss – Percy S. Zollinger. He took them into his operations room and offered them coffee. A large map covered the wall on one side, with pins and chinagraph markings, blue for own troops and red for the enemy. Rance noticed that the other two visitors took out notebooks and that, although the Americans did not actually forbid note taking, they looked discomforted. The briefing started.

'OK. This is what's happening. Here we are, at Long Cheng, the home of Major General Vang Pao, the best known Meo of them all. He's virtually king around these parts and his word is law. We work very closely as we're paying for it all. We have here some Assistant Attachés, several infantry and artillery battalions of Thai volunteers, the Thai Unity Forces as they're sometimes called. It's still all supposed to be secret. As you flew in you probably noticed a large ridge overshadowing this whole complex. That's Skyline Ridge and there's an NVA company there right now. None of us can quite figure out what it's up to and one thought is that it is on a recon in force but, quite why, we don't know. A battalion of Thais moved up yesterday and will be attacking when they are ready in position, later on this afternoon. I want to have a look so I have ordered a chopper and, as I expect you're interested, I'll take you with me for a gander. It is strange as it is too early for the normal offensive to start.'

The briefing continued and Rance, listening carefully, and reading between the lines, realised that the communist threat was greater than he had thought.

They drove down the dusty and bumpy road and reached HQ MR 2. There on the doorstep was the General, a small man with a strong, open face. Rance was introduced to him and the General hardly bothered to shake the proffered hand, let along look him in the eye. 'We're on our way to have a look at Skyline, General. Are you coming?' Zollinger asked.

The General answered in surprisingly good English, 'No, not now. I've other things to do.' He then turned to Rance. 'They tell me you speak Thai. Go and walk around the gun emplacements and meet the Thai soldiers there before you fly back to Vientiane.'

Another five minutes' drive and they reached the artillery battalion lines of the Thai secret army. A Thai Liaison Officer was there to meet them and led them through the offices. Rance spied one man tidying a desk. On an impulse he went up to him and greeted him in Thai. The man straightened up and smiled hugely. '*Sawadee krab*. How nice to see you. I never expected to see you in Long Chen.'

Rance answered him fluently. 'You were on the course when you had to fight the Viets, weren't you? I thought I recognised you,' as the Thai nodded assent. The rest of the group turned and saw the two in animated conversation. Zollinger listened approvingly because, although none of the Americans in Long Cheng spoke Thai, he fully realised how valuable it was. Daniel's face was grumpy and the Australian's vacuous.

'A friend of yours left camp yesterday evening, a Major Mana

Varamit to you but here he is known as Major Chok Di which is his secret army name. He has gone to attack the Vietnamese position. Before he left, he seemed ... he said ...'

'Come on, Jason, we haven't got all day. If you don't hurry we'll be late,' said Daniel, forcibly. The Thai's face stiffened at this rude interruption and Rance, seeing the chain was broken, sadly rejoined the others. Did none of them know that a Thai's greatest condemnation of anyone was to call him rude? *Mana in Laos? Don't tell me it will be Le Dâng Khoã next. Impossible!*

Shortly before noon they boarded a modified and armoured Jet Ranger helicopter, also flown by a CIA contract man in civilian overalls. Rance looked at the battle over which they were flying rather like at fish in an aquarium. From below little puffs of smoke from the guns were visible, as were little spurts of dust and smoke where the shells landed and exploded. The chopper circled continuously, standing off from a couple of T-28s that were pounding a hill top with 50 kilogram bombs, synchronised with the fall of the shells. Rance saw a snake of soldiers moving, hour-hand slow, toward the dust of the explosions, maybe a mile away and thought he saw men crouched in the target area but couldn't be sure as the vibration of the helicopter and the dust and smoke made clear viewing difficult.

On the ground the Thai troops worked their way slowly forward. Natural defenders by instinct, they were less sure of themselves in attack. They had left Long Cheng the day before, lightly equipped, their training and standing operational procedures laying down that they be re-supplied with food and potable water by air at various times. The battalion commander was particularly tense: this was a day for which he had secretly planned and plotted for many years. He had come to Laos in early July, soon after the last field training exercise on Thai soil in Phitsanalok had finished. His American counterparts were impressed by the knowledge he had brought back from the British Army Jungle Warfare School and had questioned him on various concepts that were foreign to theirs.

'What was the main thing they taught you there?' queried Colonel Broadus Richards, 'and how does it differ from what we teach?'

Major Mana Varamit had thought before replying. 'I think it is the emphasis they place on the individual's standard of self-dependence in the jungle, coupled with a belief that unless our own troops dominate the jungle then someone else's will. That means that the Brits place more reliance on self-sufficiency, that is carrying everything required for, say, five-day periods, combined with a high standard of patrolling, ambushing, field craft and jungle craft, jungle lore, survival, river crossing, immediate action drills and many other similarly slanted details. With a firm knowledge of procedures, they're more flexible than we are; for instance, there's seldom only one agreed school solution to a problem because they don't believe in being dogmatic. Finally, everywhere there is a ratio of one instructor for every ten men. With the American draft system, you have one instructor to one or even two hundred men except the Green Beret Special Forces.'

'We use air power to an extent those bankrupt Limeys can never visualise and our support weapons coverage is much more prolific,' chimed in Major Peter Hodge, 'and, in any case, we just don't have the time nor the need for such a rigmarole.'

Needless to say, the British ideas could not be incorporated to any great extent in the field exercise and, as the Thais now advanced in linear formation along the top of scarred and pitted Skyline Ridge, Mana could hear firing from the NVA company position. Reports reached him of his leading elements coming under long-range enemy fire and the advance slowed down, then stopped as the RLAF T-28s came in with small bombs, two under each wing, to soften up the Viet position even more. A black Jet Ranger helicopter flew in tight circles not far off, directing the fire and air attacks, blast it, presumed Mana savagely. This next bit would be tricky. It had turned noon and the last re-supply for that day was due at 2 o'clock. After that he could either wait until dark, around 6 o'clock, when he could slip away more easily or to make a recce out to a flank with his bodyguard and, having got rid of him, lie up till dark. He had put out feelers as previously told to when he first came to the Long Cheng area and had done a spell of duty in the mountains, not far from where the Viet dry-season offensive had reached. Using an agreed formula, he had had an answer back from the Viets. *This time I must try and kill that Political Commissar, Tâ Tran Quán, which I failed to do when he was with the ARVN in Vietnam.* They would stage an attack on the east of Skyline Ridge, aimed between 12 and 15 November, shortly before Mana's battalion was due to be relieved and, provided Mana could inconspicuously identify himself, the rest should be easy. He looked at his watch, saw the Jet Ranger return to Long Cheng and decided not to wait until last light but to go on the reconnaissance at around 4 o'clock.

In the NVA Company position, the military commander turned to his political counterpart, Tâ Tran Quán, and said, 'Comrade, we are too exposed in this position. Most of the natural cover has been blasted away. Water is scarce. How much longer do you want us to stay here? The Feudalists are slow but their leading elements should contact us soon. I am not questioning your decision but I must make sure we can withdraw to the main battalion position near the Plain of Jars when you are ready.'

Tâ Tran Quán looked at him narrowly then turned his gaze away. 'I want to "capture" the Thai commander. He wants our cause to be his. Watch out!' he yelled as a T-28 screamed down on them. They threw themselves on the ground until the attack was over and the plane had gone. 'Imperialist bastards, snivelling reactionary puppets and feudalist beasts,' he said as they got up again. They were dirty and the company commander saw Tâ Tran Quán move the signet ring on the little finger of this right hand to get rid of some dirt. He noticed that the dirt had left a small blue mark, almost shaped like a 9, on the inside of his finger. *Strange*, he mused … and stranger still when, thinking himself unnoticed, the Political Commissar cleaned his ring and swallowed it.

At 4 o'clock Mana called his Executive Officer and said, 'We're being slow. I don't like it. I'm going on a recce with my gunman. I want to have a personal look at the lie of the land. Stay here and I'll be back well before last light in time to give out orders for our night attack.' He called to his gunman and, in dead ground, they made their way northwards. Four hundred yards away, out of sight of his own troops, Mana told the gunman to find a place from where he could see the Viets, to observe them and to report back in an hour's time.

The Executive Officer, meanwhile, was unhappy in the way his commander had gone off. *Crazy English methods* was his unspoken comment. Those Thais who volunteered for service in Laos were given false names and false discharge documents but, even so, there was something also that did not ring true about his battalion commander whom he only knew as Major Chok Di.

Tâ Tran Quán turned to his military counterpart. 'It's 4 o'clock and the attack hasn't yet materialised. I don't understand it. If nothing has happened by 5 o'clock, put in an attack. I'll keep out of it as I want to give the Thai a chance to come over away from the actual fighting and I also want to observe the fighting spirit of our men. Uncle H is proud of the way your regiment, number 335, has been conducting itself – politically and tactically successful. I want to see if the report I'm going to submit will allow you to attain the award of Patriotic Company. I have faith in the outcome. I will move to the right, up away to the north and, waiting for our new Thai comrade to come, will be able to observe your determined efforts.'

Is he Mana Varamit or Chok Di? If the former I must try and kill him so that he will never give away our secret.

At 5 o'clock the Executive Officer of the Thai battalion said, 'Defence Squad, go and look for the Major. I'm unhappy. There's something strange in the air. But remember, I want prisoners, not dead men. Prisoners talk, dead men don't.'

Also at 5 o'clock the two forward platoons of the Vietnamese company moved west, slowly and carefully. The Company Commander went with them and Tâ Tran Quán slipped off to the north. A few minutes later, Mana's gunman heard firing and saw a lone figure moving his way. He ran back to Mana and told him what was happening. 'Go back but don't shoot him, even if you have the chance. A prisoner is valuable,' Mana said. 'Dead men don't talk,' and he laughed inwardly.

Mana then saw Tâ Tran Quán coming and realised it was time to act. He moved silently up to his gunman who was lying on the ground, watching the other man approaching him. Behind, observing and unobserved, came the Defence Squad, moving forward tactically. They saw a remarkable drama unfold. The Thai Major was creeping up on his gunman who was aiming his weapon at a baggily-dressed, unarmed Vietnamese, or was he carrying a pistol? They were unable to tell. Before their stupefied and fascinated gaze, the Thai Major seemed to be stalking his own gunman and, despite the noise of distant firing of Kalashnikov rifles and Shpagin sub-machine guns from the enemy direction and the AR-10 assault rifles and the occasional M-1 carbines from their own, they saw and heard him put a pistol shot into the back of the other man's head. The Major then jumped up and ran towards the oncoming Vietnamese who waved at him when he saw him. Horrified and smelling treachery, the Squad Leader ordered his men to fire at the Viet and the Thai. Bullets whistled over Mana's head and he jinked from side to side as he ran, cursing under his breath. More shells came his way and the Vietnamese fell, hit in the leg. Mana soon reached him and, momentarily bending over him, hurriedly looked at the little finger of his right hand, as though searching for, maybe, a ring. Tâ Tran Quán started to say something but Mana, taking no notice, moved quickly on. Four paces away, near a large boulder, he stopped, turned, thereby giving the Defence Squad time to draw a bead on him. Mana fired a shot at the wounded Viet, wounding him again. Another fusillade rang out from the rapidly advancing Thais. Mana, unable to check whether his shot had been fatal, move off fast, jinking yet again, but slipped and fell as a hail of bullets spattered around him, one deeply grazing his head. The advancing Vietnamese Company Commander saw a man dressed in Thai uniform coming from the direction his own Political Commissar had gone, so went and rescued him, carrying him away unconscious and bleeding from his head injury. The Vietnamese had no time to search for Tâ Tran Quán as the rest of the Thai battalion, attracted to the noise of the firing, had started to move forward, fast. At the same time, the Defence Squad, moving cautiously, reached the gunman who was dead. They then went on up to where Tâ Tran Quán lay and found him unconscious, shot in the leg and the chest. Heavy firing came from the Vietnamese company so the Squad Leader, remembering the Executive Officer's words, said, 'Get a move on, a counter attack's about to come in, I guess. Carry this man back, and fast, but don't bother to be too kind even when you are in dead ground. Don't kill him. Dead men don't talk.'

5

November, 1972. Vientiane, Laos: His Majesty, the King of Laos, visited his administrative capital, Vientiane twice a year, once in the spring for Constitution Day and again for the lunar festivities of early winter. It was a hectic period for everyone concerned, not least for the two British Colonels who had to continue with their own duties and, in the case of Daniel, finishing his packing.

Rance, living in a hotel until he became 'official', was dressed in his ceremonial Number 3 Dress, complete with medals, sword, spurs and white gloves. He stood to one side in the foyer, an object of many sidelong glances, until Leuam drove up to take him to the Attaché's villa. The traffic circulation had been radically changed by the introduction of a temporary one-way system during the royal visit, control of which was augmented by the Boy Scouts, whose efforts to surpass the Traffic Police in efficiency resulted in uncoordinated whistle-blowing and exaggerated arm signals that snarled up conditions even worse than would otherwise have been the case. The uncomplaining tolerance of the general public, albeit mollified by the happiness of the great *boun*, was Rance's first lesson in why the Lao had neither duodenal ulcers nor heart attacks.

'This really is the hell of a long day,' said Daniel over a cup of coffee before setting out for the first of two events. 'We have to be seated at Thad Luang by 9 o'clock for the royal inspection and investiture, "dressed in our best bib and tucker". After it is over it's back to the office and carry on with the hand-over. Then, at 3 o'clock, without sword, medals, spurs or gloves but still in whites, we have to go and watch a most ridiculous game of *soi-disant* hockey, followed by horse racing, then go to the UK trade booth and await the royal entourage, government officials, other diplomats and the general public who stream through. Stick as close to me as possible although you won't be able to sit with the other Attachés because you won't be one till the day I go. That means you won't be presented to the King until I've left. That doesn't mean much: we foreigners are miles off ever meeting him under any other conditions. And then tomorrow, while I finish off my packing, you can go and pay courtesy calls on the Big Brothers if you can fix it with the Soviets and the Chinese. At tea time there is a *baçi* in our villa to which you are invited, then, on Wednesday I'm off – thank God! – and you'll be in the hot seat. But right now it's time we were on our way to Thad Luang for Part I.'

Thad Luang proper is on the northern edge of Vientiane and consists of the wat so named and a large Buddhist school. As though the builders had hesitated to erect anything nearby, there was a large open space in front of the wat into which six rough, unmetalled tracks led, chokingly dusty in the dry season and clingingly muddy after rain. There was a shanty town collection of huts behind the temple where a group of catamites operated, silkily dressed to allure either unsuspecting foreigners or catering for the tastes of the perverted. Always a menace, they were shrewishly vindictive when roused or when paid handsomely so to be. On two sides were the trade stalls of various countries whereas on the other two sides it was open save for a wooden grandstand for spectators and a temporary throne for the King. Lining the way into the area were pairs of army cadets from Chinaimo camp, shortly to be commissioned. They faced inwards, dressed in white, and saluted the cars as they drove in, their white saluting arm looking, from afar, as if the vehicle was driving in a foam-flecked wave, an illusion heightened by the dust. All around, as everywhere else in town, red and white flags with their elephants and parasols, graced the scene. It all nicely captured the Lao sense of pomp and pageantry.

Before the royal cavalcade arrived at Thad Luang at half past nine Rance had managed to speak to the Chinese DA, who had not been at the Attaché luncheon. Everybody seemed willing to be friends but Rance noticed how the Chinese kept very much to himself. On the spur of the moment, he moved forward the six rows that separated him from the others and went up to the bland-faced Chinese and made himself known in Cantonese, adding an erudite proverb.

'Excuse me but you must speak French through me. I'm M. Teng Ah-hok's interpreter and M. Teng only speaks the national language.'

Rance turned at the voice behind him and saw a small, alert, young, bright-eyed man standing a foot away from him.

'Certainly I understand,' smiled Rance in return, amused by the other's rectitude. 'Allow me to introduce myself as the new

British Defence Attaché. I have met many overseas Chinese, as we call them, in Malaysia and Hong Kong and I always try to speak to them in Cantonese if they understand that language. It shows,' he continued, with a flash of inspiration, 'how far I have to go in understanding your perspective. May I call on you officially at 10 o'clock tomorrow morning please, when we can formally introduce ourselves.'

This was translated and the answer came back. 'Yes, provisionally. I will confirm it this afternoon. Please step over to our trade pavilion after the royal visit and I'll give you the firm reply.'

Rance thanked them both, giving them a smile and a penetrating look with his blue eyes boring into their, before turning back to his place as the senior officials, both civil and military, of the Lao Government started to arrive. Had he been more observant, he would have noticed the senior Soviet Attaché, Colonel Nechaev, eyeing him with evident distaste. It was just as well for Rance's peace of mind that he didn't.

Exactly on time those in the grandstand rose to their feet while the dignitaries got out of their cars. The King stood head and shoulders above everybody else, his Queen diminutive beside him. He was dressed in the uniform of a 7-star General and wore the red and yellow sash of the Order of the Million Elephants and the White Parasol. Rance stared hungrily at him, this his first ever view of the man he was supposed to influence sufficiently to change the course of the nation's history, his mind racing with a myriad thoughts – and echoing with hollow laughter. The absurdity of the whole business struck him even more forcibly than it had done in London now that he had had time to take the pulse of only four days. He sighed deeply and gloomily as he looked at the rest of the many dignitaries, among whom he recognised the Prime Minister, Prince Souvanna Phouma, hatless and leaning on a stick.

It was over by half past 10. 'Time for a coffee at home before we go to the office,' said Daniel as they drove away.

The Soviet Ambassador called his Defence Attaché to his office on his return from the parade. 'I know these are early days yet,' he said, 'but what have you so far for me on Colonel Rance?'

'Comrade Ambassador, he flew away with the CIA last Saturday, on a plane that was scheduled to go to Long Cheng. If it's for him the trip was laid on, then that's unusually quick off the mark. It means that he's got more influence than the other man had. Although he has not yet been reported visiting the CIA clique in their main building, he has had a long session with the US Army Attaché. That was after the attaché luncheon when the out-going man was unnecessarily offensive and I thought I could tell Rance's trends from what he said to me. And, as far as this morning was concerned, I saw him talking to the Chinese. And he started off without the interpreter.'

'All right, Comrade Colonel. I'll continue working on the Ambassador to get the right-wing reactionaries and imperialists more disenchanted with the British than they are now, and that is to include the new DA. Try and get a uniform photo of him this afternoon at the pavilion before the King gets there. As far as your own brainchild is concerned – it should be ready by now. Ask him round to the embassy for a chat and invite him to swim in my pool, changing in the special booth. By now you've had time to get all the props ready even though the whole operation is strictly speaking in the Troop Trials stage.'

The Chinese Attaché, Teng Ah-hok, was talking to his interpreter, an official in the *Gung An Ju*, the Public Security Service as the Chinese Secret Service is known. 'It's not a question of subversion, Comrade,' he was saying, 'but the overture this morning from that new capitalist-orientated English Colonel was, I thought, warm and proper. It also accords with what we have been told from our man in Peninsular Malaysia. As next in line to the doyen of the Attaché Corps, it would have been more proper still to have talked to the Filipino first but I notice that some of the Running Dogs sometimes put personal preference before protocol. What was that Cantonese proverb he used after greeting me? It sounded like an unusual five-character phrase, not the more normal four-character saying.'

The young interpreter sniffed. Although a full cadre, it irked him to be reminded that he knew the inferior Cantonese dialect. '"Feigning to be a pig, he vanquishes tigers" was what the Englishman said,' he answered. Both men pondered on the significance of this seemingly irrelevant remark.

'I think we had better cultivate him,' said M. Teng.

By 2 o'clock senior Lao functionaries and diplomats were seated in the grandstand once more, awaiting the royal presence. At half past two the same cavalcade drove up in the same sequence and, after due pomp, the King, less his Queen, sat on the forward throne, his son, the Crown Prince – to be addressed as *Monseigneur* – to his right and slightly to the rear.

From the far side of the red ground, the Thad Luang side, there emerged a group of men dressed in traditional royal red, with caps that had hear- and neck-flaps. They were the royal band and had drums, wind instruments and a large xylophone which was carried on a bier by four men, the player, walking in between the carrying handles, making the fifth. The staccato plunking was not unpleasantly atonal, at times even mellifluously tantalising. Behind them came two hockey teams, the king's dressed in crimson lake numbering about twenty and a civilian team, dressed in ordinary clothes, of double the number. They slowly walked towards the King, more or less in step and, about twenty metres away from the throne, knelt down in obeisance, hands joined together. The King responded from his sitting position. The group stayed kneeling as their leader, escorted by a palace official, went and reported to the King. There they knelt again as it was quite wrong for their heads, or any one else's for that matter, to be above the King's when they were in audience. After the King had received their report, they walked backwards six paces before turning round, bowed low once more, then rejoined the band and players, still kneeling. They stood up and continued on their gentle promenade, wheeling away from the grandstand. The band slowly plunked its way off the ground, leaving the two teams remaining in the middle. The scene was now set for the royal game of *tikhi*.

There ensued a unique version of hockey. The ball was

large, wooden and heavy. The sticks were large, wooden and cumbersome, the ground in no way marked out except for two flags, one at each end. Two court officials bullied daintily off over a silver bowl containing flowers and then pell-mell, helter-skelter, no-give-all-take, the two sides set upon the ball and each other. Rance winced as wood met shin with sickening thud but no one did more than limp heavily for a while then forget they had been hurt when the ball came anywhere near them again. The civilians scored first, by getting the ball beyond the flag at the royal end. The King's team equalized soon after. It was immediately declared half time. The teams changed ends and, in next to no time, they were at it again. This time there was a subtle refinement; whenever the ball went near the commoners' flag, a royal player hit it back into the centre again as the King was gracious and the commoners had to win, which they did shortly afterwards. The game was declared over as soon as the commoners got the ball behind the royal flag, thereby causing a greatly truncated second half. They all reassembled, bowed down, the winner's team captain reported to the King who bestowed certain presents on him for the lucky victors. They moved sedately moved off, once more almost in step with one another. The band had reappeared and accompanied the players off the scene.

Next on the programme was the horse racing and as the first six nags were being shown in front of the grandstand, Daniel turned and beckoned Rance to come down and sit with him. The wife of one of the attaché's had declined to join in the afternoon's entertainment so there was a vacant seat. Nodding at the duty protocol officer as he went down, Rance found himself next to

Colonel Gorgi Nechaev. It was the done thing for the members of the Diplomatic Corps to have a mild flutter on each of the four races, all bareback, twice round the area for the first two and three times round for the last two. Before the first race started Daniel leant over to the Russian and asked him if he would bet in pounds, dollars, roubles or the Lao kip?

'Ah, this is a decadent western capitalist sport and anyway the pound is worth nothing,' was his carping and uncompromising reply, unrelieved by a smile. Turning to Rance, he continued in the same vein. 'When your country is truly socialist, you will not need such capitalist props to society as gambling. You, Colonel Rance, don't strike me as a man that gambles, rather as a man who works on certainties.'

Rance turned towards the mocking Russian boor and coldly looked him straight between the eyes but was saved from answering as there was a great cheer as the first race started.

The riding was executed with a mixture of flamboyant carelessness and exaggerated enthusiasm. Cutting corners was a favourite tactic, resulting in some spectacular falls that brought roars of approval from the crowd. The most popular winner was the only girl to take part. With her long black hair streaming behind her, she took her horse round the three laps with superb confidence, dodging those who wanted to jostle her and cleverly outflanking the only strong contender. She used no whip, unlike the others, and her beauty was almost spell-bindingly wonderful. Even the Russian seemed interested and he turned to Rance and enigmatically asked if that wasn't better. Rance's thoughts had flown back to Golden Fairy. *What was she doing now? Where was the older sister who had sent some school books and how was he going to get the chance to meet her? What was that clod of a Russian saying? Better than what?* and to the undisguised satisfaction of the Soviet Attaché, he said 'no', thinking that nobody could be better than Golden Fairy although some could rival her. He was aware that the Russian was trying to needle him but he felt safe enough.

He was jolted away from his private thoughts by His Majesty rising to leave the grandstand for his tour of the various countries' trade stands in the pavilions. France took the pride of place and then, in French alphabetical order, the rest. Daniel told Rance there was plenty of time before the King reached their stand for them to go and visit the Soviets. It was an impressive erection, flying the flags of all the Soviet Socialist Republics and full of well-taken photographs of certain doctored aspects of the Workers' Paradise. A man with a camera asked them to pose for a picture – Daniel told him they were making it easy for him – so Rance's likeness was painlessly gift-wrapped for them. Daniel and Nechaev continued their heavy-handed badinage until, at a sigh from the Soviet, Daniel's attention was attracted by an Assistant Attaché to something else. Nechaev turned to Rance and asked, 'When are you coming to call on me at the embassy? Why not make it soon, let's say, tomorrow afternoon? After all, we are the senior military representatives for the two Co-Chairmen of the 1954 and the 1962 Geneva Accords as well as being wartime allies in the struggle against Fascism. Tomorrow, I suspect, Roger will be putting the finishing touches for his departure. You can't really start doing anything until he goes on Wednesday. Come round at 2 'clock and we'll have a talk.' As an afterthought he added, 'Yes, that's a good idea, it's still warm enough for a swim. Bring your trunks around and we'll have a dip before you leave. If you haven't got any kit, we'll provide it, a towel, trunks and a place to change in. OK?'

Rance could think of no valid reason for not accepting but he said he'd check with Daniel first, just to make sure.

Nechaev called out, 'Roger, what are you doing with Jason tomorrow afternoon? You don't want him while you're finishing off your packing, I expect. Good,' as Daniel shook his head.

'Then I'll expect you, Colonel Rance.' There was a gleam of satisfaction in his cold blue eyes as he turned away but a flash of sunlight on his thick spectacles prevented Rance from noticing.

It was then time for the British Embassy group to be lined up for presentation to the royal party in the pecking order laid down by British protocol. First the Ambassador and Mrs Taunton, then the Head of Chancery and his wife – Marie-Joseph, a French lady – and, at the end, Daniel. Mrs Daniel, physically not strong at the best of times, was exhausted by packing and had declined to be present. As Rance was not to be presented, he was relegated to the end of the queue, to the left of the Third Secretary. The royal party was dominated by the King. He was followed by the Crown Prince and the Prime Minister. Rance again studied the King intently, almost willing contact with him and comparing the remoteness of his task with his target's physical presence, regally tall and charmingly dignified. He felt a flutter of excitement as the Ambassador, in good French, started the introductions and the sincerity of purpose displayed by General Sir David Law sprang to mind. After the Third Secretary had been presented the Ambassador then invited the King to go through the British pavilion. As the King turned to go, his eyes fixed on Rance for a fleeting second but if he had heard of his niece's relationship with the new English Colonel, no sign of it was evinced. The King was led away by the Ambassador. The Head of Chancery, as next senior representative, invited the Crown Prince to accompany him, while Daniel took care of the Prime Minister. Rance, wanting to see as much as possible of what the escorts did as it would be his turn next year, was sucked after the royal entourage with the crowd of government officials, civil and military, milling along behind, feeling a little lost among so many unknown people.

After the King and his entourage had visited the British stand, Rance decided to go along to the Chinese stand. He told Daniel he'd be back soon, not to drive away without him, and walked the fifty paces to the pavilion of the People's Republic of China.

This was more in keeping with an Asian audience than was the Soviet one and Rance had not been there long when his presence was noticed by the French-speaking interpreter who went up to him. 'Colonel, how do you like our pavilion?'

'I approve of it. It is tastefully arranged and well set out,' he answered, looking around him. 'I have come here on two counts,' he continued, having ascertained that the royal visit was over. 'First, as I said this morning, I wish, if possible, to pay a courtesy call on Colonel Teng as soon as I can and secondly I am looking for a copy of *The Thoughts of Chairman Mao* in the Lao language. I asked for the former this morning unexpectedly and probably not in accordance with protocol but since then I have been approached by our Soviet counterpart to meet him tomorrow afternoon for a talk and a swim. But as your Colonel is senior in precedence to the Soviet, I feel it more apposite if I were to call on him first. As for the latter, I have an English-language version but now, here in Laos, a Lao version has the added advantage of being a most reliable text book for a vocabulary I've yet to learn.'

That pleased the interpreter, who smiled and said, 'Come along with me. We will find the Attaché whom we call Monsieur not Colonel as there are no longer any ranks in our armed forces. He will give you the answer himself.'

And so a meeting was fixed for 10 o'clock the next morning at the Chinese embassy when there would also be a Lao copy of the Little Red Book.

The white Ford Zephyr swung through gates just wide enough to let it enter. Inside on the left of the compound was a large house daubed in terracotta up to which led three steps. On the right was a small building for night sentries and beyond was an area that comprised more buildings flanked, certainly on two sides, Rance saw, by a canal. At the sound of the car two men emerged from the house and stood at the top of the steps. They were dressed in a plain blue jacket that did up at the neck and blue trousers. Rance was dressed in plain clothes because he was yet to be the Attaché so, protocol-wise, had no right to wear uniform when paying such calls. He waited for Leuam to switch off and open the door before alighting. As the door was opened a clock inside the embassy struck ten. Rance got out and went up to the Chinese Attaché at the top of the stairs.

'Good morning, M. Teng,' he said in French. 'It is most kind of you to welcome me at such short notice.' His hand was outstretched and M. Teng took it limply. His interpreter translated and then relayed the answer. 'You are welcome, Colonel. Please come in.'

The room into which he was led was large and L-shaped. Straight ahead a beautifully lacquered wooden screen divided the area into a sitting and dining room. There was another, not so pretty, screen to the right, round which Rance was led. Against the right hand wall a settee and two chairs clustered around a low table. There were three other chairs against the other walls, on one of which was a delicately executed tapestry of a bridge over an ornamental lake and, in front of the settee on the opposite wall, was the largest picture of Chairman Mao Tse-tung Rance had ever seen.

The three men sat down, Rance and Teng on the settee and the interpreter on Rance's right, on a chair. The Englishman's fascinated gaze was riveted on the grotesque picture and, as he stared at it, he realised that he must not appear brash, rude, critical or insensitive and, that, by then, he had looked at the Chairman long enough. He turned and looked at Teng then, as if by instinct, he turned back to the picture on the wall, and then once more back to Teng.

'I can't believe it: you must excuse me but the likeness to your Chairman and yourself is so uncanny I'm going to ask you if you are a close relation or not?'

As the remark was translated, Teng's eyes gleamed with pleasure. He chortled with joy as he gave his answer. 'No, no.

I'm no relation of him but, when I was small, I was carried on my father's back on the Long March which, as you know, was led by our Chairman. Of course, I have seen him since, many times, but I have never forgotten those difficult days. But for his greatness, we would all have died a hundred deaths.'

Anodyne conversation followed. A waiter brought in drinks and small eats, consisting of nuts, toffee, salty fish, a type of yam and some strange-looking brown cubes of squid. Till then Rance had managed to cope but now he found himself at a loss when Teng took one of the toothpick slivers from the tray, skewered a particularly revolting-looking piece of solidified squid and, lifting it up to his guest's mouth, smilingly indicated that he was intent on feeding him. There was an air of unreality to this pantomime that followed so swiftly and unexpectedly on the banalities of small talk but Rance managed to show no surprise. He opened his mouth and Teng popped the delicacy inside. Rance munched it nobly. The waiter brought in three cups of weak tea, already poured out, and placed them among the saucers and glasses. *What*, wondered Rance, *is the correct protocol in this case? Do I have to skewer one of the pieces of yam or squid and likewise feed M. Teng?* The decision was postponed by Teng lifting a glass containing red liquid and proposing good luck, good health and good relations between the two men and their two countries. Rance took a tiny sip and involuntarily grimaced. It tasted foul. He felt he had to take some initiative but still hung back from the sliver approach. Instead he bravely lifted the glass containing a colourless liquid and said, grabbing at a bit of their earlier conversation, 'I propose a toast to our zodiacal animals, the Dragon and the Cow,' and, as his lips touched the fiery brew, he thought to himself what an unlikely pair they were.

Under these circumstances it was not surprising no serious conversation ensued, only pleasantries and more banalities with frequent pauses.

After thanking his Chinese counterpart suitably, Rance felt it was time to leave. Glasses, cups and half-empty plates were as eloquent as any watch. As the Chinese Defence Attaché was shaking hands with the Englishman at the top of the steps, he said, 'Please think of yourself as being able to come and talk to me at any time you want – just ring first and fix an appointment. Our doors, for you, are always open. Remember, also, that the Dragon is a much more reliable animal than the Bear.'

About the same time as Rance was leaving the Chinese embassy, wondering exactly how much to read into the unenigmatic invitation that he had been given along with the warning about the Soviets, there was activity in the swimming pool enclosure at the Soviet embassy. A group of technicians was busy in one of the changing rooms that abutted from the wall of the main embassy block. To the uninitiated, the scene looked as it was meant to – a swimming pool, with a grass verge on three sides where small tables with umbrellas and chairs were laid out, a fence and shade trees – jacarandas, flame of the forests and others of the acacia variety. On the fourth side were three changing rooms and the entrance, leading in from the main block. The whole area was visible from the upper storey of the building, an obvious precaution. The changing room nearest the outside wall of the embassy was where the technicians were working.

It was a most elaborate affair, being the centre where recording, bugging, monitoring, photographing and similar activities were controlled. It was as heavily guarded as was the communications centre above it but, again in the interests of security, its staff was different. In the lower room a wide-angle lens camera was being installed, having been checked out, so that it could take a photograph of the person changing without that person's knowledge. It was set back at such an angle that it could also take enough of the surroundings to include a three-and-a-half-foot wide frame that stood eighteen inches from the ground. The surface of the frame was minutely corrugated so that any pattern on one set of ridges could be made different from that on the other set. The idea was a new one and had yet to be fully tested. Its development was of low priority and there were technical snags still to be ironed out. Even so, Colonel Nechaev, for the past five months since the KGB, briefed by M. Grambert, had been championing a ploy with personal zeal and devotion. Thus it was that a new pattern had been prepared and imprinted on the corrugated ridges, only to be visible from the wall side where the camera was. It was a picture of a nude Lao youth, golden and equivocal, lying on his back on a bed, with an erection and his mouth open. The camera was able to take a picture that included the painted boy and bed and anyone who was close enough to it. To manoeuvre the unsuspecting subject into the desired position, a shelf had been put at the far end of the frame on which a mirror and hair brushes were laid out. Below it was another shelf for a bather's personal bits and pieces and where a notice was written small enough and low enough to ensure that the person reading it would be photographed in the bending position. The genitals of the person so bending, always supposing he had previously stripped naked, would be in line with the open mouth of the painted boy. It was a clumsy way of setting a trap and one that might be unsuccessful at first but, given patience, one that could succeed admirably later if not sooner. Even so, Nechaev knew the angles were correct because he had tried to out personally, and with great pleasure on a model, on more than one occasion.

One of the technicians, smoking a vile cigarette than smelt not unlike Balkan Sobranie, was in the position the photographer required and another was ensuring the lighting was bright enough for every detail to be reproduced. The briefing had been explicit and Colonel Nechaev was to make his inspection at noon before going for his lunch – the model for the picture was now his personal servant – by when preparations were to be finished. In the event all was satisfactorily prepared and the Colonel himself both viewed the camera angle and, one again, had stood where his target would stand. As he left the changing room, he unconsciously sniffed the tobacco smell and knowing that Rance was a non-smoker, he would not need an ashtray.

At 2 o'clock Rance, driven by Leuam, motored about three kilometres from the town centre and into the drive of the Soviet embassy grounds. On the right was a lawn where receptions were sometimes held and, on the left, two tennis courts. In front of the embassy was a semi-circular car park. In the room next to the front door the duty security person, at this instant a woman, watched the car drive in. She had brown hair, porcine eyes narrowly set together, rimless glasses and a pink slash where her lips should have been. She wore cheap black shoes, thick stockings and a prim brown dress. She always felt a small thrill as another unsuspecting foreigner, and a western capitalist-imperialist to boot, was being treated differently. *Is he also one of Colonel Nechaev's sort*, she wondered?

The car stopped and she saw the chauffer get out and open the door. A tall, silver-haired man got out, said something to him and looked around, as though noticing details. She winced as his gaze dwelt longer than normal at the aerials over the corner of the embassy. As he slowly moved towards the door, she left the window of her office and went to meet him. Rance had noticed her as he drove in and was amused to see their movements synchronised. He reached the front door and there she was, prim, expressionless and, when he smiled at her, as unbending as a jail wardress.

'Good afternoon. I have come to see Colonel Nechaev. My name in Colonel Rance and I am the British Defence Attaché designate. I think I am expected.'

His piercingly blue eyes held her muddy brown ones and, although she spoke no English, she found she stuttered her Russian answer, so mesmerised was she by the intensity of his gaze and sincerity of smile. She turned to fetch Colonel Nechaev who simultaneously came out from behind a curtain that shielded a long corridor, half left across the hall from the doorway.

'Good afternoon, Colonel Rance. Welcome in.' He came across, his arm extended for the inevitable handshake. 'Come into our visitors' room and we will talk. I am so happy to be able to welcome you here this afternoon.'

They crossed the hall, the wardress going back to her vantage point of sentinel, and the Russian led the way into a musty room, in one corner of which was a settee, two chairs and a table. The rest of the room was empty. On the far wall a picture of a bald and bearded Lenin looked evilly out at them. The walls were a dull yellow and, what with only one window, the room was gloomy. The Russian sniffed and, remarking that the room was stuffy, turned on the air conditioner. It rattled into inefficient operation, exuding a cloud of surprised mosquitoes. Outside there was a banging on the roof. Replacing tiles was the explanation.

Rance was invited to sit down. On the table was a bowl of wilting flowers which Colonel Nechaev moved, thereby sending out another cloud of mosquitoes. The noise of the banging and the air conditioner did not make conversation easy to follow but, reflected Rance, obviously didn't help the bugging that he felt was inevitably under way.

'Welcome to Vientiane and welcome to the Soviet embassy. I hope our acquaintance will be fruitful.'

'Thank you for your welcome, Colonel. I am most interested to be in Laos at this juncture of history. It is a country I have often wished to visit but have never been fortunate enough, until now, to have my wish granted.'

More small talk took place as the door opened and a male Russian servant, especially chosen by Colonel Nechaev and as comely as any that could be rustled up for the occasion, more as an unconscious prop than for any efficiency but at whom Rance did not glance, came in carrying a tray bearing vodka, black coffee, salted nuts, biscuits and toffee, and laid them on the table. Rance did not remonstrate when Nechaev filled his glass with vodka. It was not necessary to swig the drink back in one and the pretence of a sip would go through enough of the motions to satisfy national pride with the added advantage of there being no room for any more liquid to be poured in. Nechaev raised his glass.

'As officer to officer, as wartime ally to wartime ally, let us drink to Mutual Understanding,' he said as he leant forward to clink glasses. 'To Mutual Understanding,' echoed Rance, lifting the glass to his lips. A trickle of the firewater touched his tongue, he swallowed, trying to hide his grimace, but blenched like a gun-shy virgin.

'Excuse me, Colonel, but I am not used to drinking. Even a touch of this with my lips is exceptional. Forgive any apparent rudeness to your hospitality by my reticence and grimace.'

'I will not force you to drink against your wish,' smiled the other. 'We have our own individual and special tastes, don't we?' The intended irony of the remark was lost on Rance who took the remark literally.

'Indeed, we have,' he countered. 'I myself prefer hot to cold drinks even in summer.' He said it so ingenuously that Nechaev changed the conversation.

'I heard you talking Lao at the Thad Luang fair. How much do you speak?'

'Not a great deal yet. I hope to continue my studies here, once I get properly settled in. I am a great believer in not using interpreters unless really necessary. I am only so sorry I cannot speak Russian to you.' A pause as Rance recalled what Nechaev had said to him the previous Thursday at the Tan Dao Vien luncheon. 'In fact, before I met you and talked to you, I had never wittingly seen or spoken to a Russian.'

More anodyne talk followed. Nechaev gave Rance a toffee. The Englishman unwrapped it and chewed it slowly.

'You have brought your bathing things as I asked?'

Rance shook his head. 'I have no trunks as my kit has yet to arrive and I never thought to buy any.'

'We can lend you some. That's no problem,' and this time, as Rance was offered another toffee, he did notice a strange gleam in the other man's eyes.

'Now then, come on, let's go, as you English say,' and Nechaev led the way out of the room, out of the front door and around the back. They entered the swimming pool area and he pointed out the booth nearest the embassy wall.

'You change in that, I'll use the one next door. You'll find what you want in there as I thought you might not have brought any kit with you.'

He opened the door, let Rance in and then went into the next room. Rance looked around. He sniffed and, in a flash, he was back in the French grocer's shop: the same smell of acrid tobacco had alerted him. He stood tensely, looking around him, wondering if the lamps, surprisingly switched on despite it being early afternoon, meant danger. The mirror over the shelf – the shelf itself. Surely there was no catch there? How could there be? A bit of toffee that had stuck in his teeth irked him. He lifted the mirror off its stand and, the better to reflect the light into his mouth, leant over the frame, thereby inadvertently shielding his face from the hidden camera. He saw the offending bit of toffee and pulled it out with his fingers. The mirror slanted downwards and then he saw part of the pattern on the frame that reflected the painted youth. Rance's adrenalin raced as he tilted the mirror sideways, left and right, and saw the extent of the picture. And then he understood: standing nude, during his changing, over the naked boy with the cock-stand ... small beads of sweat formed on his brow and his gorge rose with disgust and hatred. *The bastards*, he thought, *the rotten, stinking bastards. I'm not staying here. I'm off, here and now*. He replaced the mirror, moved quietly to the door, opened it and hurriedly retraced his footsteps. He walked round the corner to the car park in front of the embassy, called to Leuam, who had thoughtfully turned the car around and told him to start up. The watcher on the upper floor had pressed an emergency bell which Rance heard ringing in the wardress's office. He saw her open her mouth and, seconds later, a wary-eyed man, ugly as a baboon, obviously a strong-arm thug, approached him.

'You go so soon?' he asked in halting French, making as though to stop him.

'Yes. I have broken my tooth on a piece of your Russian toffee. I must go and have it seen to now. Please tell Colonel Nechaev I will contact him and explain personally why I left in such a hurry.'

While speaking, he got into his car and, in Lao, told Leuam to drive away fast. As the car turned out of the embassy ground, he looked round and had a glimpse of Colonel Nechaev, dressed in swimming trunks, gesticulating with the baboon. It was the

Colonel's bad luck that he went too far in what he said and that the baboon had a friend who had taken some of the earlier practice photos.

On his way back to the villa, feeling shop-soiled and tainted, Rance's face was concrete-hard, eyes more than usually piercing as he stared, unseeing, out of the car window. He needed every bit of self-discipline at his command just to stay silent. *Counting ten is no good*, he told himself. *Make it a hundred*, and he had recovered his composure by the time the car reached the Attaché's villa. It was there that the Daniels were being bidden farewell by his Lao friends' house staff.

Leuam drove the Zephyr into the garage. 'We'll join the others,' he said and led the way in through the back door and, seeing Leuam take off his shoes, Rance did the same. They went down a passage and into the large representational room. The furniture had been moved back and a crowd of Lao and foreigners, household staff and near friends, were sitting on the floor, not cross-legged but with one leg tucked under the other, like the King's bodyguard at the Thad Luang ceremony. He made his way to the back, unnoticed by the majority of guests. He had read about the *baçi*, a uniquely Lao ceremony of prayer and good wishes, older than even Buddhism, that was performed on such occasions as before a departure or after an illness. He had forgotten about it since that first day he had seen Daniel with his wrists tied. Now he remembered.

Towards the end of the ceremony, when the two main guests had been fully blessed, with strings round their wrists, by the aged venerable, Leuam passed a message forward to someone to send back four strings. He took two and tied them round Rance's wrists, murmuring words of welcome.

'I feel nearer home hearing you talk,' he said enigmatically.

He gave the other two strings to Rance and held out each wrist for them to be tied on. It was a gesture Rance thoroughly appreciated.

'Home,' he answered. 'Home and dry,' thinking of his earlier experience. The joke was lost of Leuam who continued to talk. 'I sense all your thirty-two *phee* body spirits were upset today. It will take thirty-two months for them to be placated. Let us start now.'

This time Rance had no answer. He was only on a twenty-four month posting.

That evening, the last in the Thad Luang programme when Daniel would be the British military representative, there was a reception at the palace. Once again Their Majesties would have to meet local and diplomatic dignitaries, shaking the latters' menfolk by the hand. As Rance put on regimental Mess Kit, his mind was torn between the times he had worn it in the past, doing a straightforward military job of work, and now, involved in an extraordinary game of ... well, what was it? He felt he were shadow boxing, having been spun round several times first to make him lose his equilibrium. Were the Chinese so subtle that they were nebulous, naïve or naturally normal? And that more than curious affair that afternoon. When Gordon Parks, the link man with the SIS, shown in the embassy staff list as First Secretary

Political, returned from a visit to Bangkok, he would talk it out with him.

At the palace, the King and Queen, with the by-now familiar retinue, came majestically across from the far side, His Majesty wearing court apparel of a white coat with his red and yellow sash and a piece of dark cloth that was wrapped around his legs, drawn between them and tucked into the waistband at the back. The womenfolk were dressed like the Queen, hair done up in a bun and tied with a golden chain on the left side of the head for married women and on the right for virgins. A pastel-shaded blouse, a skirt with a multi-coloured edge most delicately hand-stitched and a silver waist chain were worn by every lady, colours chiefly browns, blues, reds and greens. One of the royal women, with her hair done up on the right, who walked about tenth in the retinue, was strikingly beautiful. She was taller, though younger, than Golden Fairy, more slender, even more graceful, but the obvious likeness immediately struck Rance, whose gaze followed her every movement. Her beautiful smile broadened at times to reveal a perfect set of teeth. Her trim breasts exactly matched her figure, her head was carried proudly high yet with eyes demurely unassertive and her whole bearing so regal that he had to acknowledge that, in truth, she was the epitome of a King's niece.

After the formalities of being presented were over and the royal family had sat down, the others took their seats. There was then an hour's exquisite classical dancing, with the dancers' movements rippling like flowing water, so smooth were they. Rance had heard that Lao and Thai classical dancers were trained from an early age and, indeed, the complexity of their movements was matched by the perfection of the intricate pattern of the dances. He found it intensely moving but he noticed that many Western diplomats were fidgeting long before the end of the performance.

The spotlights were dimmed then turned off, the main illuminations switched on and applause resounded. The King and Queen rose and all stood. The King said something that Rance did not catch and walked into the palace. That was the sign that the guests were free to go to the tables that had been set out in the rear in the open and have their meal.

Rance moved over and watched the scene. A bar was beyond the tables and the Westerners were soon thick around it. The tables themselves were groaning with food: sticky rice, bread, many kinds of meat, vegetables, curries – European and Lao food in profusion. It was a buffet and he waited until the first onslaught had subsided before he went to collect his meal. He looked around him and saw every one of the scattered tables was occupied. At one the Daniels and the Nechaevs were talking earnestly, at another the Thai Ambassador and Attaché sat each with his wife. The French kept to themselves as though disdainful of the foreign intrusion of their former empire, while the Americans gravitated towards the Lao Generals. Rance took his plate and went to the palace side of the lawn, where he stood in the shadow of some shrubs, almost invisible in his ceremonial black Mess kit.

'Excuse me! Are you Colonel Rance?' The voice behind him was tinklingly alluring and prettily pitched. He wheeled round and there was the girl who had so bewitched him earlier. He put his plate on the ground, joined his hands together in front of his face and said, '*Men leew. Tu nong sabai di bor?*' – yes, indeed and is your royal sister well?

Her rejoinder surprised him. In perfect English but with a touch of an American accent, she laughed her answer. 'That *is* good, just like my sister Inkham said. There's no need to keep your plate on the ground and anyway your meal will get cold. Please pick it up. I am Princess Malee, or if you prefer it, Jasmine. Inkham is two above me. Maybe she told you we are seven sisters? Ouane, the eldest, is married to Prince Mangkara, the Prime Minister's eldest son, and so that joins the two royal houses of Luang Prabang and Xieng Khouang together.'

Rance smiled. Apart from being stunningly beautiful, facially and in the way she was dressed, she was so natural it put him completely at his ease.

'This is not the time to talk as I'd like to with you,' she continued. 'I live at Villa Haekham, near the Military Hospital. Inkham wrote and said I should give you practice in the northern accent. Give me a ring on 3961 any time after 5 o'clock in the evening. I'm a working girl, didn't you know? I must get to know you. Bye now.' She joined her hands in the *wai* salutation in front of her face, looked straight at Rance briefly before dropping her gaze and disappearing behind the shrubs back to the palace. Rance turned back to the throng and, feeling unexpectedly tired, finished off his meal, now cold and unappetising.

Next morning, 22 November, Rance moved into the Defence Attaché's villa, near Thad Luang, to be greeted by a rapturous dog. Villa Sinxay was a mile from the British embassy, on the edge of the town. He took over the inventory of hard furnishing from Mrs Daniel, signed up the paperwork and made himself scarce. At half past two, the Daniels drove to Wattay airport. In the VIP lounge, their houseboy, Khian An, and one of the local embassy staff, set up a champagne bar. The outgoing couple booked in, weighed their luggage, passed through emigration formalities and went upstairs to receive their guests – the Attaché Corps and any members of the other diplomatic staffs who wanted either a free drink away from their office routine or to say farewell. Colonel Terry and Mrs Jane Olsen turned up and the American Army Attaché looked in for a short while. A number of the French embassy wives came to say farewell to Mrs Daniel and there were tears as kisses were pecked in Gallic profusion, the French being more emotional than normal when one of their womenfolk is married to a foreigner. Rance gathered there was a certain amount of snob value attached to how many and who came to see off a departing member of the international community. On this occasion, it seemed that the American attitude was perfunctory, as was the Australian, the French shallow and the British bored but, as he had not attended anything similar before, he had no yardstick. There were no Soviets or Chinese there. He personally was relieved when the passengers were called forward for boarding Thai Airways Bangkok flight, TH 533. He went and gave Marie-Joseph a kiss and he shook Daniel's hand.

'Have a safe journey, Roger, and a good leave before you get back into the saddle again,' he said. 'Thanks for a good handover. I'll forward any mail that comes to you and any first-day covers for your collection.'

'Thanks, Jason. And good luck to you. Remember not to take the job too seriously. I found it the greatest fun, you know, and nobody really expects you to do anything. When I get back to London and Sir David Law debriefs me, I'll tell him that everything went smoothly between us and you're happy the way things have started – I mean those introductions to the Lao Generals I arranged for you and the excellent relations between our office and the Americans. And the house dog Singha really loves you already. I really must fly now, literally! Bye-bye!' and he moved off to board the plane.

Rance waited until the aircraft was out of sight before slowly walking out of the airport building. The week between his arrival and now seemed far longer than seven days, with the thirty-three weeks between intimation, at the Jungle Warfare School, of his new job and now, the Defence Attaché, infinitely longer than seven and a half months. The pressures to which he had been subjected were, he realised, only a small part of the whole, a beginning, no more than a foretaste. His car drove up to him, Leuam got out and opened the right-hand rear door. Rance climbed in. The door was respectfully shut and the sheath over the flag taken off. It fluttered as the car drove away. He looked out of the window, hardly noticing anything ... *The future? I can only continue as though everything was normal, well, hardly that because what was normal here? – but as though nothing was untoward. And that inner, secret, stealthy and almost laughable quest of mine?* Unconsciously he shook his head. *I'll have a long chat with Gordon Parks, the man from the SIS, otherwise where else can I turn? But at least I am here, I have seen the King and it will*

be my turn next to shake his hand. I have met Jasmine. I know
that the Soviets are gunning for me and I already know better
where I stand, as a representative, with the rest of the diplomatic
and foreign communities – even the Chinese. I will play it cool
for a while and let people get accustomed to me. That house
will take some getting used to, living alone, the entertaining, the
new routine, and, most important, the need to be on my guard
perpetually. And there was still the ring – talisman or incubus? ...
the car sped into the town, the new Attaché's face immobile but
his mind racing.

6

November-December, 1972. Vientiane, Laos: Gordon Parks was
a fat, ugly, untidy-looking man who would never have been taken
as an intelligence officer. That and a first-class brain were the
reasons why he was rated so highly by his colleagues in London
and ignored by those elsewhere who were his legitimate targets –
the disassociation of ideas working in his favour.

As Head of Station, Vientiane, he worked closely with his
opposite number in the CIA – both men using the 'need to know'
formula – and, over the years, an unusually fruitful relationship
had evolved. It was extraordinary what an English mouse could,
in certain circumstances, achieve where an American lion became
enmeshed and it was because of Laos lending itself to such
happening that Maurice Burke had contacted John Chambers to
help search for an Englishman who would have even the smallest
chance of tilting the eventual balance in favour of the King of Laos
and, ludicrously, suggesting, even in jest Operation 'Stealth'. As
he waited for Rance to return from Wattay airport after bidding
farewell to the Daniels, Gordon Parks thought of Mao Tse-tung's
aphorism, 'one spark can start a prairie fire', in relation to the
probably impossible task of contact with the King that had been
mooted for the new Attaché. He had been impressed when he

had read Rance's background details – dedicated and eccentric potential was his unspoken comment – and concerned when he read details of the Mme. Grambert episode. He felt the affair might not be entirely coincidental although, for the life of him, he couldn't see how. Whatever the reason, it might have drawn attention to Rance when such attention was least needed.

He had been away over the period of the new Attaché's arrival. This was no bad thing as Rance had a better chance of showing himself as a lost new boy, thrown in at the deep end, reacting far more naturally as an unconscious target than would have been the case had the two of them got together before Daniel left. Under these circumstances, any move against him in the first week might be the more positively identified with Rance as a passive catalyst as opposed to someone with pre-directed reflexes. Even so, it had been a gamble, as Gordon Parks realised, listening as Rance, sitting opposite him, told him what contacts he had made, what had happened at the Soviet embassy and, this last to promptings, what opinion he had of where he stood in the estimation of others now he was in the chair.

'Tempting though it be, it is difficult to pinpoint anything specific in such a short time as a week but first impressions have been indicative of what I believe may turn out to be a correct assessment of the state of the pulse politic. It is vastly different from how I imagined it would be – and I am saddened at what I have found. Between these four walls, the characters of our boss and my predecessor are such that they may have caused counter-productive results, besides being talking points everywhere and, although I've yet to hear anything definite, such signs are there.

Without putting too fine a point on it, Daniel seems to have to been taken with a pinch of salt. As for HE, it would not be too much to presume that he is the darling of the left-wing and the despair of the right, thereby making my position an unenviable one.' Here Rance told Parks what the Ambassador had told him about bating the Americans. 'By being loyal to him,' continued a worried Attaché, 'means that I'll never gain any American – and I've learnt that they rule the Lao military roost and heavily influence its politics – or Free World and right-wing Lao confidences. If I am disloyal to him, not only do I offend my own code of honour but my disloyalty will count against me with those people I must cultivate. If I show I'm anti-left which, by definition as a hater of Communism I am, I can justly be accused of only representing the United Kingdom to the Royal Lao Government when I am the military representative to the whole of Laos and that includes the Communist part of it. My strict orders are to be seen as neutral. It's a tricky situation and, quite frankly, one I'm surprised is allowed to exist by our Lords and Masters at home.'

'I completely agree with you but there's no need to despair. I appreciated before you came here that it would strike you the way it has. What with reports from London and my own knowledge of local conditions, I have been giving the problem much thought. First, behave completely naturally, impartially, disinterestedly, sensibly and patiently. Then sniff the wind – be an opportunist and do not have too many scruples. You are the target of others who think they are your target. You cannot force the pace of acceptability. Take advantage of what you can and this is particularly so with your Asian background and Asian languages.

If, as you say and which I believe, HE is the darling of the left, cash in on it. Take a leaf out of their book – remember what Lenin said in 1917: "Politics is war without bloodshed, war is politics with bloodshed". You are up against dedicated and ruthless political animals as far as the Soviets and Chinese are concerned and neither of them is our ally. Putting it bluntly, you are a boy in a man's league. As far as the Americans are concerned, they know that you've a damned hard and lonely furrow to plough. The RLG, Royal Lao Government, will be slower to make up its individual and corporate mind. Again I can only counsel patience. You have got to give them time to weigh you up and see how you behave "on and off parade". In the meantime, travel around, visiting the outlying Military Regions. You can use the Beaver aircraft whenever you want to and making new contacts in the provinces will be one cure for frustration.'

Rance grinned cheerfully at that.

'Also try and keep up to date with the various Communist pronouncements, deadly dull though they be, and study the language they use. If politics be their god, then semantics are their godlings. I'm not expecting you to like or to agree with the Communists but you'll have to talk with them at various times, at receptions if not in their offices or homes. They are like wild animals really. Don't frighten them to start with and let them see you are not frightened of them. Throw them some food and keep still. They'll choose their moment to come and take it. Throw the next lot not quite so far; wait again. And eventually, who knows, they'll take you as part of their everyday life if not actually eating out of your hand. But until then, it's routine work, blandly studying languages, never criticising, never offering advice, playing hard to catch, appearing not over-keen to get involved, even nebulous.

'You may not have realised it but the names of the Soviet Ambassador and his Defence Attaché are coincidently and ironically interesting – Bakunin and Nechaev. Their namesakes concocted a document, *The Catechism of a Revolutionist*, written in, I think, 1869. Try and scrutinise it because it shows you what you're up against – what we are all up against, come to that – and it can act as a spur to you if you lose heart at the seemingly hopelessness of your task. Try, even, to put it into Lao – you never know when it will come in useful. 'And finally, one thing is certain sure; the present situation won't last for ever.'

That struck Rance as eminently sensible – much food for thought. 'Before I go, let me say that one positive aspect is that, in London, one of the King's nieces, Princess Golden Fairy, was my teacher and, when I am settled in, I will try and ask her sister, Princess Jasmine, to help me out linguistically.' It was only afterwards that he remembered that he had not mentioned the ring.

As he had decided even before his fascinating talk with Gordon Parks, Rance started off in very low key, working from first principles like the good soldier that he was. He needed, he knew, a firm base, a workable plan and a reserve – prerequisites in any military operation of the more conventional sort. The firm base had to be his house, his reputation, his method of living, his impeccable credentials of exemplary self-conduct. His workable plan was simple enough: behaving normally, developing contacts locally as well as in the provinces, noting, observing, thinking, searching – but for what? – probing, teasing, assessing, analysing, collating, reassessing, recognising, rejecting and then seeing what was left, all within the confines and constraints of duty, tact and loyalty, never taking anything for granted. He knew it would take a long time to recognise the pieces of the jigsaw puzzle but maybe even if it was only a piece of blue sky that he found, it would enable someone else to fit it into and, who knew, complete the picture. It would take even longer to judge whether what seemed genuine fact was information or purposeful disinformation, whether it was complete in itself or only that which gave a clue to yet something else, be it a hint in a smile, a message in the eyes or an implicit warning in a tone of voice or a turn of phrase. It would take time if only because concentrating on everything at once tended to blot things out or to see them disproportionally: a nonchalant attitude, letting things sink in to be dug out later, examined and then judged as useful or otherwise, was a wiser albeit slower course of action that brash and frenetic beavering. If that was what 'stealth' meant, so be it. It would not be easy to start with, in fact he doubted it would ever be easy.

And what of a reserve? A reserve of what? He had nothing in the conventional sense. All he could do was to build up sufficient good will and trust for him initially to become known and tolerated, then accepted and finally sought after. He knew he was eccentric enough for Europeans to be suspicious of him at first but, for Asians, that was all to the good – eccentricity was regarded as a manifestation of inner strength and, provided a person was consistently different from yet rationally the same as others, he was not only accepted but welcomed. Hopefully the pattern of acceptability he would build up would pave the way for longer term benefits while taking the sting out of the current and short-term disadvantages. Nothing spectacular but all based on sound tenets, it would do for a start. Meanwhile life had to be lived, accommodating the imponderables as best possible.

'I thought you were unusually reticent after your recent invitation to Colonel Rance, Comrade Colonel, and now my suspicions are doubly confirmed.' Mr Bakunin was angrily remonstrating with Colonel Nechaev. He pointed to a copy of the *Bangkok Post* he held in his hand. 'First point: I know there is no proof as such but what did happen? Listen to this: "It is reliably learnt that the changing rooms in the Soviet embassy swimming pool area in Vientiane have much more than meet the eye, that is the eye of anyone changing there. On one wooden frame in the room next to the embassy building is a ridged covering so fashioned that a picture painted on the ridge on the side of the actual embassy itself can be photographed by a hidden camera without the person in the changing room being any the wiser. Our staff reporter has discovered that the picture is of a nude Lao boy, lying on his back with his mouth open. Of course the camera is hidden but if there were no camera, why the unusually bright cluster of lights installed there?" and a whole lot more in the same vein. The heading is an insult to our embassy: "Soviet Sex Sights Are Pooled Resources" Dateline is Monday, 4 December. What happened?'

'I've told you, Comrade Ambassador. The Englishman

suddenly left the changing room without even undressing, saying that he had broken his tooth on some toffee I'd given him when we were talking earlier on. He certainly was looking into his mouth using the changing room mirror. That we have established. The camera wouldn't have got his face even if a photo had been taken. He never gave any hint of suspecting anything abnormal but since then his manner has been much cooler than it was at first.'

'I saw you talking to the outgoing man, Colonel Daniel, at the royal banquet. What did he have to say?'

'Just that, Comrade Ambassador. I brought the conversation round to a point when I could ask him without his being suspicious. He said that Jason, he called him, had been to the American embassy Medical Unit in the "Silver City" compound and so had missed something he'd wanted to show him in the office before the *baçi*. That fellow Daniel is a stupid man, that we know, but, with his misplaced sense of humour, he couldn't have refrained from making some crack at us had he known.' Colonel Nechaev looked unhappily at his Ambassador who hadn't finished with him yet.

'I don't suppose the clever Soviet Defence Attaché even bothered to find out if the new English DA did go for treatment or not. Even if he didn't, Comrade, you will still have to be answerable, as Comrade Jan Berzin was, on my second point, which is equally serious.'

Nechaev shuddered because he had no wish to be so severely disgraced. Hard labour and exile were only acceptable when they concerned others.

'Not only did your infernal device not work out as you boasted but the lead up to it has shown what I have always suspected. Look at these!' The voice snapped rat-trap tight and Nechaev was handed several photographs of him standing naked over a nude Lao boy but this time there was no hiding the intensity of the disgusting and degrading orgy. As the incredulous Nechaev stared dumbfounded at the damning evidence, the Ambassador pressed a bell and the Colonel was taken away under close arrest by members of the embassy security guard, the 'baboon' grinning malevolently. As his Lao servant had already been disposed of, there was now only the paperwork and the permanent relief to be fixed, apart from getting rid of the deposed and disgraced ex-attaché.

Although everything in Vientiane was still new, it felt good to be travelling again. Using the embassy Beaver aircraft Rance made his duty calls at the three remaining Military Regions and returned in much better spirits.

'Welcome back, sir. Have a good trip?' Mr Joseph asked. 'I'm sure you're ready for a cup of coffee,' and without waiting for an answer, mixed a brew.

'You're only saying that, Chief, because you mean it!' said Rance with a smile as he sat down and sipped his drink. 'What's new, except me in the job?'

'Except for a juicy bit in the *Bangkok Post* I've side-lined for you, not a lot, sir. A few bits and pieces in from the other embassies. Oh yes. There was one rather strange thing that I think you should know about and is worth mentioning even though it turns out to be rationally explainable. I had a call asking for the number of your American health card as they hadn't made a note of it in their register. I said I'd ring them back, presuming it to be their office but when I did, they denied having rung in the first place and anyway you hadn't made an application. I wasn't going to have mentioned it but, on further reflection, it does seem a little odd.'

'Did you then ask the telephone operator if she knew where the original call came from? That's the only way we can trace it.'

'Yes, I did, sir, but to no avail. She'd had a number of calls coming through in quick succession and didn't even remember that one at first. Apart from this piece in the *Bangkok Post* – quite exciting, really. I wonder how the staff reporter found about it. Lucky you weren't involved. And there is this, unexpected I'd call it, note from the Soviet embassy, dated only yesterday. Quicker than usual.' He handed a piece of paper over to Rance who skim read it out loud, translating it from the French as he did. '"The Soviet embassy presents its compliments to the Royal Lao Government … bla … bla … bla and has the honour to state that the Defence Attaché, Colonel Georgi Nechaev, has been posted out and that the Deputy, Lieutenant Colonel Yuri Gorakhov, is the Defence Attaché until a permanent replacement is provided. The Soviet embassy avails itself of this opportunity to renew … bla … the assurance of its highest considerations … rhubarb … rhubarb … rhubarb",' he read.

'Now that, Chief, is indeed interesting. I'd love to know why and what's behind the bland diplomatic verbiage that covers a multitude of sins. I for one am a happier man for it. Anything else?'

'When you have read the *Bangkok Post* you might put two and two together! Who knows? Oh yes. My opposite number in the Australian embassy picked up yet another tidbit. Be careful when you walk around Thad Luang. The police have had trouble with some catamites who were organising some sort of protest to the Soviet Ambassador! Not to make a coarse joke but no one's got to the bottom of it yet. You know how vicious people say they can get, so beware! It's not that we want to lose you, sir. It's the paperwork afterwards that is so boring! Is your dog Singha in good biting trim these days?'

'Thanks for the warning, Chief,' said Rance laughingly and went to his own office. *Well, well, well. Not a break-through as such but one less danger to avoid. Is Dame Fortune going to smile on me from now on?*

At close of play that day, he rang through to the exchange and asked for 3961. A silvery voice answered, ''Ullo. Villa Haekham.'

'Good afternoon. May I speak to Chao Mali?' asked Rance, in Lao.

'Oh, Colonel. Is that you after so long? I have been waiting for you to contact me for some time now. What has been the trouble?'

'Nothing, except that I have never been able to get through to you from my home. I don't know why and that is why I'm calling from the office. But may I come round to see you, please? Tomorrow? At half past five? I hope they don't keep you late at work! I am really looking forward to it. I've so many questions to ask you. What? Yes, I came back this afternoon. Yes. See you tomorrow. Goodbye.'

Villa Haekham was an unpretentious building set back and surrounded by a walled garden. The road along which Rance was driven was tarred until it reached the Military Hospital, fifty yards away from it. The last bit was a dirt track that squirted out clouds of the finest dust when trodden on. He got out of the car and told Leuam to take the dog back home, then dismiss as he would be walking back. He watched the car drive away in the thick powdery dust, the dog looking anxiously looking back out of the window. He walked up the concrete drive and the front door was opened by Princess Jasmine herself as he reached it. His heart leapt and missed a beat, his eyes lighting up with pleasure at being in the company of such a beautiful woman. As she was a princess he joined his hands in the *wai* salutation in front of his face without waiting for a woman to initiate the gesture and, because he was a man she was learning to respect, her salutation coincided with his.

'Come in, do. Where's the dog? I hear you take him around with you. Don't look so surprised – there are no secrets in Vientiane,' and she laughed delightedly. 'Maybe next time you'll let me get to know him.'

They went inside and sat at an expensively made dining table. A paining of HM the King filled one wall. *Was Jasmine to be a conduit? Much too early now but who else?* They settled down to work, Rance asking her many grammatical questions that had been troubling him, glad that she used English when his Lao was not up to the task.

After nearly an hour he put his notes away. 'That's enough for one day. I really do thank you. It is kind of you to spare so much of your time. I've got a lot to remember from our long session.'

'Not at all. *Bor pen nyang*. Tell me, why didn't you ring before?'

'I told you, I tried to, several times from my house, without luck. I must get my telephone overhauled. Mind you, I have been settling in so I have not been exactly idle.'

'How you're finding life here amongst us? I hope you are enjoying it.'

He told her where he'd been and whom he'd met. 'I saw His Majesty at close quarters during the Thad Luang festival and his half-brother, the General at Military Region 1 at Luang Prabang. I have met all the senior Lao officials protocol requires me to.'

She hesitated before replying, then she asked, 'Haven't you been to see His Excellency the Minister of Defence yet? No!' as he shook his head. 'I'm sure he'd appreciate a visit from you. We were talking together a few nights ago and from what he said he's expecting you to go and see him. My brother-in-law, the Prime Minister's eldest son, is his Military Assistant. He'll fix up an interview if you give him a ring.'

That evening most unusually the telephone rang in Rance's downstairs room. He picked up the handset and said, '2362.'

A seductive voice cooed down the line. ''*Ullo, Colonel. Je comprens que vous avez besoin ...*' He did not let the voice finish what it had started to ask. Whoever the woman was who understood that he had a need of something, the mere fact that he put the handset down as she was talking should have spelt out that it wasn't her. He called his houseboy and instructed him to answer whenever the phone rang and, if any woman rang and did not identify herself, he was to say that the Colonel was out or busy, so not to be disturbed.

Rance had managed to arrange his meeting with the Minister of Defence at 11.30 hours on 20 December. It had not been too easy to fit it in because Prince Lanouk, as it turned out, was, in fact, the Minister of Finance and only the Delegate to the Minister of Defence, the actual portfolio being held by the Prime Minister. Lanouk was Defence in the afternoon and Finance in the morning. Rance was due to meet him in the morning so went to the Ministry of Finance, which was a mistake as that day Prince Lanouk had changed his routine so was at his office in Phone Kheng, the FAR HQ – a nice case of Sod's Law.

At 7 o'clock that morning Rance had tuned in to the BBC World Service and learnt with surprise that the Americans, tired of getting nowhere with their peace talks with the North Vietnamese and Viet Cong, had started bombing Hanoi and Haiphong again. Just before the weekly embassy meeting Rance went into the Ambassador's office to prepare himself for the briefing from the relief map there.

'Good morning, Your Excellency. May I refresh myself on your map for the briefing?'

'Did you hear the news this morning, Colonel? Did you hear it? Did you?' The Ambassador was shaking with rage and was spluttering. 'Those blasted Americans are killing innocent civilians again. It's insane and it makes me sick. Well, what do you think of it, eh?'

'I expect they started again because they became slightly exasperated at the conference table.' Even as he said it, he realised that he would be considered to be understating the case – nor was he disappointed in the reaction.

'Colonel, that's the understatement of the decade. You ... you ... don't seem to grasp how horrible it all is,' shrilled the outraged man and he was still virtually beside himself when the meeting began. 'What are you going to do this morning,' Jason was asked.

'I am going to see Prince Lanouk ...'

He was interrupted by, 'don't bother. He's mad and a war monger.'

The Defence Minister's office was on the first floor of the large building that housed FAR HQ. It was separated from Jubilation's office by a room where the secretary of both men worked together. Rance was shown into Prince Lanouk's office by the Prime Minister's son, Princess Jasmine's brother-in-law. He saluted and said, 'Good morning, Your Excellency. Thank you for sparing the time to see me, when you must be such a busy man.'

Prince Lanouk na Champassac was a tall, well-built, good-looking man in his early forties who had married a French woman and was the father of two of the most beautiful girls imaginable and one boy. He had held diplomatic posts a couple of times, in India and the United Nations, and was fluent in English and French. Rance had adjudged it more politic to use English. The prince got out of his chair, came round from behind his large desk towards Rance, offered him his hand and invited him to be seated in one of the two comfortable chairs by the far wall. He looked the Englishman straight between the eyes. 'Welcome. Your Ambassador is mad – and a pacifist.'

Rance quickly summed up the trickiness of the situation. To agree with the minister about his own ambassador's state of mental health and politics would have been as cheaply disloyal as to have denied both would have been consummately dishonest. What price being a diplomatic soldier?

'Thank you for airing the question, Your Excellency. There's no need therefore to refer to the matter again. I understand your feelings.'

They talked about the war in Laos, the renewal of the bombing of North Vietnam and the sowing of mines around Haiphong harbour. Lanouk then touched on the iniquities of the NVA's presence in Laos and their virtual colonisation of the eastern 'Panhandle'. He then asked Rance where he had been and whom he had met. Rance told him in outline but Prince Lanouk did not seem satisfied.

'Have you been to PS 18?'

'No, sir.'

'Have you been to Whisky 3?'

'No, sir.'

'Why not?'

'Because this is the first time I have heard of either of them. I don't know where they are or what they are.'

'Hmm ... well maybe these are early days yet. Even so, I am surprised.' He seemed to be on the point of saying something but, after a short pause, he got up abruptly and took a pace towards

Rance. 'Thank you for coming to see me. I don't suppose it's the last time we'll meet. I'll have to choose my moment …' and his voice trailed off as though he were talking to himself. He held out his hand as a sign of dismissal. Rance shook it, saluted and left the office. Interesting but disappointing, he mused as he drove off but how relevant was it all under the circumstances? At least he had not been snuffed or branded as an English dove – maybe that in itself was enough for one day.

On his return to the embassy he noticed a young Lao woman sitting in the foyer. She looked up as he came in and smiled modestly. The duty door keeper told him in an aside that she had come so see the English Colonel. He went over to her and she stood up to greet him. Having demurely made the *wai* salutation, unusually for a Lao woman she confidently opened the conversation in faultless French.

'Excuse me for inconveniencing you, Monsieur, but may we have a talk?'

'Certainly, Mademoiselle. At your convenience. In the visitors' room.' He ushered her in. 'Please be seated. I can spare you some of my time here and now.'

She was dressed traditionally in blouse and skirt, with nothing on her head, no stockings and thick open shoes. The inevitable silver belt was round her waist. She wore her hair tied up in a bun on the right of her head. She had delicate features, high cheek bones but, whilst attractive, was in no way pretty. She sat, clutching her black handbag, knees and heels tightly joined, feet flat on the floor. *A good parachute landing position!* She cleared her throat.

'I came to hear that you need a Lao teacher so I have called in here to see what we can arrange,' she said in French.

Rance the suspicious, the hunted, the unconventional; Rance the ever-cautious, the perturbed, the stubborn, looked back on the five weeks he had been in the country and, while he could not remember all that he had said, he knew what he had not. Apart from his acquaintance with Princess Jasmine, he had never even hinted he wanted a teacher. As his mind raced with intriguing possibilities, he stalled for time.

'Do you speak Lao with a northern accent?' he asked her.

'Non, Monsieur, but I completely understand it. For my part, I speak Bangkok Thai and Viet.'

Her use of only part of the word 'Vietnamese' to describe the language was not lost on him. It was a direct translation of what the Vietnamese people used to describe their own language.

'What dialect of those other two languages do you speak? For my part I speak Bangkok Thai and Hanoi Vietnamese.'

'I'm nearly the same, Monsieur. I speak Thai Issan, the Thai of northeast Thailand, and Saigon Vietnamese.' She used the whole word the second time.

'I'd only get muddled, Mademoiselle. It wouldn't be worth my while to have you as my language teacher. Thank you for coming round to enquire.'

He stood up but she remained seated. Was it to be a sleeping dictionary that she wanted to be? Asian women were much more decorous than their western sisters, certainly in public, so it was only when they flaunted themselves at a person that they were obviously libertine or acting a part.

'Before I finally decide one way or the other, I need to know about you. Please tell me your name, who you are and your terms.'

'I am Mlle. Kaysorn Bouapha. I am a Lao girl and spent some of my youth in Saigon when my father, an advocate, was working there during the French colonial days. I live in a house on the Avenue Circulaire. I work in the French Cultural Centre at the end of Rue Pong Kham. As regards place and times of tuition, it would be done in your villa after work, from 5 to 6 o'clock each evening. We could practise Lao on two days, Thai on two days and, if you are willing to work on Saturdays, Vietnamese on two days. I would expect US $5 for each period.'

Rance considered what she had said before replying. She was so unusually decisive in her manner that she might almost have been primed and if that was so he felt he needed to know who was running her. Even if, which he doubted, he was wrong in his diagnosis, she might have some limited uses.

'All right, Mme. Bouapha. I've got to get used to the various accents. Let's try it for a couple of weeks. It can't be every day as I will be travelling sometimes and will have to attend some soirées on some evenings.'

The look in his eyes as she came to thank him and bid him farewell was unusually penetrating. *This time*, he thought, *I'll start prepared* so, having seen her off the premises, he went to see Gordon Parks, told him about it and suggested he might like to try having her traced. Gordon agreed and, in the fullness of time, London was also appraised.

The next day Rance left the office early. He got to his villa, bathed and put on a light shirt with a sarong round his waist. On his feet he wore a pair of flip-flops. There would be time to slip on a pair of trousers when the front door bell rang, meanwhile the sarong was comfortable to relax in. He had decided that informality was required so, instead of having his lessons downstairs in the representational room where the phone was, he would invite Mme. Kaysorn upstairs to his sitting room, which he had turned into a mini-language laboratory. It was also more convenient if only to have advance warning of any other visitors. He was startled, therefore, when the first he knew of his teacher's arrival was as she appeared in front of him. His room was walled only on three and a half sides, the open side leading onto a passage off which were three bedrooms, a box-room and a bathroom with a sitting bath in it. He had no choice but to rise, dressed as he was. 'Sit down,' she commanded abruptly and then went into all three bedrooms and the box-room on a tour of inspection. He watched her, nonplussed by the unexpected turn of events – at least he was ready.

Her inspection over, she came and joined him on the settee. She sat down so close that they were touching from shoulder to leg, buttocks included. She looked at him, then at his feet.

'Your toenails need cutting. Tell me where the scissors are and I'll cut them for you.'

There was an air of unreality about the situation. He declined her offer. She got up and went over to his desk and bookcase. She looked at his books, his tape recorder and his several language tapes. Having satisfied her curiosity, she came and nestled up to him again. She noticed no mark of wearing a ring on any of his fingers.

'*Oui, très jolie*. I approve. Shall we start our lesson?'

She was an engaging and energetic teacher who knew her subject matter well. Her approach was serious as regards study but kittenish towards Rance. She had no sex appeal but, at first blush, few inhibitions either. He was amused yet concerned. His houseboy, Khian An, shutting the door behind her as she left the house an hour later, was grumpy. Not only was he suspicious of her but his professional dignity had been damaged by her having got into the house unannounced.

The next evening, 22 December, was the fiftieth anniversary of the Soviet Constitution, an occasion deemed important enough to invite the diplomatic community to the Soviet embassy in its honour. *Tenue de Ville* it had said on the invitation card and that meant white uniform for the Attachés. Rance arrived and joined the queue of people being welcomed by the Ambassador, the First Secretary and the acting Defence Attaché. After introducing himself by name and congratulating the Ambassador on his Motherland's constitutional half-century, he drifted off into the crowd that was swarming with Soviet bloc representatives. Other Communist countries' minions were also thick on the ground. Some western representation was there too as well as a token sprinkling of Royal Lao Army Generals.

Rance caught sight of his Chinese counterpart and went up to him. 'This is the first time as the official British Defence Attaché I have had the chance of talking to you,' he said smilingly.

There was a Lao in his middle thirties standing nearby, dressed in a shabby suit, so typical of out-station Communists, and Rance noticed he had been talking to the Chinese. He therefore presumed he was a member of the LPF. He turned to M. Teng Ah-hok and said, 'Excuse me, but I don't know who your friend is. Can you introduce me to him, please?'

'Certainly, I will, with pleasure.' He spoke to the Lao through his French interpreter. The Lao replied in poor French and the introductions were made.

'Comrade Bounphong Sunthorn, this is Colonel Rance, the new British Defence Attaché; Colonel, this is M. Bounphong Sunthorn, who recently arrived as a new member of the Patriotic Front delegation from Sam Neua.'

As they shook hands, Rance felt a ring on the little finger of the Lao's right hand. It was only when he let go did a crazy idea occur to him – *can this man be one of the four? No, too far-fetched* – so he dismissed it. What did surprise him was the likeness of Bounphong Sunthorn with his driver. He excused himself to the Chinese interpreter and started talking to Bounphong in Lao. The effect was instantaneously rewarding and, despite an obvious reluctance to be too familiar with a westerner, the Englishman was so friendly and had such compellingly kind eyes, that Bounphong replied with greater warmth than might have been expected for a first meeting.

M. Teng Ah-hok interrupted. 'Have you met the chief delegate of the LPF in Vientiane yet, M. Soth Petrasy? No? Let me introduce you to him now. He's over there, talking with the Soviet Second Secretary.'

The three men moved over to where Soth Petrasy was. After a slight pause to let him finish what he was saying, more introductions were made.

'So you are the one?' he asked quizzically and not unpleasantly. He seemed a kindly man somewhere in his late fifties, was slightly stooped and quietly spoken.

'That sounds ominous!' Rance's smile robbed the remark of any offence.

'No, no. We welcome an Attaché who speaks Lao. Your prowess is well known already.'

'You flatter me, Tan Soth, but I admit I am pleased. Now that I have the chance to ask you, may I come and call on you in my official capacity on Wednesday next, 27 December. I'll give you a ring before I do so I can confirm that it is convenient for you. What I really want to do after that is to invite, say, three of both your delegations, the LPF and the Chinese embassy, to my house for a meal. The only other guests would be English.'

'Will Mr Taunton be there?' The question from both Soth and Teng was almost simultaneous. Even Bounphong had obviously been briefed on this matter.

'I'll ask him as a friend not as the Chef de Mission Diplomatique so, in that way, there will be no problems of protocol.'

'We will come with pleasure,' they both said, smiling. Only the Soviet Second Secretary looked sour, not having been brought into the conversation, and feeling that the Chinese had had the edge over him in the exchange.

Watching the scene were the Soviet security guards who flanked the area. Their continued presence in the privileged position of being posted to a foreign country was consequent on their continuous alertness. They watched the western representatives intensely lest anything suspicious occur. Also watching from their protocol-ordained place of welcome and farewell were the Ambassador and the acting Defence Attaché. Both looked less pleased than might be expected on the occasion of such a political landmark.

'Comrade,' began the Ambassador in a lull when they were alone. 'That reminds me. The new Englishman, Rance, has a head start with the Chinese and the LPF. From his records he should not be ready to have made such progress. I don't really like it, however we can still play this to our advantage, maybe, if we make haste slowly. New tactics – play it stealthily.'

Rance was also observed by the Directors of Intelligence and Psychological Warfare who were among the token guests representing the royal army. As they drove away in an official black car, one turned to the other and observed, 'We were quite right to have taken the action we did. I'll tell Major General Sisavat Abhay first thing tomorrow that his suspicions were justified. It will be a great pity for our cause if Colonel Rance does turn out like his Ambassador and his predecessor, despite his almost impeccable credentials. However, it is just possible that he'll pass our test.'

On his way back to his villa Rance asked Leaum if he had any brothers. 'I had a younger brother called Bounphong whom I have not seen for thirty years or so. I don't know if he's dead or alive but if he were alive I don't think I'd recognise him now.'

'Where did you last see him?'

'In the wat in Sam Neua. I had left my village with my father and my brother. I was to do time as an acolyte monk there.'

'What is your family name, Leaum?'

'Sunthorn.'

On the Wednesday after Christmas, before the weekly office meeting, Rance went in to see the Ambassador. After ritual and meaningless formalities of greeting, he said that there was one point that he would like His Excellency's views on. 'At the Soviet embassy last Friday, I asked my Chinese counterpart and M. Soth Petrasy if they, along with the new LPF man whom you've already met, would come to supper informally in my villa sometime in the New Year. They asked if you would be there, as a friend not as Head of Mission, to avoid any pitfalls of protocol. I said I'd ask you and let them know your verdict today. In any case I want to go and visit the LPF delegation, which is something I haven't done yet. Your affirmative answer would be a good lead-in for my visit.'

'Jason,' said Mr Taunton, using Rance's Christian name for the first time ever. 'If you didn't fix something like that up, it would be a dereliction of duty. Get some dates from them for, say, two to three weeks time and let me know. We'll plump for the most convenient one.'

Rance returned to his office and rang through to the telephone receptionist, asked to be put through to the Lao Patriotic Front HQ. 'Wait, please, I must find out the number as nobody has asked for it before.' He waited, hearing the ringing tone, then a man's voice answering. Would he take a call from the English *Colonen*? Yes. One second please, connecting you now.

'Tan Soth Petrasy, *sabai di bor*?' How are you?

'*Di leew*. And how is the Tan *Colonen*?' The Lao could only pronounce a final 'l' as an 'n'.

'Well, thank you. May I come round to see you this morning, please?'

'Certainly. We look forward to your coming. What time is convenient?'

'11 o'clock. Does that suit you?'

'Yes, it does, thank you.'

'So goodbye till then, Tan Soth!'

'Goodbye, Tan *Colonen*.'

At exactly 11 o'clock, Rance's flagged car turned into the LPF compound. A sentry at the gate, obviously warned, gave a passable salute. Rance told Leuam to drive up to the front entrance. A PL soldier opened the car door: sincere or not, the gesture was a kind one. Soth Petrasy appeared at the front door as Rance reached it. They greeted each other and the Lao led the way into a room on the right of the corridor. Easy chairs, backs to the window, were at one end of long room, the other end of which had the unsmiling pictures of three founder members of the movement glowering down. The other walls were almost bare but on one was a plaque with the map of the country painted in red and blue with a white circle in the middle – this being the LPF emblem – with a white '25' painted in the centre of the circle. On asking why that particular figure, Rance was told that it merely signified a quarter of a century of struggle. On the fourth wall a number of knives in scabbards hung in clusters. Interested in national knives as he was, he asked about them. Soth Petrasy smiled, got up and, going to the wall, took one down and gave it to Rance. It was feather light, made of aluminium and, on the blade, he read the inscription: *debris d'avion U.S. Air Forces: abattu au Laos: Front Pathet Lao 1970.*

It was a difficult moment. If he declined this unusual gift of part of a shot-down American aircraft, it could be taken as a gesture of disapproval; if he accepted it, would it be putting him in the same category as his Ambassador? Rance examined it, face impassive. He then started to go over to the wall to put it back but Soth Petrasy intercepted him, telling him to keep it as it was now his. Rance, acquiescing, thanked him.

They sat down and had a fizzy drink, which was brought in by a moon-faced girl in national dress. Rance asked Soth Petrasy about the owners of the faces hanging on the far wall, the history of the design of the plaque and the aluminium knife. That led the conversation on to the life at Sam Neua, which, in turn, led Soth Petrasy to talk about the old days pre-1954 when the enemy had been the French army. Regardless of ideology, it was fascinating, Rance mentally equating what was described with the tactics he had taught at the Jungle Warfare School and whether the counter-ambush drills then practised would have proved effective against some of the more suicidal Viet Minh. He made a mental note to try and interview any of the captured Vietnamese advisers to the Pathet Lao forces who he had heard were kept at Phone Kheng. It would need official clearance and he would keep it at the back of his mind, putting his request at an opportune moment. He'd even write it up, maybe, for an article in a military journal.

Rance brought the conversation round to the party he was proposing to throw. 'I intend to invite the Chinese DA, an interpreter and either the Chargé d'Affaires or the Assistant DA. Further, as far as we English are concerned, I feel the Mr Taunton and Mr Richardson plus himself would make up the trio,' Rance explained. 'You know Mr Richardson, don't you? The Colombo Plan adviser in the Ministry of Information. He is a garrulous man, in his fifties, who has been in Vientiane for many years and speaks good Lao.'

'Yes, Tan *Colonen*, I know him well.'

'You may think me brash telling you who are to be the guests but I want you to relax and enjoy yourselves with me and this is far more likely to be the case if you are with congenial people who are your friends.' *For smooth patter, I'm doing well!* he thought, *and it seems to be working!*

'You are unusually thoughtful for a westerner, Tan *Colonen* – I appreciate your concern. I do admit it could be embarrassing to be asked to a meal with the "wrong" people.'

'As regards yourselves, I would like to invite three people. I have thought to keep numbers down for a first time. Four of you would be welcome, of course, but, apart from representation being unequal, the Chinese consider it unlucky to sit down ten to a meal. For us and the French, the unlucky number is thirteen.'

Soth Petrasy said he had not heard about the Chinese dislike of sitting down ten to a meal. He was agreeable for them to be represented by three: he himself would be happy to come and he would bring along two comrades. It would not be easy to say who they'd be. It depended on the date and who was available. Could they tentatively fix for 19 January and confirm it nearer the time? Of course.

Rance was still hopeful that he could clear up the matter of the ring on Bounphong Sunthorn's finger. Although it was only a one in a million chance that the ring would be anything like the one he had in his possession, it intrigued him enough to want to clear his mind about it. He took out a note book and a biro from his pocket and said that, as he would be sending the invitation cards written by himself and as he didn't want to make mistakes in the Lao spelling, perhaps Tan Soth would give him three names and correct the spelling? If either nominee could not come on the day this was perfectly acceptable and would not cause any difficulty. He suggested Bounphong's name and wrote it down. As Soth Petrasy was correcting the spelling, a telephone rang in the passage outside. Through the open door Rance saw Bounphong Sunthorn himself go to answer it. He heard him say '*Oui, M. Soth est ici.*' Soth got up to take the call, excusing himself as he did. Rance had a flash of an idea. Unnoticed by either man, he took the biro in his left hand and inscribed a 9 with a curly tail on the inside of his little finger of his right hand. It took only as long to do as it did Soth to reach the telephone and take it from Bounphong. Rance stood up and, as Bounphong turned, waved to him and asked him to sit with him. To Rance's disappointment, he saw that he was not wearing a ring. Ah well, a polite chat would do no harm.

'It is pleasant to meet a European who speaks Lao. Where did you learn to speak it with a northern accent?' Bounphong asked. 'That makes it more unusual.'

'In London. Someone from the embassy taught me. Princess Inkham, the King's niece, was my teacher.' Yes, the facial resemblance was strong – Bounphong and Leuam. 'Where are you from?'

'I come from near Sam Neua. It is much cooler there than here, ever though it is December and the weather in Vientiane is much cooler than it is normally, so I am told.'

'How do you like it here?' Rance glanced intently at his right hand and there, just as it had been on Le Dâng Khoã's finger that far away day in the jungle, was another little 9 with a curly tail. Rance's mind reeled as he realised he might be on the threshold of something significant that needed incredibly careful handling. Now was the moment. He heard the telephone conversation drawing to a close. He took a gamble. He took his talisman ring out of his pocket and looked at Bounphong straight between the eyes. He opened his right hand and said, deliberately and softly, 'I don't understand why you are not wearing your ring or what your mission is here but look at this. We two also have this in common,' and showed him his inked finger.

Bounphong's eyes dilated and he caught his breath sharply. 'Who are you? Can you be he? *C l*,' perhaps, he whispered.

'I'm a friend. Trust me.' Soth Petrasy was putting the telephone back in its cradle. 'And my driver is your elder brother, Leuam.' Rance's eyes bored into the other man's who, as Soth Petrasy entered the room, fell into a dead faint.

It is *that one totally unexpected chance in a million!*

7

December 1972. Vientiane, Laos: 'And then what happened?'

It was the following afternoon and Gordon Parks and Rance had been sitting together in the former's office for the last couple of hours. The new Attaché, realising more than ever before that he had to have impartial and trustworthy counsel for this extraordinary situation, had gone to see the only man in Vientiane who could give it. He had recounted everything he thought had a bearing on the matter: how courses were run at the Jungle Warfare School; how he organised that last-ever course without any Gurkhas as 'exercise enemy'; the warning from the Gurkha Officer; and, he had only just remembered, that strange remark about 'We'll win' Le Dâng Khoã had made; the quarrel between Le Dâng Khoã and Mana Varamit in the jungle on the last day of the final exercise; the ring and the small tattoo mark on the Vietnamese's finger; the incredible effect it had on Princess Golden Fairy in London; the handshake with Bounphong Sunthorn in the Soviet embassy compound the previous Thursday, hence the gamble he had taken at the LPF HQ the previous day; and his driver's background. He had gone into details of his relationship with both princesses and London's fanciful hopes of his influencing the King. Gordon Parks had asked him who else was privy to this knowledge and Rance had said nobody, he'd not even mentioned anything to his driver, even on the way back, except to learn that he and Bounphong were brothers.

'And then what happened?'

'Soth Petrasy came into the room and stared disbelievingly at the recumbent Bounphong, who was on the same settee as I was. I jumped up and told Soth exactly what had happened, how we'd been talking when suddenly the other man had fainted. Luckily Bounphong came round then, blinked at us both and scrambled to his feet. He looked ghastly and asked Soth if he could have a glass of water. Soth went to call one of the servants from somewhere in the back and Bounphong whispered that he trusted me but we both had to be more than careful. I told him that my ring had been given to me, and here I took another gamble, by Le Dâng Khoã in Malaysia, and, before Soth came back, Bounphong told me he'd contact me somehow. That was the end of our conversation as Soth was on his way back with the moon-faced girl and some water. I made the obvious type of remark and hinted it was, possibly, a delayed reaction from the change in climate between hilly Sam Neua and flat Vientiane that was responsible for Bounphong's condition and this was generally accepted. I then said it was time to leave and I'd be grateful confirmation of the 19th for my party. Soth said that he'd contact me and I excused myself and left. I can't think that Soth suspected anything untoward.' Rance shook his head in perplexity.

'What do you make of it all?'

'I wish I knew, Gordon. I seem to have become enmeshed in an acutely secret group and trusted by at least two of the four comprising it. One of the more tantalising aspects is that, whether their names are false or not, of the two men concerned – let's call them Ring A and Ring B – Ring A is a Vietnamese but Ring B a Lao. One clue is that my driver last saw his younger brother, Ring B, in Sam Neua about thirty years ago. Rings A and B are both around the same age and, from what little I have learnt so far, Sunthorn is certainly a northern family name as is Ring A. A number of Vietnamese northerners "voted with their feet" after the debacle at Dien Bien Phu in 1954, so to have a northern officer in the southern army is commonplace. That's why I speak Vietnamese with a northern accent: it is slightly easier to learn and there was no shortage of folk to practise with among my Jungle Warfare School students. If only we knew something about Rings C and D. Talk about needles and haystacks! Where do we start?' He gave a hollow laugh.

'But started you have,' countered Parks. 'Wait one. I'll call for a file.' His secretary brought it in and Gordon leafed through it. 'Ah, here we are: *It is the firm opinion of the SDECE and the CIA that, were only these sources to be found and exploited, there would be a firm lead into the Laos part of the Indo-China maze with a one-off chance of a more than rewarding result.*' He closed the file. 'It looks like you have stumbled on to what both French and American intelligence already had a slight clue about. Before your disquisition, I'd have said that the likelihood of our finding the sources were less than slim in that the chances of any European ever even stumbling onto one ring, let alone two, were even slimmer. So, by that reasoning, you've already come a long way. What have we got? Ring B here in Vientiane with a brother who is your driver; Ring A who might just be traceable through Central Training Command in Saigon. It shouldn't be too difficult to contact CTC through our channels. Princess Golden Fairy working in London and her sister Princess Jasmine here in Vientiane – what the one knows so, presumably, does the other. Even if their parents know nothing about the rings the two princesses are certainly a step in the King's direction. Who else can we think of as being useful? How about, let me think, the Chief Bonze in the royal capital? How, I wonder, could we use him?'

Gordon Parks called for his secretary again. 'Bring me what we have about the Chief Bonze, please.'

'One thing we mustn't do,' Rance said, more thinking out loud that addressing his remarks to the other man, 'is to tell HE. That'd be fatal. Just like the visit I paid to MR 2 ... Gordon ... I'm guilty of not telling you everything. I've just this minute remembered something that could conceivably be of use and have a bearing on the subject,' and he slapped himself on the forehead in disgust. 'Earlier on I told you about the quarrel in the jungle between Ring A and the Thai. Well, when I went up to MR 2, I passed through the Thai artillery lines where I met one of my Jungle Warfare School ex-students. You may think it strange that the Thais sent gunners on those courses but sometimes they did. Anyway, this man started telling me about the Thai battalion commander making the attack that we later saw from the chopper. We were interrupted by my predecessor who couldn't see why I was hanging back talking. I never learnt what it was that the Gunner Captain wanted to say although he was on the point of telling me something confidential except, and here I must apologise, that the battalion commander was none other than Major Mana Varamit under the alias of Chok Di. Surely, with your contacts, you could get some background information on him or, better still, you could fix a meeting between us.'

'Sure, I could talk to the Yanks but whether I could arrange eyeball to eyeball contact is only a remote chance. They are extremely sensitive about the Thais and I'd have to give them a better reason than the Major being a one-time Guiding Officer of yours. Leave it with me and I'll see what I can do. The coincidence is too remarkable not to pursue.'

There was a knock on the door and the secretary entered with a folder which she gave to Parks. He studied it for a short while then looked up. 'Not a lot here, I'm afraid. His name is long and cumbersome – Phra Maha (which merely means 'Holy Great') Phannyana Maha Thera. He has been in the royal capital for twenty-five years. Before that he was the abbot at Sam Neua. Your driver could, surely, be a valid link to him. Whether or not you too are allowed to have contact with him is another matter. He is getting on in years and is hard of hearing. Doesn't seem to be a great deal of scope there but, next time you're up in Luang Prabang, why not call on him. If it were possible to fix him up with a hearing aid I'd have funds to help you out.'

'Gordon, there should be no problem for my driver as he studied in the Sam Neua wat under the Chief Bonze when the latter was abbot there. I might be a protocol problem.' Rance relapsed into thought then, 'I think I've got it. We would have to wait until Route 13 is declared safe to drive along as it would invite suspicion to fly one's driver up there in the Beaver. I can't see much chance of the road opening before the ceasefire is declared but that can't be so far distant. One of the advantages of having "to dwell a pause" because of travelling restrictions is that I can the better choose my moment to tackle Leuam without forcing it – and, anyway, nothing may come out of it, so far-fetched and remote is it.'

Gordon shook his head. 'Nevertheless, it would be wrong not to squeeze the lemon dry, hoping it will be bitter for the other fellow and not for us. There's so much still left unexplained,' he said, glancing at his diary. 'Let us think about it over these next few days. Back to the present: it is nearly closing time. Have you told HE anything about your meeting with the LPF except that you wanted his permission to go ahead and fix it? No. In that case go and tell him that you've fixed the dinner and have a provisional date. Tell him the guest list isn't firm but that the LPF are happy for three of their men to come ... oh, and before I forget, the Yanks are still trying to trace Mlle. Käysone Bouapha. One woman of that name was educated in the Patrice Lumumba University in Moscow. When the CIA get any collateral, they'll go firm. Meanwhile they request you try and find out who is running her: they also said to remember one of the characteristics of a sleeping dictionary – it always opens at the same place.'

He had left Singha in his office. As he opened the door, the dog rose slowly to his feet, stretched luxuriously and came jumping up, wagging his tail in happiness at seeing the nice man who fed him, exercised him and loved him. Rance stroked his silken head.

'You may be ugly but at least you're something I can understand. Wait here, boy,' he said softly. 'I've got to go and see my boss,' and pushing the dog gently down, left the office, locking the door behind him.

He knocked on the door of the Ambassador's office and waited until he heard the nasal invitation to enter. 'Good afternoon, Your Excellency. Forgive me disturbing you. I thought you'd be interested to learn that Soth Petrasy has accepted my invitation provisionally for 19 January. He will confirm this later. I'll also warn the Chinese: I think they'll be obliging as it's to their advantage too. I'll arrange a Lao or Chinese meal, not a European one although I'll provide bread, wine and cheese.'

'Well done, Jason. This is a most welcome development. You seem to have made a good impression on these people in a short space of time. I dare say it's because you speak Lao. I hear it favourably commented on quite often.'

'Your own attitude to them, sir, is also of significance,' responded Rance equivocally.

That Thursday evening Mlle. Kaysorn Bouapha felt more confident than usual. She had been sent for and told how important her mission was. What report had she for them? Like many Asian girls not used to associating with Europeans, she had mistaken polite bonhomie for subdued passion. She therefore wrongly reported that she was not far off winning over the Englishman physically and, under the correct circumstances, could get him to commit himself. As he was a keen linguist, she had further recommended that her pupil's linguistic ability was sufficiently good for her to implement, now, the first and easier part of their plan. Accordingly, they had given her a classified manual to give to him as a present, 'to improve his vocabulary'. They would tell her further what to do after he had accepted it. It was in the bag that she carried upstairs to his room for his lesson.

She found her pupil more than preoccupied, almost hostile. Rance was torn between anger at being used and relief at knowing who was running the Lao girl even if it was those clumsy Russians again. However, he tried not to show that he had any quarrel with her as, even presuming the chain of left-wing personalities did not include Bounphong, it was just possible that their tenuous contact might be spoilt. So he smiled insouciantly at her and bade her sit. Whatever else might ensue, he still had to play his part and she was an insistent teacher.

'Did you celebrate Christmas or do you feel that *Boun Noën* is no longer apt?' he asked. If he had expected her to give a hint of any Communist-inspired aversion to that festival, he was disappointed. A radiant smile lit up her face making it almost pretty.

'Oh no, oh no. In fact I have brought you a present,' she exclaimed and opened her handbag. She gave him a small book wrapped in gaudy paper. His heart sank as he had nothing to offer her in return and being the recipient of presents embarrassed him. He was embarrassed even more when he saw what it was. He studied the title and noticed the security caveat on it – *lab*, meaning 'secret'. It was a Royal Lao Army manual on counter-subversion. She watched his expression, noticing the hardening of his eyes. Maybe it had to be the other method after all. He did not open the manual but wrapped it up in the paper and handed it back to her.

'Thank you for thinking that I could improve my military vocabulary by bringing this to me but I must return it. I am not entitled to such a publication, only the RLA is. If they were to give it to me, in my office or in theirs, it would be perfectly in order. To take this type of material from anyone who is not entitled to it, is a breach of trust, is against my charter and makes me into a spy. Tell those who gave it to you to give me what I am telling you.' His eyes bored into hers, making her drop her gaze in feminine confusion.

'I'm sorry, *Colonen*. I didn't know. Are you sure you won't change your mind? I can't believe there's any harm in what this book says. I'm sure it won't be new to you but it will be a great aid to your military vocabulary,' and she smiled winsomely.

'No. Please realise that I have no intention of putting myself in a compromising situation. Now, be sensible. Let us get on with our lesson. Today let's talk about what and where you have studied. That is going to be more use to me right now ...' but however hard he tried to bring the conversation round he could get no indication of her having been farther afield than Saigon and Bangkok.

'I've come here to give you back this manual. I couldn't make him take it yesterday.' She was almost in tears. 'He said it would make him a spy if he kept it. I did try very hard but he seemed angry inside. No, I didn't manage to look at any of his engagements in his diary this time but I did see an invitation from the Indian ambassador for a luncheon party on Sunday, 7 January. The other method, did you say? Yes, I think I know how to make him fall for me. You know his early morning walking habits over the weekends? Why not on the Sunday afternoon after the party? If you can get ready by then I'll try my best. I'll have a wooden shutter open in the bedroom nearest his upstairs study. You can put your hearing thing in one of the wardrobes. I've worked it all out. The servants in the back won't hear a thing in the morning, he'll have the dog with him and you can fix the rest, can't you? Yes, it's on the far side of the house from the main Thad Luang road. I'm sure it'll be successful this time and yet,' she snivelled again, 'he's a hard man to predict.'

January 1973. Vientiane, Laos: At a quarter to five in the morning of Sunday, 7 January, while it was yet dark and cold, Rance got up and dressed. Singha wagged his tail, eyeing him ecstatically. A few minutes later he unlocked the front door, let himself and the dog out, shut the door and disappeared into the darkness for his morning walk. Shortly afterwards a shadowy figure quietly opened the front gate and went up to the front door. He had seen that Rance had not locked it behind him when he left so presumed it could be opened. Rance had, in fact, locked himself out, as the door had a Yale lock, and the house was still secure because, being the suspicious man that he was, he had shut and bolted his bedroom windows before leaving. The man, fumbling at the door, paused as he heard a noise from the servants' quarters and, deciding that discretion was the better part of valour, left as surreptitiously as he had come, the small parcel that he had brought with him still clutched in his hand. He'd have to tell them that he'd been unable to get in, so risk their ire.

Rance always went a different route, walking or jogging. It was such an elementary precaution and he had been interested when, chatting with the new Soviet Defence Attaché had cryptically said, 'Don't forget always to go a different way when you take your exercise. It doesn't matter now, but later.' He paused and grinned. 'I know why you keep so fit! When you die, you die in good trim!' Rance had grinned at that unexpected shaft of humour and had taken the lesson to heart even more. On his return six and a half hours and about eighteen miles later, Khian An came to greet him, took a tired but happy dog by the scruff of the neck and hosed him down. That done, he was wiped dry and given his meal. The house boy said that a friend had sent a messenger during the morning and had invited him and his wife out that afternoon. The *Tan Colonel* was due at the Indians soon and the house boy's young brother-in-law, Samay, would be called over to mind the two kids, Jengko and Noi, and would watch the house, just in case, until Rance came back. 'May we have your permission to go?'

'Sure, no problem,' and Rance went upstairs to clean up and relax before his luncheon date at 12.30.

Lunch at the Indian Ambassador's residence was a pleasant, low-key affair. There were not many other guests and his host and hostess were as charming as all Indians can be when they stop trying to imitate Europeans. Rance withstood some good-natured teasing on his bachelor status. At half past two he excused himself and left on foot. It took him twenty minutes to reach his villa. The front door was open and there, on the floor and a chair in the hall, were two enormous temple rubbings of Angkor Wat in the Khmer Republic. He frowned and went upstairs to get out of his tidy clothes. Halfway up on the landing, his dog, lying grotesquely on his back, opened one sleepy eye and thumped his tail before being overcome by sleep again. Then Rance heard it, the noise of the air conditioner switched on in the main guest room. *How unusual to have left it on after its weekly cleaning*, he thought, meaning to go and switch it off when he'd changed. He went to his own room, undressed, showered, put on a casual shirt and a sarong and, bare-footed, went and opened the guest room door. He stared in disbelief as he saw Mlle. Kaysorn Bouapha lying in bed. The windows and the mosquito-proof, wooden-framed shutters were closed except for one which was just ajar, making the area around the bed brighter than the rest of the room. Rance quietly went over to the bed and looked down. The girl opened her eyes and, sitting up, pushed back the bedclothes, revealing her nakedness. She answered his unspoken question.

'You didn't take my first present so I've brought you two more. The temple rubbings downstairs and me. Both are yours if you want them.'

Her long black tresses had been undone and her hair came down to her waist. She had small breasts and her nipples stood out, firm and demanding. The vee of the vagina and thighs was matched by the larger vee where her legs were apart. All the pent-up emotions and uncertainties of the past weeks throbbed in

Rance's veins and he looked at her hungrily for a long moment. He then swiftly moved over to the opened window, shut it fast and put the shutter into place, which would have made it too dark to photograph. He glanced up at her face but, instead of encouragement, ecstasy or expectancy, she had a look of despair, of resignation. Was she acting or for real? Her face became distorted and ugly. She had become afraid.

'Who sent you?' he hissed, bending over her. 'Why all this effort and what do you want?'

Before she could answer the telephone rang downstairs. Rance went into the passage and heard Khian An answering. So he was back! A brief conversation buzzed below and then the receiver was replaced. Rance, leaning over the banisters, asked who it was.

'Wrong number,' called the house boy.

Wrong tack, echoed Rance. He went slowly back into the bedroom. Kaysorn lay where he'd left her but the window was open as it had been when he first went into the room. 'I'll try better this time,' she pleaded. She had made sure the 'hearing thing' was still safe under her folded clothes on the chair by the bed.

Rance went over to her, slapped her face hard and left the room. He dressed, putting on kit suitable to go walking in and went downstairs. He saw a worried Khian An and the two children.

'Don't worry! But why are you back so early? Your friend never invited you?' The house boy shook his head. 'No, I don't understand it either. Don't worry about me – and tell Kaysorn Bouapha never to come back. Tell her to take those temple rubbings with her. Lock the front door after her and then go and search every shelf, cupboard and drawer in the spare room.'

He called his dog and left the house. As he walked, he somehow felt he had to give his body a caning. It had taken him all his self-control not to have laid her. He was in no way averse to having a tumble provided it was discrete, decorous, non-commercial and not fraught with untoward consequences. First the European woman, Yvonne Grambert, then the ludicrous obscenity at the Soviet swimming pool – thank the Lord that nut Nechaev had been sent packing. And now this creature. His feet led him towards a rice swamp, wide and deep. He started to cross it, feet instantly filthy with black mud, bare legs scratched by coarse grass. *But it would have been easy to have had her, you nearly did. Are you chicken?* one part of him queried. *Yes, I suppose I am. If it is a question of a dirty weekend, there's always Bangkok. I've always been averse to dirtying my own door step.* He sent Singha in front. Where he did not have to swim, Rance followed. When he saw the dog swimming, he tried another tack. *But why was the window open? Peeping Tom with a telescope or camera? Well, you shut it, didn't you? Yes, I did – second nature. But why did the house boy come back so early? Didn't you hear him say that his friend knew nothing about it? Balls to them all. What do the Chinese say when the enemy's not identified? – Clear spear, easy rattle – dark arrow, hard beware. Too erudite for me. Get on crossing this swamp.*

Just before dusk, Khian An peering worriedly into the gloom, was relieved to see man and dog turn into the gate but shocked at their mucky, muddy state. He hosed them both down.

'I am sorry to tell you that I was couldn't get him to commit himself. We were interrupted by a telephone call. Only the lad Samay was there and there were no difficulties with the props.'

'Did you try as hard as you said you would and we think you could?' she was silkily asked. 'Answer me truthfully.'

She momentarily hesitated and said, with eyes downcast, 'I did my best.'

'Go in and see the Doctor. Don't worry. It won't hurt. You can go home after that.' A few minutes later she reappeared and was dismissed. After she had gone there was silence for a while then the Doctor appeared.

'I don't know which way you wanted it, but she is still a virgin.'

Monday, 8 January, was the first working Monday of the month, was always the day for an Attaché lunch and the host today was the South Vietnamese Attaché, Colonel Chi.

Rance arrived at the Colonel's house shortly before 1 o'clock and told Leuam to take Singha back to the villa before breaking off for his own meal and that he, Rance, would find his own way back to the embassy afterwards. At the luncheon there were no Communists, only representatives of the Free World and some RLA Generals, amongst whom was the Deputy Commander-in-Chief, Major General Sisavat Abhay, who glanced at Rance on his entering the room. Rance wanted to ask him about visiting one of those captured North Vietnamese Army advisers that Colonel Chi had previously mentioned when they had met at the Prime Minister's New Year party. *Now's not the time or place.*

'I was at the Jungle Warfare School in Malaysia about six years back, first on a course, then as a Guiding Officer but never got a graduation brooch!' Colonel Chi had then said to Rance's surprise. 'After that I went as a tactics instructor at the NCOs' School at Nha Trang, on the coast, to the northeast of Saigon.'

'Yes, I've been there,' the Englishman had answered, smiling. 'Before coming here I was the boss of the Jungle Warfare School. I'm wanting to contact my last Guiding Officer, Major Le Dâng Khoã. Do you know him? My predecessor also mentioned that there were some captured North Vietnamese advisers to the Pathet Lao who have turned "rallier". Do you think you could use your good offices in getting me an interview with any of them? Or, if not, who do you advise I should contact?'

Colonel Chi had looked hard at Rance before replying. 'As for your first point, there's no difficulty. I have a friend in the CTC and I'll send him a signal. If he sparks, I'll let you know on Monday at the lunch. If you want to write to Major Le Dâng Khoã give me the letter to post as foreigners' letters don't get delivered to our servicemen. But your second point: this is a tricky one, Jason, as officially such people don't exist although you and I know that they do. My advice is to see Major General Sisavat Abhay. Don't rush the conversation but ask him if you could possibly have permission to talk to a new man who was brought in six weeks ago. His name is Tâ Tran Quán. Tell the General why you are interested and remind him of your previous dealings with the Vietnamese at the school and that you wish to update your tactical knowledge and send the British Army your findings.'

Pre-lunch drinks over, they sat down to eat in strict protocol pecking order so Rance found himself at the end of the table talking to the garrulous Gurganus. Opposite him was the Thai Colonel. After lunch, coffee and liqueurs were offered and Rance had a chance to talk with General Sisavat. 'I would like to come and pay my New Year's respects to you, General, if I could. Would tomorrow suit you?'

'No, please come on Wednesday if you can. I am busy tomorrow. Come to my office at 10.30.' The General soon departed and soon afterwards the other Attachés made to go. Rance made sure he was the last to leave.

'Goodbye, Colonel Chi. Thank you for a superb meal. Before I go I would like to present you with this,' and he took out of his pocket a small brooch with the Jungle Warfare School emblem on it; an upright No. 1 Mark 3 bayonet on a green background. 'You said you never got one of these when you graduated. I found I had this one so please accept it. I am sorry you were so long without it.'

Rance pinned it on, Chi standing formally to attention. This American habit had spread to the School and, such was its reputation, US-orientated students were proud to be presented with one when they 'graduated' at the end of their courses of instruction. Chi thanked Rance effusively.

'I didn't forget about the man, Tâ Tran Quán, who has not yet got "rallier" status so he is referred to as a "prisoner". I mentioned it to General Abhay but obviously I can't promise you anything. As regards Major Le Dâng Khoã, I've had a reply from CTC in Saigon. Central Training Command could get no details but they regret he is listed as "Missing in Action". Apparently it happened not long after he was with you.'

Before he left the embassy that afternoon, Rance called in on Gordon Parks to give him the latest news. He described the relevant details of his confrontation with his teacher and discussing possible implications, he continued, 'I have also arranged to call on General Sisavat in two days' time. I've had odd glances and snide remarks about being the "official spy" from various senior officers of GHQ recently and, hyper-sensitive though I may be, I'd hate to think it was anything to do with my relationship with what the Yanks call "Brother Gook". So I am going to see him and put my cards on the table and tell him about the party I'm giving for the LPF and the Chinese. I gather it's an Attaché first and he'd be bound to hear about it and probably equally bound to draw some unflattering conclusions.'

Gordon Parks thought about it for a few seconds and said, 'There'll be no harm in that and who knows but some good may accrue.'

'My other piece of news is that Ring A is reported Missing In Action. As far as we are concerned that is of academic interest only although, remembering it was he who started all this off, I personally am sorry that we'll never have the chance of meeting up again. It would have been interesting.'

On Wednesday morning at 10.30 sharp, Rance was shown into the office of the Deputy C-in-C RLA at Phone Kheng. He was bidden to sit down and coffee was brought in. Conversation was banal and the General seemed content to wait for Rance to give his real reasons for coming to see him. To use the occasion for such greetings, even though it was not the Lao New Year, was certainly a polite gesture but it could have been made at the Prime Minister's party ten days previously. In fact, he was glad that the Englishman had asked to come and see him as he had something he wanted to say and this neatly gave him the opportunity without having to take the initiative. In any case these contacts were sometimes interestingly fruitful.

'General, you must forgive me for intruding on your time in this fashion and approaching such a busy and important man as yourself directly but, under the circumstances, I feel that you will understand my reasons when I have explained them to you.' Rance looked the General straight in the eyes and the General looked back unflinchingly. *I've a hard man in front of me*, each thought to himself. Then they both smiled simultaneously and so dispelled what little tension had arisen.

'You are always welcome, *Tan Colonen*, and I appreciate your concern,' purred the General. 'The British are different from the French and the Americans.'

'I find myself in a new and strange position,' Rance continued. 'I have been active in fighting Communism in Asia for nearly twenty-five years. I find their way of life totally unacceptable and I'd do almost anything I could to frustrate their expansion and intolerance of individuals, yet here I find that, as the accredited military representative of my government to the Kingdom of Laos, I must behave neutrally. As a soldier it used to be my duty to operate against them in the jungle, killing or capturing them whenever possible. Now, no longer, but, as second best, I would like to debrief a "rallier" so that I can update my own tactical knowledge and send the British Army my findings, sources guaranteed but unnamed. Compared with my dealings with the Communists before, the situation here is quite different. My policy is, and must be, one of non-interfering and never criticising, and this applies to both sides, the Royal Lao Government and the Lao Patriotic Front. The quarrel is amongst you Lao people; it is not mine. This means that I have to conduct my dealings with both sides along the same lines. I aim to get to know everybody as well as I can and this has led to contacts with the LPF, the Chinese, the Soviets, even to the extent of inviting them to my house. What I want to tell you, General, is this.'

As Rance spoke, the General's eyes narrowed and bored into his with ferocious intensity. If Rance felt discomforted, he did not show it. 'I want you to understand that, however much I might contact them, my sympathies are wholly on the side of the non-communists, despite the contacts that I make. I want you to believe that I am not trying to do what the English describe as "running with the hare and hunting with the hounds". I have also now been here long enough to have understood the situation in my embassy as it was before I came here and, in one respect, as it still is. I know it is probably not normal for an Attaché to say such things but, for me at least, few things are normal – yet. Perhaps they will be one day.'

The General's eyes lost their fixed intensity and he paused before replying. 'My friend, thank you for that. Indeed this is a curious situation for you but, remember, it is almost second nature for us Lao people, so long has it been continuing. Whole families have been split with brothers taking opposite sides but, we, the Lao people, have our own way of conducting our affairs. Brother will still meet and talk with brother as father will to son despite politically being divided because our blood is thick – thicker at times than is our skin.

'Sitting here I have watched you, so to speak. I have had my doubts and I have to be careful. I know you British still value loyalty and I know your standards are high. That is why even a small deviation from them is noticeable. What did I read in a recent edition of the *Paris-Match* journal? Oh yes; "A high standard brings its own penalties of expectation",' the General quoted in French. 'When my worries overcame me I had to check – the language teacher whom I sent returned the manual and is still a virgin – and I am now satisfied that what you have said is so. It was your astuteness that got Colonel Nechaev removed, so I learnt,' he continued to Rance's amazement, which must have shown in his face as the General smiled, 'and as a reward you may have access to the latest North Vietnamese prisoner, Tâ Tran Quán, who came into our hands after he was picked up wounded on 18 November, in the Long Cheng area. My records tell me that you visited there on the same day. You can fix a meeting through the Director of Psyops, Brigadier General Etam Singvongsa.'

John Chambers picked up the report that had reached him in the first bag of the year. He sat in his under-heated office in the nondescript building near the south bank of the Thames and, from time to time, looked up from the paper and through the window, as though contemplatively regarding the dismal January scene of dank cloud, sombre buildings, hurrying pedestrians and the unending stream of London traffic. But he was lost to the outside world, excitedly engrossed with the piece of paper in his hand as he tried to grasp the tremendous implications of what he had read: '... the new DA, in the five weeks since his arrival has again been the target of Soviet efforts to compromise him, is currently being targeted by a native female operator who is being monitored. He has managed, by an amazing coincidence, to be in a position not only to help penetrate the LPF movement but also, albeit just a remote chance, to reach the King as well. Before these events and hopeful future trends are expanded on in detail below, it is germane to mention that the "Soviet Swimming Pool Saga" which led to the summary dismissal of Colonel Nechaev was only due to Colonel Rance's alertness and his giving me enough details to work on – as previously reported. Also, at present, it is difficult to see how his contacts with the LPF can best be utilised. What is now needed is a slow and careful period of consolidation.'

There followed descriptions in detail including a short paragraph mentioning the coincidence of the one-time Guiding Officer of Thai students being at Long Cheng when Rance visited and the unfinished conversation with the ex-student, the Thai Major's treacherous behaviour, the report of his death but the inability, later, to find his body although a search was made. At the end of the letter were a summary of events, a strong plea not to let anyone outside SIS and CIA know about the rings and the strange signs until cleared by Head of Station, Vientiane, and as many personal details of relevant characters as were known.

It was tantalising not knowing any more but it seemed a

vindication of the trust Maurice Burke had put in the Brits. At their next meeting they would have to decide how best to put their strange demand to the many archivists who would have to cast a wide net for any morsel about the background of the case to be discovered, as requests for matters not obviously connected with the politics of the moment would be contested.

Rance was greatly relieved to learn who had organised his language teacher and why. He must tell Gordon Parks about it and that it was not as the CIA had tentatively thought, even though there had been no collateral evidence – but fancy General Sisavat linking him with the posting of Colonel Nechaev!

'Leuam,' he called to his driver, 'go to my villa not the embassy.' It was time for a talk with Ring B's brother.

Leuam Sunthorn was a quiet, unresponsive man who kept himself to himself. He had been the DA's driver since 1956. Living near the embassy with his wife and seven children, he was one of the more fortunate citizens who had escaped the war and could live in relative security. Rance thought that the man was slightly deaf and had no imagination, yet he was happy with the prestige that went with a flagged car; in short, an ideal man for the job. With, at last, the tide seeming to be turning in his favour, Rance decided it was time to tackle Leuam and find out, if possible, how he fitted into the pattern. At the villa the car was driven inside and the front gate shut. Leuam momentarily demurred when invited upstairs for a chat but Rance insisted. As the driver was taking off his shoes, as the Lao did when they entered a private dwelling, Rance quickly went ahead into his bedroom and, taking the ring from its hiding place, slipped it into his pocket. Leuam came upstairs and the two men sat down in the open-sided room where Rance had had his Lao lessons. He called to Khian An for two soft drinks and, when they came, he drank a silent toast to 'Dame Fortune, that fickle lady'.

'Leuam, welcome to my house. I am new to this country and want to learn as much as I can. This takes a long time and, now that I have met most of those with whom I have to do my official work, I want to learn about my staff. You told me about the time when you were a boy and went to the wat in Sam Neua. I understand the system how most Lao boys spend a year studying under the bonzes. Can you remember the name of the abbot under whom you studied?'

'Yes. Phannyana Maha Thera.'

'Where is he now? Still in Sam Neua?'

'No. As far as I know he is in Luang Prabang.' Rance heaved an inward sigh – almost of pleasure. Luck seemed to be running his way.

'How far is the wat from your village?'

'Not very far. About two hours' walk.'

'When did you enter the wat?'

Leuam pondered. 'Let me see. I went to the wat when I was about thirteen years old. I went for one year but the abbot kept me there for three. I left in about 1949 when I was about sixteen. That's how old the bonzes told me I was.'

'And where did you learn to drive?'

'After leaving Sam Neua I went to Hanoi and joined the French army. They taught me at their driving school in Hanoi.'

'How long did you serve the French as a driver?'

'Until 1954, the year of the battle of Dien Bien Phu. That was the end of the French army and as I had no love for the North Vietnamese Tongkinese, I managed to run away back to Sam Neua and, not knowing anyone except the abbot, I went to him for advice.'

'Why didn't you go home and settle down in your village?'

'Because by that time I had no village, no home and no parents. My mother was dead and my father had disappeared.' As Leuam did not choose to elaborate on this bald statement, Rance paused before asking a question on a less painful topic.

'What did the abbot say when you asked him for advice?'

'He said I should try and find work, marry and raise a family. This was important as too many of my people had been lost already.'

'What did he mean by that?' Leuam again paused and looked distressed. Once more Rance did not press him for an answer. 'Did you then come to Vientiane?'

'Yes. I was lucky. I couldn't go back to my village although it was so near as there was nothing left of it. I had to start afresh somewhere else.'

Yet again Leuam gave the impression of unwillingness to give details ... it seemed that he had drifted southwards managing to get enough work as he went to keep him alive. He was lucky to have been employed by the British embassy and, a couple of years later, had saved enough money to marry and start a family.

Rance had noticed Leuam's resistance to talking about his childhood and this could be put down to some nameless disaster if not to faded memory.

'Tell me, Leuam, about your brother. You said you had a younger brother but you didn't know whether he was dead or alive. Was that the war or was he too young to be involved in the fighting?'

Before Leuam could answer, Rance took his ring out of his pocket. He slipped it on the little finger of his right hand and, saying nothing put his hands on his knees, fingers splayed so Leuam had to see it. Leuam saw it, looked at Rance, who took the ring off and gave it to Leuam to examine, which he did intently. He was obviously awe-struck.

'Did my brother give you that?' was his surprising question, asked in a husky whisper.

'No, Leuam, he didn't, but he knows that I have it. One of his three other friends gave it to me.'

'Is that why you have come to Laos as the Defence Attaché?'

'No, but it's why I'm asking you these questions. First your brother is using your family name and calling himself Bounphong Sunthorn. He is part of the LPF political team in their HQ near the Morning Market. I have spoken to him privately but for less than a minute. I learn from General Sisavat that brothers talking to each other in this country is natural. I hope your brother comes to a party here on 19 January. I want you to be here to open the car doors and help with the parking. I know the three LPF guests will bring a PL escort but that makes no odds. I believe he would be willing to use you to talk to me but, in some ways which I do not yet understand, he is not his own master.'

Rance paused to let Leuam take all that in and was relieved

when his driver slowly nodded assent. 'He knows that you are my driver and so will be prepared for your presence. Will you tell me, if you can, how it is that your paths have led so differently?'

'I am about five years the elder. As you know, every Buddhist boy is supposed to spend a year of his life in a wat and it had been decided that I should go when the Japanese allowed me. They came to rule us when I was much smaller and then they suddenly left so my father went and spoke with the abbot. The day before I went from my village at Ban Liet, I remember some strangers came from the east. Some of them and some of us went to the wat in Sam Neua the next day … then some men came and killed some of us … and burnt down the village and killed all the villagers … and the abbot then took my brother and three other little boys, with my father and their fathers, inside the wat. Two days later the others left. My father called me over and before he said goodbye, he showed me a ring like yours. I'd never seen the inscription before but that's not surprising. Rings are often worn by Lao and Thai men, as you will have seen for yourself, so they excite no comment. But the abbot swore me to secrecy never to talk about my father, my brother, the others or the ring to anyone, except a person who was wearing one like that which you are wearing. This is the first time I've seen one since then. I've never mentioned any of this to anyone except when I passed through Sam Neua again and the abbot spoke to me about the secret.'

'Why did you stay three years and not one year? Was that because you had nowhere to go?'

'Yes, that's right. Also I had no one I could go to. By the end of the first year it seemed natural that I should stay at the wat. I was young and the significance of losing all I had only struck me when I left. I don't think the abbot really wanted me to go but he saw that I'd made up my mind and he let me. I don't know anything else. Can I go now?' he ended abruptly.

'Wait a moment, my friend. Don't worry that I will betray your secret. I won't. Thank you for telling me so much. When eventually Route 13 opens, you will drive me up to Luang Prabang. There you can meet your abbot, now the Chief Bonze. I also hope to meet him. I'm sure he will understand. But, please, feel free to come and talk to me whenever you have anything on your mind. There are many aspects of this that I don't understand. One day I hope to: until then you and I will act as if the abbot had sworn both of us to secrecy.'

'So it was the right-wing, not the left who put the woman in your path. I admit I wasn't expecting that, I must say, but I'm glad that you have squared your pitch, so to speak, with Sisavat and his lot. I'll tell the Yanks about the woman not being who they thought she was. By the way, I did tell you what they had found out about Mana Varamit, didn't I? I thought I had. As regards Leuam's story – that gives us some new and useful background information. It will also make a meeting with the Chief Bonze infinitely more positive. It could also provide a motive for what we've yet fully to get to grips with, namely revenge for this catastrophe that seems to have hit the village of Ban Liet. This gives us a whole lot of eggs to tread on,' observed Gordon Parks.

'Yes,' answered Rance, 'and that will make them even harder to hatch. It doesn't bring Operation Stealth any closer, does it?'

'No, I can't see that it does unless your talking with the Chief Bonze somehow helps and it looks as if you have an embryo Operation Four Rings as just a high priority."

Jason shrugged.

'Play this just as close to your chest as you can and leave me to tell London what is happening.'

On the evening of Friday, 12 January, Rance went round to Villa Haekham. He felt he could lose nothing by bringing up the topic of the ring. Remembering what her elder sister had said in London, it might be awkward but Jasmine was so friendly and natural a person that whatever transpired would probably be genuine. She met him by the front door and they ceremoniously greeted each other, she breaking into English as she did from time to time.

'Why, *Tan Colonen*, it's good to see you. How are you?'

'Well, *Tu Nong*. And you I hope.'

'Yes, please come along in.'

They sat down at the highly polished table and Rance got out his note book. 'I've learnt a lot recently, not all of it language. I had to sack that paid teacher I told you about. She was being devious and embarrassing.'

'Oh, that's dreadful. I must admit that the attitude of some of my fellow countrymen and quite a lot of foreigners to women have meant that a single man is an obvious target. If he is a diplomat, rich and single, even more so. I take it that your teacher is unmarried. I'm glad for your sake you've avoided what could have been a trap.'

'What I'd really like to ask you, *Tu Nong*, is to tell me the significance of this,' and he wrote a letter that looked like a 9 with a curly tail.

She looked at him for a longer time than a normal question would have warranted, then answered him as he thought she would. 'I thought you knew about our silent consonant and the "or" sound having the same letter,' she said. 'Why do you ask what you already know?'

'I'm interested because I've come across it in strange circumstances. Twice on the inside of the little finger of the right hand, almost as though it was a code mark, once on a Lao's hand and once on a Vietnamese's. Both were men of around the same age. And *kha* on this,' and he dramatically produced the ring from his pocket and put it on the table in front of her. He watched her reaction intently.

She stared at it, fascinated, then picked it up – almost with revulsion – and examined it closely. She gave it back to him, clearly agitated. 'How many people know you've got hold of this?'

'Only a very few. For instance, the man who gave it to me and your sister in London. I have learnt it is not a thing to flash about the place.'

'You have somehow been dragged into something that I have only seldom come across. It is a sign that could be innocuous because it is rare and only our royal family and a few bonzes of a particular sect know about it. It so happens that the Chief Bonze now in the royal capital is of that sect. But combined with *kha* meaning "kill", it takes on a most sinister aspect. It was taken as a secret sign of revenge in olden days. It fell out of use when the French came on the scene. I don't suppose more than a handful of important people know its real meaning, people like His Majesty and the Chief Bonze. If they saw it they'd suspect something drastic as the wearers, by tradition, are either killers themselves, as Buddhists sometimes are, or the target to be killed. It is not my place to advise a man, especially a man like you who has earned himself a name in high Lao society already but please, *Tan Colonen*, keep extra alert, always – and what I have said is a secret. I trust you.'

'If I had not trusted you with all my heart, *Tu Nong*, and if I had not the greatest respect for you, I would never have done what I have. Having told me so much, it almost seems unfair to ask you more – but may I?'

She nodded meekly and he continued. 'What I don't understand is how I came to be given this ring by a Vietnamese. I know two other men who know I know about the ring – both are Lao. What do you make of that? Also, would you expect Communists or non-communists to wear it?'

'That aspect would never have occurred to me had you not mentioned it. The tradition of the rings and the signs is so much older than modern politics. What I can say is that, whatever the partnership, even if it is non-communists who are involved, they will bind them far harder than the Communists bind each other together. As far as the other wearers are concerned, the fact that you are wearing it will mean that you have identified yourself with them to the extent that your other loyalties now take second place. That is the true implication of the ring. If His Majesty knew that you were in possession of a ring like this, he'd be most upset. I hope he never knows about it. But, please, one thing I beg of you.

Feel free to come and talk to me whenever you have something on your mind. Now shall we get on with our lesson?'

On Wednesday morning, 17 January, a staff officer from GHQ rang Rance in his office. 'Is the *Tan Colonen* free tomorrow, 18 January, at 11 o'clock? Good. Well, drive round the back of the main office block and park the car there. Someone will come and meet the *Tan Colonen*.' The caller rang off without identifying himself.

Rance put the ring in his pocket – *just in case*, as he said to himself. At GHQ, he was met by a squat Major, a Tai Dam, or Black Thai, who inhabit the general area of Dien Bien Phu and are so called because of their black clothes. 'Follow me,' he said and went in front to a block out of sight of the main building. A sentry armed with an M-16 rifle stood guard outside and a Military Policeman, who was carrying a captured Russian Makarev 9.5-milimetre pistol, unlocked the door. They went inside a small room with barred windows, used for interrogation of prisoners brought down from the main jail.

A man in his late thirties got up as they entered. His movements were slow as though it hurt him to move. He looked pallid but composed.

'*Chào Ông Tâ Tran Quán.* This is *Dại Tá* Rance, the British Defence Attaché. He has come to talk to you and he will explain his mission himself.'

Rance then explained, in Vietnamese, what his previous assignment was. 'I have come to discuss tactics with you. Please do not regard me as an enemy. I am like a doctor who is interested in the disease more than in the patient.'

The prisoner nodded, showing neither curiosity nor concern. The three of them sat around the table and started talking. Rance was glad the Black Thai Major was so fluent a Vietnamese speaker as some of the prisoner's military terminology baffled him when the conversation became involved in various types of patrol and ambush procedures. Rance was surprised at the prisoner's lack of detailed knowledge about tactics so asked him what his task had been.

'I was a Political Commissar.'

Rance recalled the cumbersome command structure and asked the Vietnamese if he could explain it. To demonstrate the better, he splayed out his fingers and the Englishman momentarily froze as, scarcely able to believe his eyes, he saw the sign of the 9 with the curly tail on the inside of the little finger on his right hand. The Major, slightly bored, noticed nothing, neither did the prisoner who was watching where his fingers were on the table. Rance turned to the Major.

'Would it be a nuisance to ask you to get a piece of paper and a coloured pencil? I'm afraid I haven't brought any and this is proving interesting enough to write down.'

'No problem. It'll take about five minutes to get the pencil,' he said, giving Rance a piece of paper. 'I'll go, as the guards don't know their way about. Just keep on talking.'

He got up and left the room. Rance took the ring out of his pocket and, out of sight under the table, slipped it on the little finger of his right hand. Covering it with his left hand he put both hands on the table. He looked at the Vietnamese straight between the eyes, a smile playing on his lips.

'Friend Tâ Tran Quán. Be not afraid. To prove I'm a friend, look here' and he revealed the ring. Tâ Tran Quán gazed at it fixedly then took Rance's hand, pulled the ring off his finger, looked underneath, sighed deeply and contentedly, and gave it back.

'The Thai shot me so I couldn't shoot him. I was slow because he used the name Chok Di, not Mana Varamit. By the time I recognised him, it was too late, otherwise I'd have killed him. He's the traitor,' was the completely unexpected answer – *the traitor?* – and, before Rance could find an answer, came another question. 'Did he die too?'

'I think he did but I'm not sure. No body was found.'

'Yes, it was a risk. I took it but he shot me before I could shoot him ... who gave you the ring?'

Rance had only time to say 'Le Dâng Khoã gave it to me.' before the Black Thai Major returned. Rance slipped the ring back into his pocket and found the rest of the interview an anti-climax. Nevertheless, he thanked both men most sincerely when he left.

The supplementary telegram from Head of Station, Vientiane, to London was decoded by the secretary and brought in to John Chambers during the weekly session with Maurice Burke. John read it, grinned and handed it over to the American to read. 'Take a gander at this, Dally lad. It's veered away from an Operation Stealth, which is where it ever was, almost a non-starter, and is morphing into something of an equally unexpected nature.'

The message was basically factual, giving details of Leuam's story, Princess Jasmine's reaction and the meeting with Tâ Tran Quán, Ring C: it stated a further situation report would be sent after the dinner party with the LPF and the Chinese. It also mentioned the end of the Mme. Bouapha story. It concluded by saying that a lot more thought was needed before advantage could be taken of the situation and no contingency plans had yet been made. It further cautioned that the link so far was tenuous in the extreme and it really did seem that the four rings were all part of the same plan. Hugely exciting! Ring D was not yet accounted for nor the King in Luang Prabang, even though the new Defence Attaché had established a good link with two of his nieces.

Maurice Burke read the message twice and whistled through his teeth. 'We've got to watch this like a cook watches milk on the boil – timing will be everything. But, Jiminy Cricket, it's fraught with difficulties.'

On the evening of 19 January, as previously arranged and duly confirmed, Mr Taunton and Mr Richardson, the garrulous Colombo Plan adviser, came round to the DA's villa shortly before 7 o'clock. The Chinese, in two cars, arrived at two minutes past and, as they were still getting out, the LPF group arrived, jam-packed in one car with two armed PL soldiers sitting in the front with the driver. Leuam slipped unobtrusively out of the shadows and opened one of the back doors. Rance opened the other and Soth Petrasy emerged first. Rance peered into the car and saw Bounphong Sunthorn sitting in the middle. Rance caught his eye and motioned with his head that he should get out of the other door. As Bounphong inched his way along the back seat, Rance stood by, looked over the roof of the car and saw that Leuam was ready. Rance turned and paid attention to the other guests, ushering them indoors. As was customary, they were asked to sign the visitors' book on the hall table. With good-natured courtesy, the Chinese had let Mr Taunton take Soth Petrasy inside and, once he had written his name, Soth turned to introduce the other LPF guests to the British Ambassador. Bounphong was not in the queue waiting to sign the book and Soth, obviously agitated, went outside the front door to see why he had not come into the house. Rance followed him and saw Bounphong come forward smiling happily.

'Comrade Soth. What do you think? After twenty-seven years I've found my elder brother!'

Rance turned and broke the news to the others. As the guests crowded round Bounphong and Leuam, congratulating them, he slipped the ring on his finger and, waiting until the rest had finished and drifted away inside the house, went up to Bounphong with his hands outstretched so the ring could be seen, took the other's right hand with his left and gave it a double shake, thereby effectively hiding the ring from any onlooker's sight.

'Thank you, thank you,' breathed Bounphong.

'*Bor pen nyang*,' answered Rance, using the almost meaningless 'never mind' phrase if only to cover the necessity of saying anything else. 'We'll meet again, won't we?'

The other man nodded his head imperceptibly and both men moved into the house, saying no more, to join the rest of the guests. The Englishman had taken off the ring by the time the others saw him. What with the hubbub of conversation and happy badinage which ensued, the evening passed quickly and successfully, although, for Rance, it was another anti-climax.

'Comrades, welcome to this serious meeting. You have been called together so that we can review our glorious revolutionary struggle in the light of our comrades' victory with the signing of the Vietnamese peace talks in Paris on 20 January 1973 and the progress we have made in the last quarter of 1972. All our work we had called Operation Stealth has now come out into the open, certainly as far as we are concerned but not yet as far as the rightist running dogs are concerned.'

Nga Sô Lưư, the Political Commissar of Office 95, was addressing a group of cadres not far from Dien Bien Phu. 'The fraternal socialist struggle in Indo-China between the glorious workers and the imperialist Americans and their lackeys has been so intensified on the political front that in Paris we have won a great victory. When the imperialist Americans started bombing Hanoi and Haiphong to try and lessen our resistance and conviction in the justice of our cause, they found our resolve, far from weakening, was being strengthened, so they called off their criminal and barbarous bombing attacks on 31 December. We fully believe it will not be long before we have won further victories by achieving the ceasefire in all Indo-China on our terms, when we will consolidate our victory by political and military action.'

He looked up at his audience most of whom were repelled by his dark, glassy eyes behind which were vacant pits where his soul should have been, and continued, 'As soon as the ceasefire is signed in Laos, there also will our struggle be continued in accordance with the latest directive. Of the greatest importance in achieving complete political victory was the appointment of four comrades who have been picked by the Central Committee of the Politburo. Two have yet to be put in position, one is already in his new location and one has, recently, been reported dead. Now we are one highly energetic revolutionary comrade short. The plan is that Comrade Le Dâng Khoã will be the military commander of the Lao Peoples' Liberation Army battalion that moves into Vientiane once that town has been neutralised, as we have insisted it will be. In fact, the protocols that will be the basis of what will be known as the Provisional Government of National Union, the PGNU, include that clause.

'Comrade Bounphong Sunthorn is already installed in Vientiane and, as well as having the correct relationship with our Soviet comrades as Co-Chairman of the Geneva Accords, has an equally correct relationship with our Chinese comrades. He has also established a healthy contact with the British Defence Attaché, so it seems – based on post-Nechaev policy – and as a result of what the English know as a Fellow Traveller, the Ambassador, Mr Taunton. Also the comrade's elder brother is the British DA's driver. We in Office 95 will exploit this relationship by sowing dissention and mistrust between our side and the right-wing clique. This we are working on.

'Comrade Thong Damdouane will move from northwest Laos as the Lao Patriotic Front representative on the neutralisation of Luang Prabang and take up residence there. His task will be equivalent to Comrade Bounphong Sunthorn's in Vientiane. It is with sadness that I have to report the death of Comrade Tâ Tran Quán under strange circumstances in the Long Cheng area. Briefly we have been successful in recruiting a new Thai comrade, once Major, now plain Comrade, Mana Varamit. Regrettably, his actual crossing over was clumsy and attracted the attention of some of the feudalist mercenaries he had been in charge of.' He took a piece of paper from one side of his desk. 'This is what the medical report has to say about the cranial wound he suffered: *the bullet's penetration subcutaneously bruised the thalamus and hippocampus fibrous regions.*' His audience stared at the Political Commissar with blank incomprehension so he hurried on with, 'What is not yet clear, and our Soviet friends are also concerned in this connection, is how it was Comrade Tâ Tran Quán so exposed himself to get shot and killed by the enemy. It has been found impossible to get confirmatory details from our military commander as the battlefield confusion was considerable. Unfortunately, our new comrade has yet to be fully debriefed because of his severe head wound. He was unconscious when picked up and is still suffering from severe amnesia. We had been expecting some communication of particular importance from him but until he recovers his memory, we must control our impatience. You may be comforted to know that, in other respects also, we are not unprepared as we have many comrades bravely struggling in the enemy's camp. For instance, we can monitor the US Army Attaché, the Air America airline office and the Australian embassy because their telephone operators are ours. As for the movements and schedules of the English Defence Attaché, they are all logged but, so far, we have yet to find any weak points that we could exploit. Some of the other Attachés, though, are disgusting,' he prudishly denounced.

On 20 February Rance made the discovery why he could never telephone anyone from his house: the dial had been set in such a way that it activated the wrong numbers. Subtract one and the system worked for all digits less one. And, from the ridiculous to the sublime, on 21 February, the ceasefire between the Royal Lao Government and the Lao Patriotic Front was signed in Vientiane.

8

April 1973. Laos: Once the cease-fire had been signed Rance felt it safe to motor to the royal capital, an all-day journey. He booked a room at the Phou Si hotel. 'I'll come back after my meal,' Leuam said as he locked the car, parked in the hotel compound. 'The car will be safe here. I have a friend in town I will stay with.'

Up in his room Rance stood under the cold water shower getting the grit and dust out of his hair and skin The hotel rooms were boastfully optimistic in that the taps for shower and basin had 'chaud' and 'froid' marked on them but it was never a question of 'hot' and 'cold' but water or no water. Luckily the system was working and, half an hour later, dressed in plain clothes and feeling fresh, he was sampling a venison steak at the outside rotunda. The Vietnamese manager, ears razor-sharp when foreigners talked among themselves, left him alone in his silence.

At 8 o'clock Leuam returned and came up to Rance at the counter where the Englishman was still silently sitting. Rance offered him a drink and he asked for a fresh lime. Both taking a full glass, they went and sat on a bench out of earshot.

'I think it's best if you try and see the Chief Bonze in your own right, by yourself,' Rance began. 'Try and meet him today as we have to return to Vientiane the day after. If you do regain contact, bring the conversation round to me. If he will deign to see me as a student of the Lao language or an admirer of Buddhism or just as a straightforward simple searcher for truth, I'll be more than pleased. I fear there may be a language problem.'

'I'll try my and come back here by noon.'

Being out of earshot, the Vietnamese could only guess their conversation. They had said that this Englishman was different so he went over to them quietly, see if more drinks were required, and overheard Leuam say, 'Great Master.' That did not strike him as strange, but, even so, to be on the safe side, he logged down the time they spent together.

Leuam met Rance as planned. The weather was hot and sticky, with the rains not far away, so they sat under a tree in the shade. After a long pause, Leuam said, 'I did meet my master this morning. I went to the royal wat and reported to the duty bonze telling him who I was. I prayed in the wat and the Chief Bonze came over to bless me when the others had left. "I knew you'd return one day," he said. "You're not alone are you?" and I said I wasn't.'

Leaum paused, recollecting how old and deaf the Chief Bonze had become. He still looked serene and placid, with close-cropped head and saffron robe. He had not been surprised or, if he had been, he'd hidden it well. 'The man you came with, an Englishman, told you to meet me, didn't he?' the Chief Bonze had asked, almost as though he knew the answer. 'You look unhappy. There's something on your mind. Tell me,' he had coaxed gently. 'Is it your oath from Sam Neua that is troubling you? And in a way that you could not foretell?'

How had *he known?* Leuam asked himself; *how* had *he remembered after all these years when there was so much else to be done?* He had nodded 'yes', tears pricking at the back of his eyes. 'Don't worry about talking to the Englishman. That way you haven't broken your oath. Any other way you would have ... and still will.' A pause. 'Come round today at 3 o'clock, my son. Come as a tourist with the Englishman and go to the Phra Boun wat over there,' and he indicated which wat he meant. 'I'll join you. Now go.'

Leuam looked at Rance. 'I'll take you so see him this afternoon. Bring the ring. I didn't broach the subject but he knows,' was his only comment.

'What about the language problem? Normally those who can't speak the monks' special dialect have to have an interpreter, probably one of the other bonzes.'

'I expect he'll dispose with that formality in your case but you'd better learn how to greet him and address him. I can teach you that much.'

By the time they were due to make a start, Rance had learnt by heart what little Leuam had considered necessary and had committed to paper a few extra snippets. He also rehearsed what he would say if he happened to be asked to comment on the situation as he saw it. They got up and left together, passing the rotunda, watched suspiciously by the Vietnamese manager.

'Now it's cooled down a bit I'm going to be a tourist and visit some temples,' called Rance. The manager smiled affably. There was nothing unusual, either, about a Lao and a European walking together. The free and easy Lao way of life made visits to temples commonplace. *No, nothing wrong there*, he thought, *but I'll still have to log that up also. They'll have to know. They have to know everything.*

At five to three they were outside the appointed wat. Leuam said, loudly enough to be overheard, 'I'm going in to light some joss sticks. Come in with me, do.'

They took their shoes off and went inside. Around the walls were depicted various stages of man's travail and, always interested, Rance went to examine a picture-like painting at the far end where, at exactly 3 o'clock, Leuam opened a door in the wall and made obeisance. He turned and beckoned Rance to follow him. Inside, on a raised dais, sitting in the lotus position, was a rigid-backed, stern-visaged old man, dressed in saffron. Rance went over to him, raised his hands in the *wai* salutation and formally greeted the Chief Bonze as he had been taught then waited to be bidden to be seated. The invitation came.

'Sit down and talk in simple Lao. So *you* are the one,' not said as a question but rather as a statement of affirmation.

Rance sat down cross-legged on a rush mat and looked at the Chief Bonze. 'Am I?' he asked.

'If you know about the rings, then you are. Only that could have brought my chela here. Only that has brought you here. Let me see it.'

Leuam, silent and subdued, had seated himself next to Rance, who felt in his pocket and produced the ring, holding it out to the Chief Bonze. That being contrary to protocol, Leuam took it from him and put it on the ground near the Chief Bonze's right hand. The stiff-backed old man picked it up, examined it and put it back on the ground, signalling Leuam to give it back to Rance. He sighed and repeated himself. 'Yes, you are the one. Who else are you? Tell me about yourself.'

Rance told the Chief Bonze in the detail he presumed was wanted: an Englishman, forty-eight years of age, unmarried, long service in the British Army in Asia, a Christian, a teetotaler – a man whose main task over the years had been fighting Communism which he hated as he felt that such a system was nothing but the denigration of human dignity. Some of the aspects of his long answer to the Chief Bonze's question bore no immediate relevance as a direct answer but nevertheless seemed to please the old man for, at the end of the description, he again said what he had said earlier on, 'Yes, you are the one. Now tell me how the ring came into your possession. There may be details that are important to me.'

Rance then told the Chief Bonze how had been given the ring, referring to Le Dâng Khoã by name, even mentioning the tattoo mark on the inside of the little finger of his right hand. The Chief Bonze's eyes lit up. 'Yes. I know him by his other name best,' a remark lost on the British Colonel. 'An impetuous youth!' the Chief Bonze added. 'What else do you know?'

Rance described how he had started learning Lao in London with Princess Golden Fairy who had first alerted him to the significance of the ring, then to what Princess Jasmine had said, on to the news that Le Dâng Khoã was reported by the South Vietnamese Army authorities as 'Missing in Action' – 'A "cover up", I expect,' the Chief Bonze had interpolated – to how he had met with Leuam's brother, Bounphong Sunthorn, now a political representative for the Pathet Lao in Vientiane, and Tâ Tran Quán, who had been wounded and captured. Finally he said that they spoke of a fourth man.

'Is that all? Is there no one else to tell me about?' queried the Chief Bonze.

'Well, I don't know if it has any bearing on the subject but there is a coincidence,' and Rance explained about Major Mana Varamit's being at Long Cheng, his disappearance and the strange query of Tâ Tran Quán, 'Did the Thai also die?'

A protracted pause followed and Rance, excusing himself, stood up as his legs were aching. The Chief Bonze told him to sit with his back to the wall and stretch his legs out straight if that would help him but not to point his feet in his direction. He then started to talk.

'Since you know so much, oh Englishman, and since I adjudge you sincere and in some danger; since you have been wise yet rash, and since you are the one, you must know all' and the Chief Bonze told Rance about the Ban Liet massacre of 1945 and how the way to salvation was in the hands of four people; Le Dâng Khoã, Bounphong Sunthorn, Tâ Tran Quán and Thong Damdouane. There had also been a fifth boy, a Thai named Mana Varamit, a quizzical and resentful lad who had deep-set eyes that were slightly flecked. The boy's father had disappeared as had the boy himself the next day, during an initiation ceremony. The divinations had foretold that there would be a traitor amongst them, so Mana Varamit was the danger. The other fathers, who had indoctrinated their sons so successfully, had had to take new identities, and the crunch was still to come, some two years away. That much the divinations had been firm on; not before thirty years were up and only twenty-eight had so far elapsed. The divinations had further prophesied that, although the path to salvation was almost certain after thirty years, yet another thirty years must elapse to make sixty in all before the country could find peace with itself.

Rance sat riveted. He made a rapid calculation – 1975 to 2004 AD and 2518 to 2548 BE – marvelling at the strange mixture of ancient and modern, at the utter sincerity of what the venerable man was saying, at the incredible intertwining of fact and fantasy. The Chief Bonze came to the end of his disquisition.

'Have you understood what I have said? Good,' as Rance indicated that he had. 'And now have you any questions to ask me before we end this meeting? It won't be easy for us to meet often.'

Rance's mind raced. 'Your Serenity. I do not need to remind you that my official position forbids me to criticise or interfere but, under the circumstances, I must be explicit and frank. Please bear with me. What do you advise? I must determine my future actions within the balance of my potential and your expectations. Help me please.'

Before the old man could give an answer came a knock, made in a special way, at the door. 'Come in. Are we called one stage further?' he queried.

'Prince Sainyavong and the Princess await your pleasure,' came the voice.

'I attend them.' Turning to Rance, he answered him by saying, 'my advice, oh Englishman, must be for you to follow the dictates of your heart but,' and his face was wreathed in a beatific smile, 'your heart will be the wiser if you follow me. Come,' he bid, rising stiffly. 'Start following me now.'

He led the way down the steps, followed by a wondering but an utterly fascinated Rance and a docile Leuam. Prince Sainyavong Hatsady, the Englishman recalled, was the King's only full brother and the father of Princesses Golden Fairy and Jasmine. He shivered with tension.

The wat they entered was more ornate than the one they had been in, with intricate decorations on the wall, columns, ceiling and beams, beautiful to behold. The Chief Bonze went to a door in the far wall, opened it, and spoke to somebody in the outer section. Leaving the door ajar, he came back and was followed by a couple whom Rance recognised, having been introduced to them both at the banquet following the last royal boat races. Unusually, the Princess had come up to him and told him that she was Golden Fairy's mother.

'I thought it must be you from the description in her letters. Tell me, when did you last see her? How was she? Do you think she is eating enough?' she had asked him, full of motherly concern. She had shown much interest in Rance as well, asking him about his lessons, and had then taken him over to meet her husband who, as President of the King's Council, was busy with certain protocol matters. They were both charming people, friendly, happy and obviously devoted to each other.

Now, as the royal couple came into the inner room, Rance and Leuam both gave them the *wai* salutation, they, in turn, similarly saluting the Chief Bonze. As was normal, the gesture was not returned by the monk; Rance had early on noticed that none wearing the saffron robe ever made the *wai* gesture. As there were no chairs, they made themselves comfortable on some low wooden stools. Rance sat to a flank, wondering what was expected of him. Leuam's face was an impassive mask in the presence of such exalted dignitaries.

The Chief Bonze looked at the four people in turn and then started proceedings; 'This is an unusual meeting but we are living in unusual times. You may not realise,' this to Rance, 'that your reputation has preceded you. To be on good Lao-speaking terms with two of the Prince's daughters, who are the King's nieces, is in itself a noteworthy accomplishment. That said, and because we in high-class society still believe that an Englishman's word is his bond, and because time is running out, we are meeting today.' He bowed slightly in the direction of the Prince.

The King's brother, looking less cheerful than Rance had previously seen him, challenged Rance with his eyes. Rance faced him, serene and unworried, his momentary feeling of tension having quickly dissipated, and smiled. Prince Sainyvong broke the silence.

'Oh English *Colonen*. In this wat let us be united and, under the guidance of His Serenity, let us follow the precepts that have guided right-thinking men for centuries. To emphasise his greatness and also his humbleness, the Chief Bonze is today wearing the saffron robe and not his white robe of the highest rank. Are you willing to help us? We believe you are. If you're not, we are wasting our time.'

'Royal Father, will you please excuse me not speaking to you in the royal dialect that strict protocol dictates?' The Prince nodded assent and Rance continued. 'May I say, besides being most honoured to be in your presence, that of course I will help you to the limit of my ability and authority. As I have already pointed out to His Serenity, I am bound by the strict rules that my Government has laid down for the conduct of Attachés and this bond I cannot break, nor would you want me to break it. If I were willing to break faith in that context you could not expect faith unbroken in this.' The royal couple and the Chief Bonze nodded understandingly. 'May I quote two Lao proverbs which come to mind? "Listen to others and you will be unhappy" and "When the water level falls, the ants eat the fish: when the water level rises, the fish eat the ants". In this situation everybody you meet has his own vested interests and, I fear, it is more than likely that you will be unhappy in any case. Also, never was matter more serious and less favourable to you.'

After a short silence, during which this enigmatic reply was digested, the Princess looked across at Rance and smiled at him. 'As a woman, I hope I can reach the depths of what you've got to say. From what my daughters say, I trust you though I may not fully be able to understand the implications of your message,' she said.

Rance smiled back at her, glad that she had made that comment. He looked enquiringly at the King's brother and the Chief Bonze. 'How do you think I can be of help to you? As a soldier I can only offer advice of a military nature.'

The Chief Bonze answered. 'Everything that I have ever

stood for is at stake. From what I have heard of you I gather you have intelligence and ideas; from what I know of you, you have courage and contacts. If you can see your way to linking these, anything I can do to help will be done. We want advice on how to combat the menace to our way of life.' The Prince again nodded his assent. 'Give me your ideas.'

Rance felt another momentary flutter of butterflies in his stomach: the practice for the heats was over, the heats were being run in earnest, stealthily no longer. Would he reach the finals, let alone stand a chance of winning them? He collected his thoughts.

'Your enemies come in the guise of friends,' he started and went on to explain what was, in essence, *The Catechism of a Revolutionist*, which he had painstakingly mugged up, simplified and put in an Indo-China context. At the end of about twenty minutes, he said, 'In Laos there is only one person who can hold the people together – a crowned King. He must convince the neighbouring Chinese that Soviet influence, which is what the North Vietnamese will bring, will be kept to a minimum, and that His Majesty can become crowned before the forces against him and his kingdom can prevail. His Majesty must play along with them, always trying to be one jump ahead of them until he judges his moment.

'You know better than I can ever know who of the Pathet Lao leaders are pro-Chinese and who are not: I believe that the only chance your country has of retaining its traditional identity is to act along the lines I have explained – using those who can help you and discarding those who either can't or won't. I have nothing more to offer you, except to remind you that security is of paramount importance if success has any chance of being won. If, in what I have said, I offended you in any way, I apologise. This is the first time that I have been called on in this fashion. And, as a final thought – when those who try to convince the rulers of this fair land that what I have been saying is untrue, please remember that Communism, as practised by the Soviets, is the Twentieth Century's most successful and biggest confidence trick. Thank you for listening.'

Prince Sainyavong Hatsady sat with his head in his hands, motionless. The Chief Bonze also stayed as he was, rigid-backed on his seat, with a look of a man far away with his thoughts. The Princess fidgeted slightly with her hands, bird-like in her delicacy of movement. Leuam looked strained. Silence held them in its thrall. Rance suddenly felt exhausted. He again thanked his lucky stars that he had bothered to read up what Gordon Parks had advised and that he had spent considerable time in rehearsing that long and dreary spiel in Lao to himself on his long weekend walks, never dreaming such an opportunity as today's would come his way.

A good five minutes later the Prince stirred. 'So be it: to bend is not to break and to bend in the direction you have outlined will not be easy but to bend in any other way will be fatal. So ... we must try it. Thank you, oh Englishman. I will pass your message on. I believe, in your position, you may be our only link.'

The royal couple stood up, Rance and Leuam following suit. All four saluted the Chief Bonze and, as the Prince and Princess turned to leave the main door, His Serenity beckoned the other two over to him. They stood within arms' reach of the old man who leaned forward and touched each on his head, lightly – a rare gesture, made with dignity and serenity. Rance felt a glow of powerful reassurance surge into him and looked up at the Chief Bonze, being rewarded with the ghost of a smile that momentarily made his face lose its look of ineffable sadness. 'The white from the west: at least that part is correct,' was his one and only remark, enigmatic and lost on Rance.

The two visitors left for the outer temple, being met at the other side of the door by an acolyte who led them to where their shoes were. Without even a backward glance, he turned and abruptly left them to put on their footwear and walk slowly back to the hotel in the cool of the evening. The Vietnamese saw the Englishman take a ring off his finger but thought nothing of it, presuming he wanted to clean it.

After Rance and Leuam had left for Vientiane the Vietnamese in the Phou Si hotel filed their departure time in his log as meticulously as he had their arrival. He had noticed that the Englishman was on friendly terms with his driver but, as he was on friendly terms with everyone, and as the search of his baggage had revealed nothing suspicious, he did not consider it necessary to check his daytime movements. He had already collated the descriptions of foreign visitors to the brothels and Rance was not one of them.

Meanwhile, on the return journey, Rance was trying to think of ways and means of implementing what had happened the previous day. Having been thrashing around on the outer fringes, he now had been offered the chance of closer liaison with what he regarded as his royal target. He had been most surprised to find the King's brother and sister-in-law the previous day and only hoped that what he had said would somehow work the oracle. Although outwardly charming, the Lao had an obstinate, even vicious, streak in his character that only manifested itself well after the cause of irritation had been forgotten by the perpetrator. The meeting had been arranged at short notice, and here he grinned to himself, his eccentricity had obviously been a point in his favour. How long would his rapport last and would he recognise the next approach? *Sufficient unto the day* ... he thought to himself as Leuam stolidly and efficiently drove the white car with its fluttering flag along the winding hill road. He was still deep in thought when they reached Vientiane late that evening, dusty and stiff, to be greeted by an ecstatic dog. There at least was something genuine and uncomplicated.

Nga Sô Lựu looked at the file on the office table in front of him. It was marked secret and contained the details of the conference that was being held shortly and he was chairing in Office 95. The visitors from Hanoi had been with him for four days already and had inspected his training and operational programme. They had attended a seminar only the previous day and had seemed tolerably well pleased with everything. The seminar had broken up as a message had been received that two more visitors were to attend the main conference. He glanced at his watch and almost immediately afterwards heard the noise of an AN-2 overhead. There were only six such planes in the Hanoi squadron, three piloted by North Vietnamese and three by Cubans. They wore the markings, however, of the Lao Patriotic Front. He glanced at his watch once more; they would be another half hour or so before getting to the office, time enough to read the signals that had accumulated during the morning.

Much of what came into him was concerned with trivia and, were the truth known, boring, but he was a conscientious little man and he felt that whatever he did helped the cause. He also felt he ought to know if there was anything that would be prudent for him to know about before the main meeting began. However, the signals were of a routine nature except one, nearly at the bottom of the pile, that did catch and hold his attention. It was from his agent in Luang Prabang: Route 13 was being used once more by civil traffic and it cited the case of the British Defence Attaché who had recently driven up unescorted and spent a couple of days sight-seeing in the royal capital. *Western playboy* had been his unspoken comment. *But not for much longer. We're not quite ready yet,* he thought, *but we soon will be and the meeting today should hasten the time when we will have taken the whole country over.* He put the signal down and glanced through the remainder. Nothing there. He got up. *Sight-seeing! If that was all the new British Defence Attaché could find to do in the how many?* – he flicked his gaze up at the Attachés' roster on a notice board on the wall – *seven months he has been in the country* ... Initially the Englishman had seemed puritanically different from the others. Close monitoring had revealed no vices and considered opinion had been that he might be a hard nut to crack. *But sight-seeing after seven months. No worry after all* ...

He went into the conference room, gave the orderly some last-minute orders then went to escort the Hanoi visitors from their quarters to the meeting. He found them sitting inside, talking with the recently arrived dignitaries, whom he had yet to meet.

'Comrade Nga,' said the leader of the Hanoi delegation, blenching slightly from the Comrade's inscrutably dark, glassy eyes, 'Before we go in I'd like to introduce you to the doctor and the political cadre who have just arrived.' Introductions over, the leader continued, 'I had hoped the doctor would bring with him our new Thai comrade, Mana Varamit, but regrettably he is still suffering from amnesia.'

Nga Sô Lựu nodded. He had followed the case with great interest and much concern in that he had had more than a hand in its processing. 'The doctor will tell you why we have to delete the item concerning him and our plans for him from our agenda.' He turned and invited the doctor to carry on with the topic.

'Briefly, Comrade Mana Varamit sustained a head injury on his way over to us from the lackeys. I am a neurologist and I have been dealing with him ever since I first saw him, ten days after he had been hit. He regained consciousness whilst at the forward field medical unit but,' and here he paused, 'as he had lost his memory – I won't bother you with technical terms – and forgotten his identity, it took more time than I would have liked to get him to proper care. He may, in fact he probably will, get better but we have no idea of knowing when. He will be no use to us as long as he cannot recall who he is.'

'Who does he think he is, Comrade Doctor?'

'Someone called Le Dâng Khoã.'

Gordon Parks met Rance in front of the embassy as they arrived for work simultaneously on the following Monday morning. The SIS man's brows raised themselves slightly and Rance nodded.

'Yes, I've got to talk with you, Gordon. I didn't bother to come in over the weekend having got back on the Friday evening after office hours. I'll have to look at the bumph that is bound to have accumulated during my Luang Prabang visit and I'll come along later. That'll give you time to do what you have to do first.'

'Fine.' They strolled to the entrance. 'The dog pleased to see you?'

'And how! Kipling's "eternal covenant – four legs behind" I think it was he wrote. If only he'd been brought up better he'd be easier to control – the dog I mean, not Kipling – and yet if Roger Daniel had not treated him so badly, he'd not have reacted so positively to me. It's an ill wind, so they say. Come on, Singha.'

They went inside, Rance smilingly greeting the doorman, the telephone operator and the British security officer. *Charm the hind leg off a clotheshorse*, thought Gordon Parks, noticing, not for the first time, the happy reaction that was always forthcoming. Rance peeled off into his clerk's office, holding the door open for the dog. 'In you go, boy, and say good morning to Mr Joseph.'

'Good morning, sir, welcome back,' said Mr Joseph. 'It's nice to see you still in one piece. I rather wondered how you'd get on. Was it a success? I hope so.'

'I could only say "not so dusty" after I'd had a marathon wash,' grinned Rance. 'Seriously though, it was well worth the effort but I'm glad I don't have to do that journey every day. I'd much rather be a long-distance runner than a long-distance lorry driver! When the road gets entirely safe I'll send you and Mrs

Joseph up in my car.'

They chatted desultorily for a while then Rance asked Mr Joseph what he had in store for him. His clerk pulled a long face. 'The Desk Officer wants us to give an appreciation of the situation if the ceasefire gets out of control to the extent it has done in Vietnam. What options have the right-wing got? Government in exile? Capitulation? Fighting spirit? Political bargaining counters? Relative strengths? PL sympathisers? And a lot more I can't remember off the top of my head. I'll fetch it from registry as soon as you're ready, sir. The rest is reading material, a couple of dispatches that might interest you – the other bits are routine crud.'

An hour later Rance pushed the last document away and stood up. 'Come on, Singha, let's give the draft to the Desk Officer's query to Mr Joseph along with the rest of the bumph, go and talk to Gordon and sign the London stuff in time to catch the bag later. The answer I've given them is a tame affair from what it could be – none the less welcome, I hope.'

Singha looked up devotedly at the sound of his master's voice, thumped his tail on the floor and yawned. Rance gathered up his papers, called the dog, locked the door and gave the papers to Mr Joseph, telling him he was going to pass the time of day with Gordon Parks. 'I'll come back and sign that report in time to send it off.'

He strolled down the corridor towards Gordon's office, glancing up at the photographs of the past Ambassadors lining the walls. *The FCO has to make bricks with volunteer straw, same as the peace-time armed forces do*, he thought. *In neither profession can the young entrant ever know if his dreams of greatness will come true. Just as well, maybe.* He stopped as he noticed for the first time the photograph of Mr Taunton that had been hung up. He hoped it meant that the man would soon be on his way. Still didn't know what he would be doing when he had gone on retirement. It had been on the tip of Rance's tongue to suggest that he go into the Church because only the Almighty was compassionate enough to offer him a job, but he had refrained. He knocked on Gordon's door; normally the FCO never bothered to knock as they went into their colleagues' offices but he had yet to lose the habit.

'Come on in,' called Gordon and half an hour later he had brought the SIS man up to date. 'Congratulations, Jason. Operation Stealth can only have advanced significantly. Luck and judgement, I'd say, have repaid your efforts, especially linguistically, in spades. This is fascinating and it makes sense. Now we have the cause of this strangeness and know the actors, it all adds up. It's like a thirty-year time bomb ticking away but without, so it seems, the chief actors having any fixed idea of how it will pan out or whether conditions will be back to something like normal in sixty years' time. And yet, in their eyes, you must be a gift from Providence. Are we now looking at the two sides of the same coin, I wonder?'

'Too early to be definite, Gordon but, yes, I'm still amazed by it. I shall have to pick my moment with the "avenging four" terribly carefully. I'll have to have a lot of help and advice if I can be "fusion and fission" so to speak. There are some grey areas I'm concerned about: Major Mana Varamit, his behaviour and disappearance; and the beeline that the Soviets seem to have been making against me. I now know that Mana was the fifth boy, was abducted somehow from Sam Neua and is now a converted Communist, a long-time mole – a sleeper – and that he either suspects me or fears me. In any case he most certainly recognises all four rings. What are your views, Gordon?'

'It is indeed a worrying puzzle and what you suggest could well be the correct answer. Now that you've voiced your doubts, Jason, I think I must concentrate on Mana as a target. The CIA might have some useful hints or even the Thai Intelligence Service might help. They have links stretching a good long way into that corner of Asia. You concentrate on your side and I'll see what I can do on mine.'

Next week John Chambers handed a report to the lugubriously expressioned man opposite him. 'Have a gander at this, Dally, then call off your search of the archives.'

'Jiminy Cricket!' The American whistled through his teeth as he came to the end of his reading. He lifted his bulk off the chair and danced a small jig for joy.

John Chambers later had a session with General Sir David Law who was similarly pleased with the Attaché's unexpected progress. 'John, mouths duck-arse tight on this one,' was his startlingly basic riposte.

The day of an unsuccessful coup, 20 August 1973, was the day of the arrival of the new Ambassador, Mr Cameron, who had decided not to fly to Vientiane but travel through Thailand by rail and cross the River Mekong by boat. The crump of bombs was heard to the west and the far-off stutter of machine-gun fire as, seemingly unperturbed, a small motorboat was seen coming across the river with a European couple as passengers.

Introductions were soon over, reassuring remarks and brittle jokes helping to cover the new arrivals' concern. They got into their cars and, Rance leading, drove as fast as they safely could back down the road, reaching the embassy without any incident. By midday it had sputtered to a close, a dismal failure, the non-event of the year.

News of the *coup manqué* spread round the world and newsmen in Southeast Asia who had flocked ghoulishly into Vientiane when a coup was first rumoured and who left in disgust when nothing happened, flocked back again, disgruntled that they had missed a scoop. A curfew was imposed that night and the crews of the boats that had rowed the rebels over the river during the previous night, blissfully ignorant that it had finished so quickly and so ignominiously, crossed the river once more to collect their pay that had been promised them and were promptly arrested for breaking the curfew.

The next morning Rance thought it would be opportune to visit the LPF HQ near the Morning Market and see their reaction to it and also to say that Mr Cameron would be making contact with them after his credentials had been presented, before the week was out, so the Protocol Department had announced. Anyone reading the diplomatic tea leaves would have seen so quick a replacement being in post as an unspoken apology for past personality aberrations and for the Head of State to call the new man to present his credentials within a week of arrival would also be seen as appreciative reciprocity. Thus, lest the LPF felt that the British would now be less than even-handed, it would be politic and do no harm for a visit to be made. Rance judged that, as well as being frightened by the previous day's events, the Communists would make as much political capital out of it as they possibly could.

And he was correct! He drove through the gates of the LPF compound, unannounced, but the sentry on duty merely gave him a passable butt salute. There was another diplomatic car in front of the entrance – 124 CMD 01 – the Soviet *Chef de Mission* number plate that showed that the Ambassador was already inside. No one greeted the Englishman nor came to the door as he got out of his car, wondering whether his visit was, in fact, inappropriate. He decided not to ring the bell but to stand outside and count a hundred. If no one had come by then he would leave and come back later. As he turned away having slowly reached the magic number, he heard footsteps in the passage. He turned back and there was Bounphong Sunthorn, smilingly holding out his hand in welcome. Communist protocol did not allow them to make the *wai* salutation.

'Come in please. I'm so glad to see you again. It's not easy to meet together. I've been thinking so much about what we might do nearer the time.'

'I'm also worried. There are so many unknowns and we daren't make a mistake.'

They went inside and sat down on the same settee as before. From the nether regions came the voice of Mr Bakunin, talking French, drawing cheers as, presumably, he thunderously fulminated against the lackeys of the imperialists or the neo-colonialists, or whatever the current in-phrase was, and their barbaric disregard of the people's legitimate socialist aspirations.

'Sit down and listen,' continued Bounphong Sunthorn, having made a scathing gesture in the direction of the noise. 'We haven't much time to talk and now is an opportunity to cover some ground,' and he went on the tell Rance that Le Dâng Khoã, Tâ Tran Quán and Thong Damdouane, Rings A, C and D, had been working together for a long time and had managed to keep in contact – how, he did not explain – until recently. It was not easy for them to meet that often these days.

'What do you know of us?' he asked.

Rance said that he had visited Tâ Tran Quán in Phone Kheng and that he had heard that Le Dâng Khoã was missing in action.

'Don't you believe it,' smiled Bounphong. 'He is to come here, probably with another name, when Vientiane is neutralised and will be in charge of operations leading up to its political liberation. As far as Thong Damdouane is concerned, he will be posted to Luang Prabang as soon as the accords and protocols are signed for the formation of the Provisional Government of National Union. His role will equate to that of Le Dâng Khoã in Vientiane. He knows about your special relationship and is prepared for a visit when the time is ripe.'

He looked at Rance. 'I invoke the ring,' he said, his face paling with emotion. 'You are the one on whom we four must rely to defeat the Vietnamese takeover of Laos: we have our own personal scores to settle and, if during this settling, we can bring retribution on the Vietnamese for what they perpetrated in Ban Liet, so be it. We will try and manoeuvre a situation to allow what will amount to a counter-coup, not like that sad, botched affair of yesterday, but we four will be insufficient to arrange the correct setting by ourselves. If, at the same time as we prepare ourselves, you can somehow use your diplomatic contacts to announce that the King's coronation will take place in the not-so-distant, well, the not-so-very-distant future so as to get the population that is sympathetic to him and I must protest to you, *Tan Colonen*, as the military member of the Co-Chairman that the right-wing clique be kept under control and that you will try to exercise your position of Co-Chairman of the 1962 Geneva Accords more strictly in future.'

His voice had not changed in pitch, tone or flow. Rance nodded in sympathy and glanced up, hoping that he was not showing surprise, and there was Soth Petrasy standing at the entrance of the room, where neither door nor curtain blocked the view.

Rance stood up, smiled and approached the other man with his right hand extended. 'Congratulations on coming through yesterday unscathed,' he said. 'I was calling by to let you know that my new Ambassador, Mr Cameron, also reached his residence safely, having crossed the river on the Nong-Khai-Tha-Deua ferry then driven through the fighting. He sends his regards and says he will be making contact with you as soon after presenting his credentials as his programme allows. We fly to Luang Prabang tomorrow, the 22nd, and perform the ceremony the day after – unusually quick, I'm sure you will agree.'

'Thank you, *Tan Colonen*, for your support and forethought in coming round ... perhaps you will excuse us. We are busy today.'

'Certainly. Of course. So am I,' replied Rance. He turned to Bounphong Sunthorn and, after thanking him for allowing this unscheduled visit, took his leave. The two Communist officials watched his car drive out of the compound. Bounphong was sorry that he had not been able to finish his conversation and Soth glad that a rebuke was being given in accordance with policy. They both turned back to continue listening to the Soviet Ambassador.

That afternoon Rance held another long conversation with Gordon Parks, bringing him up to date. Later on during the day yet another long coded signal went to London. John Chambers, on reading it, sighed deeply and happily but was surprised to find he had unconsciously crossed his fingers as he thought of how far they still had to go.

Mr Hamish Charles Cameron was a breath of fresh air. He had sent for his Defence Attaché during the latter's visit to the LPF. On finding Rance away he told his secretary to fix up a meeting that afternoon. On his emergence from Gordon Parks' office, Rance was waylaid by the secretary who told him he was wanted by the new Ambassador. He found himself talking to a tall, dark-haired man of his own age. Mr Cameron was, in fact, a wartime naval officer who had not let himself go to seed despite some London postings. He looked fit and lean, giving the impression of quiet authority and had, so Rance had learnt, more than once proved himself in the past.

'Your reputation reached me in London,' he began, having invited Rance to be seated. 'Both the Director of Intelligence and your Desk Officer, who gave me a detailed briefing of the unusually confused situation here, led me to believe that you have made many useful contacts. They both rely heavily on your judgement.'

'Thank you, Your Excellency. That is comforting news. It is certainly a slow game and, like making friends with a cat, one where you can't force yourself on others. The slowness of my start here had me worried but your words give me comfort and confidence. This is a strange set-up to get used to.'

They talked on generalities for a while then the new man said, 'I'm taking you up as part of my team when I go to present my credentials. I hope to take you if and when I get around to being invited to the Plain of Jars and Sam Neua. In any case I'll want you with me when I make my first tour of the provinces. Initially, however, I don't want to go into military details: aid, political and our miniscule trade affairs need to be tackled first, along with the need to get to know people. Go your own way; I'm sure you know what you're doing – and keep me informed of any major item of interest.'

They were met in Luang Prabang by a member of the Protocol Department who had flown up the day before to arrange the ceremony of presenting credentials with the palace officials.

On the morrow, at ten to eleven, three protocol cars and four police outriders came to escort the British group from their hotel to the palace. Inside the leading car was the ADC to His Majesty, a Brigadier General, and the Protocol Officer. The cavalcade drove off, police outriders' motor cycles' sirens shrieking and red lights flashing. They drove into the palace grounds, past an Honour Guard of a platoon of the King's Bodyguard, dressed in red jacket and white trousers, and ascended the steps into the ornate chamber. Hats and gloves were taken from them. They talked among themselves in subdued whispers, the atmosphere a trifle tense. The large doors were open into the passage across which thick curtains were hiding the throne room.

'Come this way, please, Gentlemen, ' said in French by a court orderly in traditional Lao court dress who formed them up ready to enter the Presence. The curtains were drawn back and there was His Majesty, King Savang Vatthana, sitting on his throne with the Crown Prince, *Le Prince Héritier*, to his rear right. The Queen was not there. Six paces, bow, another six, bow again. Stay there. Mr Cameron walked another three paces towards the throne, bowed, took out his prepared speech and began to read his message of loyalty in a firm voice with no trace of nervousness. As he finished an orderly stepped forward with two silver bowls, one for the speech and the other the letter from Her Majesty, Queen Elizabeth II. They were put on a table to the side of the throne. The King stood up and took three steps forward towards the group. He shook hands with the new Ambassador, congratulating him.

'May I present my staff, Your Majesty?'

'*Si vous voulez,*' and Mr Cameron called his Head of Chancery forward. A bow, a handshake, a picture taken by the court photographer, another bow and three steps back – over and done with in a trice.

'And now, Your Majesty, my Defence Attaché, Colonel Rance.'

Rance walked three paces forward, bowed, put his hand out in answer to the King's and, as his hand was shaken, they glanced at each other. In commoner Lao, the King gently murmured, 'I have got your message. Thank you,' unheard and unseen by the others. They let go of each other's hand, Rance bowed and stepped back his three paces.

He did not take much interest in the rest of the ceremony: the walk back out of the room, the *vin d'honneur*, the standing to attention as, in front of the Honour Guard, the national anthem of both countries was played, the handshakes with the court officials, the drive back to the hotel, still escorted by outriders. He was his normal courteous, charming, smiling self but he was also smiling inside as he recalled the King's words: 'I have got your message. Thank you.'

9

September-October 1973: On 19 September a Provisional Government of National Union, PGNU, was established in Laos, its seat in Vientiane. A Communist and a non-communist alternated throughout, so that there were an equal number of Communist and non-communist ministers, deputy ministers, assistants, down to the lowest functionary, with the Health Ministry being given to the Neutralists. The torpor that always affected any government decision, royal or Communist, became more noted, otherwise, to the outside world, no change was discernible.

On the previous Thursday evening, a car drove into Rance's villa compound as he arrived back from the office. Seeing it was an LPF car, he stayed outside to welcome it. Unusually there was only one man in the back and Rance saw Bounphong Sunthorn open his own door and get out before the armed and uniformed escort sitting in front had time to get out and open it for him.

'Good evening, *Tan Colonen*. May I take up a few minutes of your time?'

'Certainly Comrade. You have obviously come on business. Is there time for me to get you a drink of something while we talk?'

'No thank you. I'm in a great hurry and have to be back within a certain time. I'll pop inside and tell you about it.' He turned and addressed the driver. 'Turn the car round. I'll be ready directly.'

They went inside, leaving the front door open, and sat down away from doors and windows. 'Our Neutralisation Forces begin their airlift from Hanoi tomorrow morning and the first two planes land at Wattay at 10 o'clock. Please, as the Co-Chairman's military representative, come to the airport and see them in,' Bounphong said.

'This is the result of the signing of the protocols for the PGNU? Presumably you are going to neutralise Luang Prabang also?'

'Yes. The Soviets are flying in the Vientiane Neutralisation Forces and the Chinese the contingent for Luang Prabang. Now I must rush. Have you anything for me?'

'I have. I've had an audience with the Chief Bonze – who well remembers you four – and the King's brother. The King, who told me himself, is fully aware of the importance of his coronation. There's no need to go into details now.'

'Wonderful news. I'll choose my moment to contact you stealthily. Wait, and have patience. About two years have to run before our strike deadline is reached. Remember, Le Dâng Khoã is the commander of the Vientiane Neutralisation Forces but using a Tai Dam name to disguise his real place of birth. Don't try to contact him and don't expect him to recognise you as he passes through Wattay airport. Give him, and me, time. Oh yes, when you do go to Luang Prabang, go and make contact with their Political Commissar, Thong Damdouane, the fourth ring. He is expecting you. Now I must go.'

The car had turned round and was ready with the escort, holding the nearside rear door open. The driver looked up as the two men emerged from the house. Rance said, 'I'll certainly be present tomorrow morning. Thank you for coming round to tell me. Where are you off to now?'

'I have to go and tell representatives from another five countries about this matter. That's why I'm in a hurry. Thank you, *Tan Colonen*. Goodbye.' He turned, shook hands, Rance feeling the ring on his finger, and got into the car. The escort hurriedly got in and the car drove off.

Back in the house the telephone rang. The French DA was on the line. Was his English colleague going to the airport tomorrow? Right. Would the representative of Her Gracious Majesty go round by way of the French embassy so they could go together? *Merci. A bientôt.* Rance put the telephone back. *I'll only find out tomorrow why he wants to go with me*, he thought, as he sent his houseboy to arrange for Leuam to pick him up in the morning. He had not planned to use him as it was an official holiday on the Friday: the end of the three months Buddhist Lent. Maybe the French DA had sent his driver away to celebrate?

All was abuzz at 10 o'clock at Wattay airport the next morning. The visitors' gallery was full and a large crowd of Communists had gathered in front of the terminal building: apart from the Pathet Lao, there were Soviets, Chinese, North Vietnamese, Poles, Czechs, and, although not Communists as such, the Indians who were the Soviet-leaning neutral Head of the International Control and Supervision Commission. Only the British and French

Attachés represented the non-communists. The latter had been told by his Ambassador to represent the Common Market – a bizarre idea at the best of times – and keep with the Englishman but, being protocol-minded, was sulking as he had been longer in Laos than had Rance. The Englishman wore uniform but his French colleague was in plain clothes with a homburg hat pulled over his eyes and a shabby mackintosh, no better dressed than an out-of-work jobbing gardener. *As the sole representatives of the so-called Free World, we don't make a particularly inspiring couple*, thought Rance.

By a quarter to eleven no plane had arrived. The chief of Aeroflot, a member of the KGB, walked up to the Soviet Second Secretary and said something to him. The word spread that the time announced the previous day was only the time the first of the two aircraft was due to take off from Hanoi where the Pathet Lao troops had to be mustered for processing before flying down south, as the strip in Sam Neua was too small for the type of aircraft being used.

At a quarter to twelve a cry went up as the noise of an aeroplane was heard and five minutes later an AN-21 landed and taxied as near the terminal building as it could. The crowd surged forward, a Lao policeman trying to prevent people from getting too near. A sallow-featured, bearded French journalist pushed his way forward but was stopped by the policeman. The Frenchman shouted something insulting and laughter arose from the crowd because the policeman wore the uniform of the normal police force, not the LPF, so was regarded as an unrepresentational nuisance. The journalist was seized by two others who had come up behind him as he tried to strike the policeman and was carted off, protesting. The French DA spat with disgust. 'Some pig from the newspaper *Humanité*. They're all the same, that crowd.'

By then the aircraft's propellers had stopped and the rear compartment opened, revealing rope-bound stores. A full five minutes elapsed before the side door opened and two PL guards emerged, blinking, to the top of the portable steps, completely unnerved and unprepared for the heroes' welcome they were getting. They quickly popped back inside and the cheering stopped. There was an incongruous, ludicrous and unrealistic air about the non-event.

Rance turned to the Frenchman and said, 'Look at that crowd. They are like a lot of mechanical sheep. They were told to cheer the first plane in so they cheer the rice or whatever the stores are and the sentries. The powers-that-be in the north could have made an impression of efficiency on the people in the south with a modicum of slick stage-management but, no, they prefer to muddle along with bureaucratic inefficiency. They pay lip service to social democracy as being the people's wish but when it comes to the crunch and the people would wish something with a touch of panache, what happens but a shambles? You know, only our two countries are enlightened enough to be able to have the political elasticity to withstand and accommodate to the pressures of what the majority want: that should be what the word "democracy" means. This disorganised bumbledom and political mockery is a far cry from anything like that.'

Steady. Keep your cool.

The second AN-21 came in forty minutes after the first but by then it was an anti-climax. Rance counted seventy-eight passengers including seven women. The men, in equal numbers, wore civilian clothes or uniform of a nondescript green, representing functionaries and soldiers; however those uniformed men not carrying weapons were believed to be policemen. Counting these people as they streamed by him had a mesmerising effect. He saw and recognised Le Dâng Khoã – *so he has come back to haunt me* – and, as he continued to count the passengers, his mind switched to that scene in the jungle with Le Dâng Khoã, Mana Varamit and the grizzled Sergeant Major. It had since struck him as strange that he should have been given a ring that seemingly had to be worn by the original owner and not given it away to a stranger on what was, on the surface, a comparatively minor incident. Had the Vietnamese somehow recognised in Rance some*one* that he was looking for or waiting for rather than some*thing*? He could not have known about him before coming to the Jungle Warfare School. What was that word uttered as the ring was given to him? Yes, that was it. *Có lẽ* – 'perhaps' in Vietnamese. Perhaps what? Perhaps I am the man the omens in Sam Neua had proclaimed? From what the Chief Bonze had said, yes, I am. Would …

His companion laughingly dug him in the ribs. 'Wake up, dear colleague, they finished going by minutes ago! You were miles away then, weren't you?'

Rance grinned back sheepishly, slightly embarrassed that he had been caught out. 'I'm sorry.'

Rance dropped the French DA off before driving to his villa, wondering if he could last out the rest of the two years of his tour of which one year had almost elapsed. But hadn't Leuam once spoken of a thirty-two month stay in Laos … ?

The day's historic events were noted in the capital of many countries. Some were optimistic, others not. The BBC was factual, the Voice of America plaintive, the French scathing. The Soviets, Chinese and North Vietnamese gloated and stressed fraternal solidarity, the people's wish and inevitable Socialism. But behind these bland announcements more specific matters of moment were discussed.

Somewhere deep inside the Kremlin a senior official of the KBG was dilating to an equally senior member of the Foreign Affairs staff. 'Yes, that's the beginning of the end. Only two more years to go. Carrot and stick. False hope and genuine fear wear the others down and keep our own side alert. We'll get what we want in Laos fairly soon after victory in Vietnam. I'm annoyed that we couldn't get into Luang Prabang but we can still influence and hoodwink the King from our Vientiane base. We'll have to watch the Chinese. Regarding one minor matter, I wish that the Thai I was telling you about would find his memory but that is not critical now. He was watching our interests in South Vietnam on and off and, for a short while, in Malaysia, as indeed was – what was his name? – Le Dâng Khoã, I think it was. We've yet to get to the bottom of what happened to him, really our Vietnamese friends can be most inefficient in some of their routine work. There was something that didn't ring quite true; one of the two got his knife into the other but I could get nothing out of the Viet who seems to have disappeared from the scene – unless Office 95 has him under an alias. We'll get news as soon as the Thai comes round. There's enough time yet. He could just conceivably have been wrong about that Englishman but I've yet to be convinced. As I said, there's time enough yet to make absolutely sure. In any case the Englishman is expendable, hapless sod that he is.'

Somewhere deep inside the Palace of Heavenly Peace in Peking a senior cadre of the Public Security Service was talking to his political superior. 'So far we've beaten the Soviets to it in Luang Prabang and, in the long run, will do so for the rest of Laos, to say nothing of the whole of Indo-China and Southeast Asia, our Nanyang territory. Our policy of *taoguang yanghui*, concealing our own capabilities and biding our time, is our secret weapon. The inevitable American defeat, the way they have backed those regimes without a firm political base and their sordid habits are a pointer to our incalculable advantage. Foreign devils in Asia, from now on, will be the lesser because of our victory – only two more years to wait for it – and their defeat and, although they don't see it yet, that includes those expansionist, imperialist Russian bears. By the way, did you know that the British Defence Attaché in Laos is anti-Russian but seems to be on good relations with our men there? We could use him if we are clever even though that would make him expendable. "Feigning to be a pig, he vanquishes tigers ...".'

In Sam Neua an elderly and zealous party worker was updating a policy draft for consideration by the Politburo. He read, '... your main weapon is absolute terror, so destroy everything and everybody except one or two people who can help spread terror by rumour. It has always worked in the past, so make it work again in the future ...' *That was the way we did it then*, he mused. *That was what we did in the wat after the Ban Liet foray. Pity we had to kill that Thai man when he tried to escape – he'd have been useful if he'd been more cooperative. But the boy was good ... trained him and sent him back. Basically not much has changed but nowadays we have political refinements and disinformation to keep people unsure of themselves. We'll get our allies to play up the King's coronation. We've heard quite a bit about that during the past couple of months or so. We'll even get him to visit Sam Neua to discuss it within the framework of the situation prevailing at that time, whatever it may be. Lull them and then it can't help but be ours. Twenty-eight years gone and only two remain ...* He chuckled in anticipation. ... *as for that expendable, sight-seeing Englishman ...*

The meeting in the annex of the American embassy in Grosvenor Square coincided with the announcement that the commercial capital of Laos, Vientiane, and the royal capital, Luang Prabang, had been neutralised by being divided into two, one portion being under the control of the forces of the Royal Lao Government, the Royal Lao Army, and the other under that of the Lao Patriotic Front forces, the Pathet Lao. John Chambers and Maurice Burke now felt that it was more than necessary to have an in-depth meeting on how to play Rance's unbelievable nearness to the King and his enormous progress with the wearers of the rings. Could an operation could be mounted, with resources of both the SIS and the CIA, to take maximum advantage of what he had managed to orchestrate.

The full extent of Rance's contacts, after being presented to the King, had been reported on a wider but most carefully controlled distribution but, even so, it was a jealously guarded secret. Now the matter had to be aired and discussed at a level where the political consequences had to be fully analysed before final authority to proceed could be given, in other words, let many more people into the secret. A position paper had been circulated at 'top secret' grading containing enough data and possible courses of action to merit the holding of the meeting with departmental representatives being fully briefed of background, possible scope and probable consequences.

The SIS fielded John Chambers and his immediate superior, one Bill Hodges, and the CIA had Maurice Burke and the Regional Controller, Ed Murray, flown in from Bangkok. They had been joined by no less a personage than Lieutenant General Sir David Law, representing the MOD and the FCO was represented by Mr Gerry Elwood, Head of the Southeast Asian Desk – a select band.

Proceedings had been opened by Ed Murray who had rehearsed the background to, reasoning for and constraints imposed by, their original request for a special British DA whose unofficial aim had even had its own special name, 'Operation Stealth'. First of all the meeting was briefed at how this had progressed and how it was hoped it would develop. Those not already in the secret gasped on hearing the story.

After that had been discussed, Bill Hodges, supplemented where necessary by John Chambers, had described why Rance had particularly been chosen, how he had originally stumbled on one of the 'miniscule group of four men' that both the CIA and SDECE had had rumours of – and what had happened since. The military man and the FCO man listened attentively, occasionally jotting down notes. It was an amazing story by any standards. A large wall map made it easy to follow the political implications, whether one was a domino-theory man, who believed that, once a country had been taken over by the Communists, its neighbours would topple, or not. John Chambers' thoughts turned to the sadly too many of his political superiors left-wing leanings, their innate dislike of anything unorthodox and the best method of convincing them before they, in turn, would even contemplate taking the matter any higher.

'And so,' Bill Hodges summarised, 'in a nut shell, we have the DA in an incredible position: tenuously open lines to the King, to the Chief Bonze, to the Communist hierarchy and the senior right-wing brass, despite a background of, initially, somewhat unusual personality circumstances' – and here the FCO man winced at the oblique reference to the late Ambassador – 'and the Attaché himself being a target on two separate occasions. It would, to my way of thinking, be folly not to take every advantage of the present unique circumstances.'

'Hear! Hear!' echoed the two Americans.

'So, gentlemen,' continued Bill Hodges after a meaningful pause, 'the crunch is – what advantages shall we try and take, and to what extent are we prepared to go to press them? In other words, do we continue with "Operation Stealth" as well as launch an "Operation Four Rings"?'

Mr Jerry Elwood looked uneasy as he turned to the General and asked him his opinion. The General shot him a glance of distaste before replying. 'In the normal course of events, the DA, having prepared the ground to such an extent, would stand back and let other agencies follow up on the latter proposition were such to be approved by the appropriate authority. However, in this case, I cannot see anyone else who could take over contact with the palace and the four rings although our combined resources' – and here he looked at the SIS and CIA men – 'could no doubt mount an operation against any worthwhile targets that were presented like, for instance, kidnapping the Thai, re-infiltrating the wounded and captured ring, or the disruption of any plans the Communists have for their eventual take-over of Laos. But with Colonel Rance in post, the Soviet and Chinese elements could be played to our greater advantage; the DA seems to be the meat in the sandwich there.

'Rance must be particularly lonely out there but I fear he has to remain so. We simply cannot afford to let the present set-up slip out of our grasp. I must ask him if he is willing to extend his tour from the normal two year one by another eight months to make it a thirty-two month stint. He has painted himself into a Southeast Asian corner and he might as well stay there till the paint dries. As I see it, he must continue to be our link for as long as possible. "Operation Four Rings" must be definitive but might well have to be mounted against an opportunity target if one crops up whatever the planned contingencies. What do you think, Elwood?'

Mr Elwood looked unhappier than he had done so far.

'I'm sorry to say so but I don't think you would get any official blessing for any project such as "Operation Four Rings". The Cabinet won't countenance anything that distracts us from the forthcoming referendum on Europe, oil, Ireland and financial survival. You may keep this man Rance, purely in his official capacity, for as long as we have an Attaché in Laos – and this aspect will be discussed at our next meeting concerning our role as Co-Chairman which is due soon – but in no other capacity whatsoever. As for continuing his unofficial, unauthorised and completely unorthodox quest to talk to the King, it must stop. If Buckingham Palace were to hear of it, Her Majesty would be most displeased., I am sorry, Gentlemen, if I disappoint you. That is final.'

Stunned silence greeted this bombshell, then Ed Murray innocently asked, 'So you wouldn't mind if we continue using Colonel Rance in an unconscious role, always provided he keeps within the bounds of official constraints?'

'Of course not, but nothing more.'

Another uneasy lull followed as the implications of this bleak prospect sank in. *It's impossible that Rance can be used unconsciously when he has such a personal rapport with so many folk who would never agree to work with nor even trust anyone else. It's not only criminal but it also shows up how sick our own society, or maybe western bureaucracy, is not to take advantage of this unique opportunity of thwarting the prospects of the Sick Society*, General Law savagely thought. *And how will the hapless Rance like to be told that all his unique efforts will have to be water under the bridge?* However, neither the MOD nor the

FCO could dictate government policy, only try to influence it, so as loyal government servants, they could do nothing but fume privately. The Americans looked on uncomprehendingly at this feeble outcome.

The meeting broke up, with Mr Elwood leaving first. As the General left with the two SIS men, Ed Murray came up to him and invited the three of them to come to his private office. Maurice Burke was also asked in. It was an unhappy, hard-eyed group of men who kept quiet until they had a cup of coffee at their side. The General then spoke.

'Well, that makes it so much the harder now. Sometimes I think we're so wet you could shoot snipe off us. With them it's policy, project, plan; with us it seems to be view points, vote catching, vacillation. They work at long-range targets. We don't, the more's the pity. I believe not only we here regard the Communists as our implacable enemies but that Rance does also. Provided we work within the ambit of what Mr Murray said, there will be no comeback officially. Yes, no?' He quizzed the CIA men with a brusque look and got affirmative nods in return. 'In that case, I have the genesis of a plot which I'd like you to listen to and give me your initial comments on now. If you agree we can work out details later. What this means is, unhappily, that Rance is now much more vulnerable than he ever was. Here we are, safe in London, while he, poor toad, is fighting a one-man fight, virtually blindfolded with his hands tied behind his back, so to speak. That just about makes him expendable. As far as "Operation Stealth" is concerned it always was more than a million-to-one chance of any success, but end it must. I'll let Rance know.'

He looked at the others and asked, 'Can we really let it end like this?'

Heads shook.

'Very well, then. Let "Stealth" become unattributably even more stealthy and start an unattributable "Operation Four Rings". This, in broad terms, is what I have in mind ...'

Colonel Jason Rance's exploits in Laos continue in ...

Operation Four Rings

After the ceasefire in Laos in February 1973, London forbids Colonel Jason Rance, the British Defence Attaché in Laos, from continuing his search for four Lao 'moles', who work within the Communist Party and wear a dedicated ring as a talisman.

Unsanctioned contingency plans are therefore made by others for Rance to continue his work with the moles, the 'Four Rings', in an unattributable Operation Four Rings. But Rance remains ignorant of the plan and does not know he is in imminent danger.

The communists now suspect the Four Rings as well as Colonel Rance and they launch their own Operation Four Rings: to kill the four moles and the British Defence Attaché. The tightest of races ensues.

Based on historical fact and the author's personal experience, Operation Four Rings is the fifth in a series of books involving Gurkha military units and includes Operation Black Rose, Operation Janus, Operation Blind Spot and Operation Stealth. The author, a retired Gurkha colonel, draws on real characters and events he witnessed across various theatres of war.